SOUND OF BLUE THUNDER

A.J. DOWNEY

BOOK TEN

Published 2022 by Second Circle Press

Text Copyright © 2022 A.J. Downey

ISBN: 978-1-950222-37-7

~

Editing & book design by Maggie Kern @ Ms.K Edits

Cover art and Indigo Knights logo by Dar Albert at Wicked Smart Designs

DEDICATION

For all the relationships that don't look like the others. Your relationship is beautiful, your relationship is valid, and love, no matter what form it takes, is pure. Love is love. Happy Pride 2022.

PROLOGUE

*D*riller...

"This whole thing is bullshit," Oz declared, throwing his tie down on the boardroom-like table in the fishbowl. I leaned way back in my seat and sighed, locking eyes with Narcos across the table. His were guarded as he looked back at me.

Something silent and heavy passed between us. He simply nodded and glanced past me out the glass and what I presumed was the knot of women at the table out there... I didn't turn to look. I knew he was looking at Everleigh, his woman, that he so graciously shared with me.

I would be lying if I said I wasn't scared to death of going away. Hell, *I wouldn't* go to prison. I'd shot the guy that'd I'd *thought* had shot me – but the reporters had gone buck wild and the gun hadn't been found – and *shit...* it'd gotten ugly. One big tangled mess and *it was bad*. Now I was on trial, and I didn't know what the fuck was going to happen, but I knew one thing – I would die first before living the rest of my life in a fucking prison.

I closed my eyes and sighed, shutting my brothers around the table out as they went back and forth over the day in court with a play-by-play as if I hadn't been the one sitting at the fucking defendant's table, my ass on the line.

"Guys, I think he's had enough. Let's table the play-by-play for now," Skids declared from the other end of the table.

Coco breezed in with a tray and sat a plate in front of me.

"Eat up, boys. Reflash is in that kitchen, worrying you're all wasting away. Worse than the lot of your mothers," she said as she went around and set plates in front of everyone else.

"I shot the wrong kid," I said, staring at the food in front of me. "The people out there aren't wrong about being pissed about it."

"You shot the shooter's cousin, who was acting as a lookout. You'd just been shot yourself and were running on pure adrenaline. Haitian kid, standing in the alley his cousin had just run through, actin' as a lookout, dark green hoodie, black pants, Nikes – same height, same approximate weight, at fuckin' night. Suspect was wearing a black hoodie, dark-colored jeans and wearin' the same kicks. How the fuck were you supposed to know the difference in that set of circumstances?" Yale demanded. He railed on...

"It's a fuckin' joke that this even went to trial. Our office recommended against it. The only reason you're in the defendant's seat is because the mayor insisted on it. It's a goddamned election year. We barely even got the indictment. This farce should have stopped there!" He shook his head and had a righteous anger about him.

"I thought it was him," I said... but that still didn't make it right. Didn't absolve me of the fucking guilt I felt. The guilt I would live with every day. The shot I fired still echoing in my head with the sound of blue thunder every time I closed my eyes. Every time I had to see the school photo of that smiling fifteen-year-old fresh-faced kid. A kid that barely spoke any English, who was here with his single mom, just trying to live the American fucking dream.

"And the jury will see that," Blaze declared to a round of snorts and noises of derision from every cop and lawyer around the table.

"You hose boys are so cute," Golden said sarcastically. "Dumb as fuck sometimes, but cute. Like a Labrador puppy or some shit."

"Man, fuck you!" Blaze declared, but he was sorta grinning.

I looked across the table at Narcos, who tossed back the rest of what was in his glass and looked back at me with grim resignation. I nodded.

He knew as well as I did, as well as any other cop seated at this table, how fallible the criminal justice system was from first contact with one of us, all the way through the juggernaut that was the court system.

About the only thing that was remotely saving my ass was some grainy-ass surveillance footage of the alley I'd turned into.

God, this was all such a fucking mess, my fate in the hands of twelve strangers. Twelve people set on the whims of their emotions as much as their ability to logically and critically think through all the evidence and spin surrounding the case.

"Eat something," Skids ordered me and I looked from him to my plate.

I really wasn't hungry, my stomach in knots.

"Eat," Narcos urged finally, picking up his own fork and digging in to whatever Reflash had made up for all of us special. It certainly didn't look like a menu item.

I sighed, picked up my fork, and moved some of the food around on my plate.

Closing arguments had been today and would bleed into tomorrow a little bit before the jury was sent off to deliberate.

All any of us could do was hope that they got it right. I just kept going back and forth on what "right" was in this case.

I didn't want to go to prison. I wouldn't go to prison... but there was a big fuckin' part of me that felt like I honestly deserved it.

I guess if I did, that would be what would happen. Wouldn't it?

1

*T*eresia...

I lowered the paper in my hand with the official court proceeding script I'd been asked to read along with our verdict, and I didn't exactly feel good about it. The defendant, a police detective accused of shooting a young man in a moment of confusion, was practically sagging with relief and turning to hug his lawyer as the courtroom burst out into a frenzy of shouting and outrage.

We'd done our duty, and yet still, finding the man "not guilty" left a bitter taste in my mouth for the boy's family. From a legal standpoint and the evidence presented, we couldn't determine beyond a reasonable doubt that the defendant had the intent required for a conviction. As much as it pained me for the boy's family, it just wasn't there.

I was a little numb and a little scared as I filed out of the jury box last, following my fellow jurors into a back hallway as the judge banged his gavel and the angry shouts of the gallery rose fierce and white hot behind us. The anger was punctuated by the absolute heartbreaking anguished wailing and weeping of Témaël Etienne's mother, aunts, and angry shouting from his uncles.

He'd only been fifteen, just a baby, serving as a lookout for his older twenty-two-year-old cousin Juste Baptiste, the man who had shot Detective Stahl and run. He had already accepted a plea deal for that, and somehow, while we had done the right thing here, it all seemed so very wrong and didn't seem fair.

I was unsettled as the doors to the courtroom swept shut behind us and the din was hushed by its closing.

I took in a shuddering, fortifying breath as we all faced forward in our single file line and listened to the court officer at the front.

"Alright, now! You all will be taken back to your hotel to gather up your belongings and then will be transported back here, where you'll be free to go. It's almost over for you guys and the court thanks you for your service. So, if you'll all just follow me down to the vans, we'll get you all over to the hotel to get your stuff. Come with me, now!"

We followed the bailiff, Randall, down the corridor to the service elevators at the end. The vans would be waiting, as they were every day of the trial, off a secure loading dock down in the depths of the court's underground parking garage, where the media had no access.

The drive to the hotel was a somber and quiet one. I don't think any of us felt very good about things. If anything, we were all some form of afraid. Afraid of what the fallout would be. Riots were commonplace when it came to acquittals like these, and I honestly couldn't fault people for being angry.

It was all so unfair. Years upon years of it, day in and day out, so many people just so... tired.

I couldn't begin to understand their lived experiences. I knew precisely how privileged I was with my blonde hair and blue eyes, my white skin. I was of Swedish ancestry and as Nordic as they came— the perfect ideal, according to some white supremacist asshole subsets, which honestly made me nauseous to think about.

I mean, gross. No one was any better than anyone else in my eyes. Differences are what made the world such a beautiful place. Sameness would all be so disgustingly *boring.*

The drive to the hotel was short, the trip up the elevator took what felt like forever, and finally, Rita, my roommate for the duration of the trial, and I were let into our room to gather our things.

I sighed, and she gave me an empathetic look.

"That was hard," she said, patting the back of her gray, perfectly coifed hair, her clouding brown eyes looking worried.

I nodded.

"Yes, it was," I agreed in a murmur. We packed up our belongings into our suitcases silently, a pall hanging over and between us.

"What do you think is going to happen now?" she asked, and it broke my heart a little. This older woman, who had clearly seen far more than I in her lifetime, sounded scared, and that scared me.

All through the difficult trial, Rita had been the one to keep all of our spirits up at shared meals and the like. Now she looked at me, her eyes beseeching me for answers I didn't have, for optimism and comfort, but I just... I couldn't lie to her no matter how much I wished I could.

"I don't know," I said. "Your guess is as good as mine."

She looked troubled and nodded once. We set about, finishing up gathering our things. My car was parked back at the courthouse parking garage. It had been over the weeks of the trial.

As much as I wished I could just go back to it, climb inside and drive myself home – go back to my life as though nothing had changed, I didn't think I could. Things *had* changed. Irrevocably.

I just didn't know how much yet. I wouldn't know. I couldn't know. All that I could do was go back to my home, my life, my breads and pastries. Catch up on all the things that'd been neglected during the weeks of trial. All I could do was hope for the best and prepare for the worst, but that was sort of impossible, especially not knowing what the worst would be.

I shouldered my purse and extended the handle of my carryon suitcase and looked around the room for anything I may have forgotten.

I waited for Rita and held the door for her, looking back at the lonely hotel room and wistfully wishing that I could stay for just a little longer.

It felt like… it felt like the calm before the storm.

2

*D*riller...

I didn't much feel like celebrating.

Was I relieved? Fuck yes, but nothing about this warranted a celebration.

Still, the guys and their women wanted me at the 10-13 and I didn't want to dampen their moods or whatever. What I *did* want was out of this fuckin' monkey suit and onto the back of my bike. So I took my ass home with Narcos and Everleigh.

Once inside the door, my longtime partner and brother from another mother turned to look at me. I was tugging on my tie, trying to get the stranglehold it had me in loosened up, but somehow, even though the tie got looser, my throat got tighter with the look Narcos was giving me.

He stood staunch and silent, and just opened up his arms. I hugged him tight, pounding him on the back even as he rattled my fuckin' ribcage with the blows he landed on mine.

"Fuck, I was scared shitless, bro. Not gonna lie."

"You were scared?" Everleigh's voice was soft but thick with tears from nearby us. I sidestepped just enough and opened up one side between me and Narcos for her to burrow in and make three sides to our little triangle.

It was the best I was going to get for now, but I needed her softness right now.

Her lithe, lush body fitted to my side and her slim arms went around my waist. She tucked her head against my shoulder. I looked to Narcos, who smiled wryly and said, "I think you two might need a little while alone. I'm going to go grab a shower and a change of clothes. I expect if you're still going, I'll join you."

"Right on," I muttered, transfixed by Everleigh's green eyes framed by all of her wild auburn hair.

She stood on her toes and put her lips against mine and I obliged her, devouring her mouth like a starving man. It hit me then, how I'd been so close, *this close,* to never tasting another woman again. How if things had swung the other direction, I'd be in an orange fuckin' jumpsuit and headed to Oz's jail in chains right now. Awaiting processing… then prison… *fuck.*

Everleigh jerked back as my breath hitched and she looked around to make sure that Narcos was out of sight.

She nodded at me and whispered, "It's okay. You're home now. You're safe now." She wrapped her arms around me. I buried my face in her hair and breathed her herbal, flowery scent in, and I mean my breath *heaved* as the panic swept through me and I tried like hell not to fall apart.

"It's okay," she soothed, her hands smoothing over my back. "You're home now, with us. Everything is okay."

It wasn't, though, at least, not really.

The illusion was pretty much shattered for all of us. Any of the boys in blue really, but especially me...

We were on our own out there. The brass didn't have our backs, and it was one split second, barely any time at all, that things could, and would, turn on a fucking dime and we'd be taking a perp walk of shame like I had. That all of this, everything I'd built with these two, could be ripped away. I had been so close, so fucking close to losing it all, to losing any chance I had of finding a pretty princess of my own.

Everleigh stepped back and dragged me not to her room that she shared with Narcos, but to mine. She got up onto my bed and walked across the king-sized bed on her knees, dragging me by the hand up after her. She turned and dragged me down with her so we were lying together, then held me tight, held me close, my head pillowed on her breasts. She pressed lips to my forehead and with a steel I didn't know she possessed, she ordered me, "Let it out. I'm here for it." Who was I to deny a direct order like that?

Besides, I'd been holding it in for far too fucking long. Permission granted, I lost my shit and stopped holding shit back, the flood of emotions and tears hitting me like a tempest. One shuddering breath out and I sobbed into Everleigh's chest, knowing that my secret was safe with her.

3

$\mathcal{T}$eresia...

"I just don't feel right about it," I said with a heavy sigh, looking across the worktable at my mother and grandmother. Our family run little Swedish bakery wasn't open yet. We were in the back, preparing doughs and kneading breads, the ovens going and the back window propped open to vent some of the heat that liked to build up back here.

"You did the right thing," my mother said breezily, and it felt so... dismissive.

"Did I, though?"

My grandmother, my mother's mother, looked at me with sympathy.

"The whole thing was tragic, just tragic," she said, her English still accented with our family's Swedish origins. It was my grandmother and winter nights spent baking all sorts of breads, cookies, and cakes that had inspired me to go to culinary school and to open this bakery. When my mother retired, she'd come to work with me and my grandmother insisted on being a part of things from the word go.

We had always been a close-knit family, hadn't always had all the things we wanted, but had always managed to find the things we needed. My grandmother, the tie that bound us, the glue we'd always been able to depend on to hold us together. My mother had been young when she'd had me – only sixteen. My father no where in the picture and as far as my grandmother had been concerned – good riddance to bad rubbish.

My grandfather had passed two years ago in a blow to our little family and it was just us girls now.

"Yes," I agreed dully. Guilt still riddled me, but I had done everything to the letter of the law. I still couldn't help but feel like the law was broken.

"Stop beating yourself up," my mother said, hefting a tray laden with unbaked loaves of Vetebröd, a cardamom bread that was traditionally made during the winter months around Yule and Christmas. We had started making it year-round due to its popularity. It had become the signature of the bakery. We sold out very nearly every day, and I was proud that it was my grandmother's recipe.

My mother went over to one of the standing ovens and my grandmother rushed over, wiping her hands on her apron, to pull the doors open for my mother to slide the tray inside for the loaves to bake.

"Thanks, Ma," my mother muttered as she pressed buttons on the oven to set the time and temperature.

I sighed and dusted the flour from my hands, dropping the loaves of dough I was working into their baskets and covering them to allow them their final rise.

Tensions in the city were rising, and I was afraid that normal was going to be a long way off. It'd only been three days since I'd been able to come home and I'd been notified last night of, and I quote, "credible threats made against the jurors in the People vs. Stahl case," and that was absolutely bone chilling.

I mean, there was a defense attorney who had been shot in her own home after trying the Maguire case in recent memory. It'd been all over the news with its own hashtag, "where's Tina," for weeks.

I shuddered, afraid, and had asked what to do. All I'd been told was not to worry about it, that increased patrols would be made through my neighborhood, at home, at night and to basically call if anything happened.

Not. Very. Comforting.

Protests had turned into violent clashes with police last night and I'd been half afraid to even come into the bakery this morning, wondering if our windows would be intact. But the protests had been in the heart of the core of downtown, near the courthouse and the prosecutor's office.

My little corner of the old city had remained untouched and for all that, it was mere blocks from the major unrest. Everything here was idyllic and untouched.

"Teresia," my mother called, and I shook myself as though waking from a dream. I turned to look at her and my grandmother, who both wore crumpled expressions of worry.

"Are you alright?" my grandmother asked.

"Yes, why?" I asked, immediately moving to take off my flour-doused baking apron to swap into my seller's apron that was embroidered with the shop's name – *Swede Dreams*.

"Are you sure?" my mother asked. "It took me like six tries to even get your attention just then!"

I rolled my eyes. She probably called out to me twice. My mother was always prone to exaggeration like that.

"I'm fine!" I cried over my shoulder as I headed for the shopfront with a tray of rolls for the front case. "I just have a lot on my mind!"

All of it came to a screeching halt and collided with the glass of my shop's front door, crashing and shattering into many points of glittering light. I cried out in surprise and no little panic as I ducked down behind the counter. A person all in black with a black ski mask covering their face, a black bandana tied over the lower half of their face, and big black wraparound sunglasses over their eyes stepped through the door. Whoever it was, had on bulky black gloves and so busy was I with trying to get a physical description of them having *just* been through a trial where the importance of *that very thing* had been drilled incessantly – I missed the big square bottle in their hand at first. The big square bottle with the rag stuffed in it. The rag that was ablaze with orange hellish light.

I screamed. They shouted something – in my terror it didn't register exactly what – and they launched the bottle in my direction.

I was lucky and ducked in time behind the glass case that held all of my breads and pastries. The bottle clunked against the case but didn't shatter. Rather, it fell to the ground in front of it as the person dashed back out the front door. I grabbed the nearest fire extinguisher around the back of the counter and heard my mother and grandmother shouting from the back.

I went around and doused the flame from the improvised wick, all the while adrenaline with the sour edge of fear pounding in my temples and coursing like battery acid through my veins.

The noxious cloud from the extinguisher did what it was supposed to do, sucking the oxygen from the air, the white powder instantly drying all it came in contact with – including my nose as I accidentally breathed some of it in.

Oh, no!

"Gramma, get back! Don't breathe!" But it was too late. My grandmother, who was severely asthmatic, already had her hand to her chest and was struggling.

15

"Mom, get her back!" I cried and jumped as another bottle, a smaller one, thank God, crashed against the tile floor of the bakery front. I jumped and turned to let loose in its direction, but this one *had* shattered on impact and flames were spreading and leaping.

Just when I nearly had it under control, a brick crashed through the display window and another bigger bottle followed. It also broke and the flames leaped.

"Teresia!" my mother screamed from the back and I had to abandon my efforts, the flames leaping and growing, the hellfire all consuming.

"Emergency exit, through the kitchen! Out the back!" I cried, covering my nose and mouth as the acrid smoke began to rise with the bitter tang of burning plastic and likely a ton of carcinogens from the old building beginning to fill the air.

I ducked back into the kitchen and pulled the fire alarm along the way. It started clamoring, drowning out the angry incessant roar from the hungry flames, which were building, building, building, rising higher and higher, chewing up the wall to taste the ceiling. The stupid sprinklers weren't coming on!

"Teresia!" my mother screamed again, and I turned from the horror blocking our way out the front and ran into the back, the smoke pouring after me and giving chase. My grandmother was next to the back door to the kitchen, leaning heavily on the stainless-steel table. My mother tossed her phone aside and using both hands on the handle of the metal door that exited onto the back alleyway, wailing in frustration.

I went to her, confused, and wrapped my hands around the door handle and jerked. There was a heavy rattle of chain against the other side and an ineffective clunk.

Oh, my God... they chained the door. We're going to burn to death – suffocate! What the fuck?

"Mom!" my mother cried, and she grabbed for my grandmother, who was struggling to breathe and slipping to the floor. I heard a distant squawking, and I picked up my mother's forgotten phone and started pouring out the story – the description – anything to the recording I knew was on the other line, talking over the man's voice on the other end.

"No, you listen!" I snarled into the line. "We're going to die and I want you to catch the bastard!"

I could hear the distant wail of sirens over the rush of blood in my ears, but my grandmother was already unconscious. The tears poured down my mother's face, and I was helpless in the moment to do anything... anything at all, except speak.

My voice would not be drowned out! I would be heard! If it was the last thing I ever got to do.

4

*D*riller...

I closed the door behind me, my captain on the phone.

"Uh-huh," he said, and distractedly opened up one of his desk drawers. I held my breath as my badge and service weapon appeared in his beefy hand, over the lip of his desk's top. He faltered, grabbing for the phone cradled between his ample chin and his big-ass shoulder. He tilted his head up and scowled a bit and said, "Ain't that some shit?"

He reached out with my gun and my badge and set it on the edge of his desk, closer to me. It took everything in me not to snatch it up and hug it, for fuck's sake. I picked them up and set about clipping both to my belt in their respective locations.

"Yeah, alright. Yeah." His watery blue eyes flicked up to mine and his expression turned a bit grim. "I got just the man for the job," he said. "He just walked into my office."

I raised an eyebrow quizzically.

"Yeah, alright. Mm-hm." He hung up the phone without so much as a goodbye and fixed me with a plaintive look.

"Welcome back, Stahl."

"Thank you, sir," I said and cleared my throat some, a little uneasily.

"Sit down," he said.

I took a seat. He sighed.

"A lot of pressure from the mayor's office to have you quit or resign – barring that, they want me to find a reason to fire your ass."

I went still and sighed, leaning back in my seat heavily. I mean, it hadn't exactly been unexpected. Still, it was disappointing.

"What'd you tell them?" I asked.

He chuckled, and it held a darkling sort of mirth, something truly evil as fuck. I felt my eyebrows make for my hairline.

"Told 'em they didn't get to tell me what to do with my division and that their grandmother could suck eggs," he said.

At that, my eyebrows met my hairline, and I felt my lips twitch into a smile.

"Did you now?" I asked, and he gave a curt nod, leaning back in his own seat.

"Damn straight. This is my domain. I get enough shit from my HOA tellin' me what to do with my own shit – they can fuck off. How do you kids nowadays say it?" he asked.

"Uh, they can fuck all the way off?" I asked.

He laughed. "Yeah, that's it."

My captain honestly should have retired something like a fuckin' decade ago. He was as old-school as they came and was in his seventies, but like most Boomers, he just didn't know when to quit. To hear him say it, he wouldn't know what to fuckin' do with himself if he *did* retire. His wife was gone, and so he didn't exactly have any pressure to quit. He said he didn't feel like rattling around their house all alone and that he preferred to die with his boots on like some old cowboy. I mean, he was originally from Texas. Moved out this way because of his wife, who wanted to be near their son and their subsequent grandkids.

Personally, I was grateful to have him as my captain. He was probably the only reason I still had a job right now.

He sighed and his expression shifted as he stared off into space, the wheels in his head turning.

"It's a real shitshow out there because of this whole thing," he said. "At the very least, I figure it'd be best if we kept you on a low profile, if you know what I mean..." he trailed off and looked at me expectantly, taking my temp on the subject.

"As much as I hate the idea of it, I'm afraid it's probably what's best," I agreed. "What are you thinking?" I asked. "Desk duty?"

He huffed a bit of a chuckle and said, "I *was*, but the call that came in might just be what the doctor ordered for you, son."

"How's that?" I asked, equal parts suspicious and curious.

He took a deep breath in through his nose and let it out through his mouth.

"There's been a series of attacks on several of the jurors from your trial."

I stilled in my seat, the hair raising on the back of my neck.

"What kind of attacks?" I asked.

"Bad ones," he said. "Enough that protective custody is definitely called for at this point."

"Okay," I drawled out slowly.

"It's scut work to an extent," he said with a sigh. "But it's something that's still field work and not desk work, and I definitely don't want you on the front lines in riot gear out there. They figure out it's you and you're probably as good as dead at this point. People are angry..." he trailed off. "Real angry."

"I can't say as I blame them," I said honestly with a one-shouldered shrug.

He nodded slowly. "We've certainly been painting folks into a corner for centuries," he agreed, and I didn't say anything. While it was true to an extent, I knew what he was saying didn't apply to *us* personally. Neither of us were cut from that particular racist-ass cloth. Still, we were only a couple of dudes, cogs in the oppressive machine whose foundation was built on oppression. It was nuts. It needed changed, but I didn't know how to affect any of that change on a bigger or broader level; on the *national* level, let alone just the ICPD's city wide plane.

I felt gridlocked and powerless, but there were certain things I still had the power to do. I could still protect and serve. I could still do some good, and I would continue to put whatever good I could out into my city and into the world until the day that I fuckin' died.

"Guess if you wanted to say thank you, now's your opportunity," the captain said as he leaned forward in his seat. He scribbled down some info for me onto a bigger than average, lined sticky note, and tore off the page from the pad.

He handed it across to me and I took it, reading the name, *Teresia Ehrling, Trinity General Emergency Department – being held for smoke inhalation and emotional distress, accompanied by her mother and her grandmother...* just what the fuck had happened?

"Captain?" I asked, and he raised an eyebrow and cocked his head.

"Detective?" he drawled.

"Just what the fuck happened to these women?" I asked.

"Guess you better get your ass to Trinity Gen and find out," he said. "Time's a wastin'."

I stood up, and he said, "Welcome back, Detective... dismissed."

"Thank you, Captain. Off I fuck." He chuckled, and I got the hell out of there, taking a car from the motor pool, just about every Tom, Dick, and Harry from the department congratulating me and welcoming me back as I passed and made my way through the place.

I had mixed feelings about that. I didn't feel like *congratulations* were in order. I mean, yeah, I was grateful I wasn't going to prison, but that didn't negate the fact that a boy was dead and I'd been the one to kill him. It also didn't negate the nagging worry in the back of my mind that if it came down to it again that I would hesitate to pull my weapon and fire.

I mean, it was one thing if I was going to be the only person shot dead in that scenario – Hell, maybe I even deserved it. I couldn't guarantee that would be the case, though. I mean, what if my hesitation got another motherfucker killed?

Shit...

I had a lot of thoughts on my way to Trinity General Hospital, on the edge of downtown, and chief among them was *maybe desk duty would have been better...*

I had a funny feeling in my chest, like a pressure or a weight as I drove through downtown traffic and found a spot in the garage across the street from the hospital. It took me a while to get there. Streets were closed from protests and marches. Tensions were high as I passed by mobile command units and a few pockets of officers in riot gear, their helmets off, hair sticking to their heads and soaked with sweat as their partners emptied bottles of water over them in an effort to cool them down. This summer heat was no fucking joke to have the riot gear piled on.

I kept turning the name on the note over in my mind. *Teresia Ehrling, Teresia Ehrling...* I didn't know which one she was. There had been five women on the jury and all in varying ages and height/weight descriptions, but the one that'd captured my attention the most had been the blonde foreperson.

She'd had wide blue eyes and a steely resolve. Her face had given nothing away during the entire trial. I had to admit, her strength had radiated from her and it'd been attractive.

Trust me, I knew there was no way I should have been thinking that way – especially at a time like that – but it wasn't like it was the forward most thought in my mind the *entire* trial. No, it hadn't been the totality of my focus, far from it, but it'd been there in small part.

I half wondered if I would encounter Pasquale, but I doubted it. He was rarely in the emergency department and would be occupying one of the floors – typically ICU or one of the general admission floors when he was rotated out of ICU. I guess they rotated nurses like they did homicide and undercover officers and detectives. You could honestly only handle so much.

Shit, I'd never in a million years thought I would catch a bullet or draw down working fucking *robbery*.

I sighed and waited for the crosswalk light to cross from the garage to the emergency department's entrance.

I wondered like hell what to expect out of Teresia Ehrling when I got to her. I definitely wasn't expecting gratitude for my presence. I don't think the captain thought this entirely through all the way.

I mean, she wouldn't be here if the jury had convicted me.

Or maybe she might.

You never could tell when it came to these white supremacist yahoos out there. If I'd been convicted, they could and would have likely stepped in; the fuckin' jack wagons.

Y'know, I didn't have the full story on just what the fuck was going on yet, but that uneasy feeling of shit just being *wrong* or *out of place* kept intensifying with every step I took in Ms. Erhling's direction.

"Help you?" a harried front desk person asked, as a clearly mentally ill and homeless guy raised a ruckus, surrounded by hospital security in the waiting room.

"Yeah, I'm Detective Sam Stahl with the ICPD here for Teresia Ehrling. Can you point me in her direction?" I half-shouted over the man's ranting, flashing my badge.

The woman at the front desk craned her neck back to peer up at me.

"You're taller than what I thought you would be, from on TV," she said, and her mouth thinned down in a definite set of disapproval.

"Yes, ma'am," I said neutrally and politely.

She clacked away on her computer terminal's keys and rolled her eyes up to me, catching me looking. She immediately glanced back down.

She was a pretty young thing, thick and with a crown of glorious soft curls held back from her face by a navy-blue headband. Her rich, mixed-race, golden-brown skin holding a smattering of darker freckles across her nose and high cheekbones.

"Here." She snatched a printed visitor's badge sticker off of the thermal printer that spit it out. I took it and peeled it off, sticking it to the chest of my dark blue polo. I wasn't exactly happy in it, but it beat the full-on monkey suit I'd been trapped in for court.

"Through there. The nurses will direct you," she said, and she pointed at a pair of doors to the back. "I'll buzz you through."

"Thanks," I said with a nod, and booted feet thudding against the high shine of the linoleum, I went the way she'd indicated. The door's locking mechanism made a mechanical *ka-thock!* And they smoothly swung open for me.

"Hey!" one of the security guards shouted from behind me and the homeless nutcase came barreling full tilt in my direction. I caught him, swinging him wide in an arc and fetched him up face first against the wall before he could cross the threshold into the treatment area of the ER.

"Thanks," one of the guards muttered in consternation, taking over.

"No problem," I said as that same guard insisted the man had to wait his turn. The man wailed about some gibberish or other.

I sighed and went through and waited until the doors swung shut behind me.

"Help you?" a nurse asked.

"Yeah, I'm here for Teresia Ehrling. She's being treated for some smoke inhalation?"

"Bay three. She's alright – her mother is a little rougher and her grandmother? Well, all three of them are pretty lucky to be alive."

"You know what happened?" I asked.

The woman raised a red eyebrow and asked, "Don't you?"

I gave her a flat unimpressed look, and my patience getting a little tested, asked, "If I did, would I be asking you?"

A light lit up outside one of the walled-off bays and she gave me a shit-eating, dirty little grin and said saccharine sweetly, "Duty calls."

"Bay three?" I called after her and she pointed in a general direction. I grunted with a sigh.

I headed that way and skimmed the numbered plaques outside each room, finally finding the one Teresia Ehrling was in.

"I want to see my grandmother," she argued with someone, and I knocked at the edge of the doorway.

"Yes," a weary male voice called out.

I whisked the curtain aside, past the sliding glass door, and lo-and-behold, it *was* the blonde from my trial.

She turned those fiery blue eyes on me and they went from heated to absolute *glacier* as soon as she registered it was me.

"What do *you* want?" she demanded, the fury evident in her voice.

"Ms. Ehrling, I'm Detective Stahl. I'm your protective detail," I said steadily and noncommittally.

"You're my what?" she asked, rearing back a bit and blinking slowly.

I sighed inwardly and hoped she wasn't stupid. I could already tell I was at a disadvantage here.

Fuck. My. Life.

5

*T*eresia...

"Ms. Ehrling, I'm Detective Stahl. I'm your protective detail," he said, and he sounded... bored.

"You're my what?" I asked, as it took a moment or three to register just exactly what that meant. But to be fair, I'd just been through *a lot*.

"I said I'm your protective detail," he echoed. "And while I'm at it, I might as well get your statement if someone hasn't done it already."

"I'm sorry?" I stammered, the enormity of what he was saying crashing into me.

"Your statement," he said, pulling out a notepad and a pen from the back pocket of his jeans.

"You don't know what happened to me?" I asked, stalling for a little time to get my scrambled brains around things.

"I have other patients," the doctor, who had been arguing with me that I needed to stay put, said. He buried his hands deep into the pockets of his white coat and looked from me to Detective Stahl, to me, and back to Stahl before taking a step back from my bedside, going around Stahl and batting the curtain aside to go out onto the rest of the floor to do whatever.

That left Stahl and me to just stare at each other.

"There wasn't time to get the full story from my captain. It was kind of imperative that I just get here. I was informed they were treating you for smoke inhalation and that was about it." He put a hand down on a stool and wheeled it up to the side of the bed and took a seat. "The city is in chaos. Shit's gone crazy out there. The force is a little disorganized as a result. Some apologies for that – now, has anybody taken your statement?" he asked.

"No," I said, and I felt as though I spoke into a vacuum. Like the word should somehow echo in the ringing silence that hung between us.

He clicked the button on the back of his pen and let the nib hover over the page in his black leather-wrapped notepad.

"What can you tell me?" he asked. "Take it from the top."

"This is all your fault," I whispered, horrified, and I could swear something flashed in his eyes.

"What happened, Ms. Ehrling?" he asked me, and his tone was... I don't know... cold somehow.

"I want somebody else," I said, and he shook his head.

"We don't get to choose," he said. "Like it or not, it's me or nothing and nothing isn't an option given that you're here right now," he said, glancing around the hospital bay. "You don't have to like it, but I'm your huckleberry."

I was angry, and he was... he was a convenient target for my helpless rage at the situation. I sniffed, eyes brimming with tears I was just so overwhelmed with emotion, chief among them fear and anger but as much as I wanted to scream at Detective Sam Stahl to get out, get out, *get out!*

28

I couldn't.

"Uh, we were finishing up the day's baking. I went up front to..." my voice shook and I sniffed. "I went up front to fill the case with some stuff from the back."

"Okay, then what happened?" he asked, scribbling in his notebook.

"The glass on of the door of my bakery shattered and a person – I couldn't tell you if it was a man or a woman – came through with a big bottle, rag sticking out and on fire. They threw it at me."

"Shit." He looked up at me. "You, okay?"

I stared back at him. I mean, did he really just ask me that? Sitting in the hospital, my gran... my mom...? Fresh anger welled up, and I bit the inside of my cheek.

"Do I *look* okay?" I demanded, the rest of the story pouring out of me in a biting, angry tirade. He stared at me the entire time as I railed at him and finally, growing angrier by his stoicism, I snapped, "...and it's all your damn fault!"

He cocked his head and didn't say anything despite the flinching around his eyes at the jab.

"You're upset. Emotional – and with good reason!" His voice rose, cutting off my protest. "I get why, believe me, and no matter what you think about me – I'm here to do my job and to help, Ms. Ehrling. So, after you put out the undetonated Molotov, what happened next?"

Undetonated Molotov... I shuddered at the thought. I hadn't really looked at it with that particular perspective. You know? I mean, I'd literally just survived an attempt at burning me to death, by people throwing *Molotov cocktails* at me through my business windows, all because I legally couldn't convict the man sitting in front of me.

"I think I'm going to be sick," I uttered as the sweat prickled my forehead and that funny metallic taste flooded my mouth – the precursor and first warning sign that my stomach was about to rebel.

He snatched an emesis bag from the holder on the wall; you know the ones, blue with a blue plastic ring to hold it open, and I threw up into it. He calmly pressed the button on the side of my gurney to call a nurse and tried to comfort me, putting a hand on the back of my shoulder. I jerked it forward out of his grasp violently as I heaved again into the bag.

There wasn't much to come up, and I absolutely *hated* how my eyes watered.

I didn't want him to think I was crying.

"Just take it easy," he said. "Take your time."

I rolled my eyes, unsure that he could see them as my stomach clenched again.

The nurse came, and she called for the doctor and tried to soothe me and clean me up where I missed, kicking the detective out of the bay and kindly telling me that enough was enough. She was going to see about the doctor giving me something to calm my nerves.

They put it through my IV that they'd given me fluids to ward off shock when I'd arrived. I'd been wholly resistant to taking anything mind altering up to this point, but I had to admit defeat. I absolutely abhorred throwing up. It was the actual *worst*, and I didn't want to do it again.

I was given a fresh gown, the nurse spotting me as I changed into it, and the blankets were whisked away and fresh ones brought from the warmer.

I was calmer, the Ativan or whatever they'd pushed through the IV taking effect and smoothing things out. I would have been unhappy about it but good ol' benzodiazepines, they were a great chemical lobotomy when the occasion called for it.

I tried not to think about my father or my brother right now. I didn't need my misery compounded any more than it was by the family crazy.

They let Detective Stahl back in and he retook his seat, asking, "Better?"

I managed a scowl at him and he gave a nod.

"We can continue this later," he said, closing his notebook, and I laid my head back and closed my eyes.

"Everything you could possibly want or need to know about it is probably on your 9-1-1 recording anyway. Go check with your dispatch or whatever," I said coldly. I got the sense by the rustling sound of his clothing that he leaned back some or nodded.

"I'll do that," he said. Then he said at the soft tread of the nurse's sneaker on the linoleum, "About when do you think she'll be getting out of here?"

"Not until I see my mother and my grandmother," I said as sternly as I could manage.

"Where are they?" he asked, before the nurse had a chance to speak.

She sighed out and said, "They're being admitted, fourth floor. They'll be sharing a room. Just overnight for observation."

"She being admitted too?" he asked.

"I don't know. I'll check with the doctor." I opened my eyes to the nurse fiddling with buttons on the IV stand.

"I won't be admitted," I said. "I'm going home."

"We'll see what the doctor says," she said kindly, and I raised an eyebrow.

"Doesn't matter what he says," I said. "I'm not a danger to myself or others and you have no reason to put me on a seventy-two-hour hold. There's nothing physically wrong with me, and I want to go *home*."

"Okay." The nurse gave a nod. "I'll let him know."

"Thank you," I said.

She left, and it was just me and the detective after that.

A long silence stretched between us before he finally asked, "Somebody in your family a frequent flier? A spouse maybe?"

"None of your business," I muttered.

"Got myself detective of the year with that guess, huh?" he asked and I turned away from his smile. "Okay, fine. None of my business. I've got it."

"Do you?" I demanded. I don't think he did. It wasn't like any of this was affecting him. He'd gotten off scot-free. I was the one living the dire consequences, damnit.

"Shouldn't you find out who burned down my bakery?" I demanded tiredly a little while later, not enjoying how my head felt muzzy and how it'd been entirely stuffed with cotton.

It was hard to really think through the haze of drugs, and even harder to feel.

"I told you, I'm your protection detail. I'll pass what info I've gathered from you to the detective assigned to your case for the arson and assault – not sure who's caught it, yet."

"Wonderful, just splendid," I muttered with a heavy edge of sarcasm.

"It'll get figured out," he said, and he sounded so sure of himself. I wondered vaguely if he was so sure he would get off when I'd been sitting in the jury box. I didn't remember him being so confident then.

Maybe the civil rights groups had it right. With every cop let off for shooting a man, it sent the message that they themselves were bulletproof, so to speak.

My doubts on whether I had done the right thing were seriously beginning to haunt me, especially the more I worried about my damn grandmother since no one would tell me anything.

6

*D*riller...

She slept for a while. She lucked out in that the emergency department, for the time being, wasn't batshit fucking crazy like it usually was. They let her rest for a bit, and I sat by, staring at her soot-stained face, breathing in the sterile hospital smell with the faint undercurrent of char emanating from the open bag of her belongings under the gurney.

She'd been through it, and while it was a reason for her biting remarks in my direction, I didn't think it was an excuse. I couldn't say I particularly liked the woman right now, but I didn't get to pick the vic. That wasn't how police work worked. I texted back and forth with Narcos. He thought she was kind of a bitch too, and that the goodwill she'd had upon my entry to the hospital bay for refusing to convict my ass was close to used up.

Thank God for Double Jeopardy, I thought to myself… but I also couldn't help but feel vaguely guilty.

I mean, she didn't ask for this. She'd simply been called in to do her civic duty and had drawn the short straw of having to be a juror on my trial of all the trials to be on.

I shot a text to Youngblood and asked if it would be appropriate or not for Chrissy to reach out at some point. I laid out the circumstances to the best of my ability, all the while trying to figure out why I cared.

I'd done some more texting to the club's group text, letting them know I was back in the field and on assignment already, protecting one of my jurors, while she was out. Backdraft had hit me up almost immediately in a window separate from everyone else. He'd been on the scene and got to fill in some of the missing pieces for me. Namely, the one about how someone had chained the emergency exits shut with some heavy-ass galvanized steel chains. I'd called him then, and he'd told me about how he'd been the one to cut through them. He told me for as long as he lived, he wouldn't forget the sounds of the trapped women pounding on the door and screaming from the other side.

He said it was a new low, even for him, what people could fuckin' do to each other. I was right there with him on that one. I thought I'd seen and heard it all… but that? It made me vaguely sick just thinking about it. He said he'd be at the 10-13 tonight for sure, hugging Lil extra tight as he downed a few extra to try and scrub his brain clean.

I'd looked back over my shoulder through the gap in the curtain at Teresia Ehrling's unconscious form and had pretty much absolved her of most of what she'd cursed me with. I mean, I could understand being a convenient target for all of that fear, rage, and pain with no place else for it to go. She'd said she didn't even know if the person who had come in through the door, hurtling Molotov's, was even a man or a woman. She couldn't tell if they were white, black, or purple – but that kind of rage and extremism?

Shit.

I couldn't imagine how traumatized she must be, but by God, she held it together. Holy fuck was she holding it down.

When she roused, the doctor came around and performed some vital checks, let us know what room her grandma and her mom were in, and gave us carte blanche to get the fuck out of his ER to make way for whoever needed to come in next.

"I'll wait outside while you get dressed," I muttered, and she looked up at me.

"You're serious about sticking around?" she asked, kind of incredulous.

"I'm your protective detail," I reminded her. "Kind of hard to protect you if I *don't* stick around."

I went out before she could say anything else and thought it kind of sucked that the hospital couldn't provide some kind of burn cream for the psyche. Her caustic words of earlier were burning my ass up from the inside out, worse than fuckin' Taco Hell.

I had to give it to her, though. She was feisty, stubborn as hell, and ready to fight. Gotta like that. Whoever had come after her had gone hard and ended up walking away empty-handed when it came to their objective, which had *clearly* been to kill her. What a way to go, too... burned alive in her own shop, doors chained like that? Man.

She wouldn't hear of leaving the hospital until she saw her mom and her gran, which I couldn't say I blamed her on that one. The nurse wasn't about to let her walk, so to speed things along, I said I'd push her damn wheelchair and fuck trying to find some volunteer or whatever.

I shot the nurses a little salute as the elevator doors closed, and Ms. Ehrling demanded, "Can I just get up now?"

"No," I told her with a smirk behind her. "Consider it the price of getting what you want. Last thing I need is any of these nurses up my ass because you got woozy and decided to face-plant on me."

"I'm fine!" she said tartly, and I grunted non-committedly.

The doors whooshed open on the fourth floor, and I steered her around and pulled her out over the elevator threshold backward.

She tsked, but I ignored her.

She got really quiet and somber when we pulled up outside her mom and grandma's hospital room. Both the women appeared to be sleeping as she leaned way forward to look through the door. I went to push her forward into the room more but she hissed at me, "Wait! I don't want to wake them up. I just needed to see that they were okay. We can go."

"You sure?" I asked.

"Yeah, I'm sure. I can always call later," she said.

"Okay, where to?" I asked.

"I don't know," she said. "You tell me. I don't know how this whole protective custody racket goes. Are we supposed to go to a hotel or something?" She craned her neck way back to look at me. I looked down at her and wrinkled my nose at the acrid tang of burned building coming off her soot-stained clothes.

"I wasn't given a directive to take you to a hotel or anything. City is on a budget," I said. "I'm just supposed to take you home and sit outside until relief watch shows up."

"Oh," she said and sat back a little deflated. She worriedly looked back into her mom and grandmother's room.

"Do you think they'll come after them?" she asked.

"No," I said. "You were the target. I think they were just collateral damage."

She shuddered and muttered, "Bastards."

"Yup," I said with a big sigh. "I'm not supposed to make promises, but we'll get them. Somebody always fucks up somewhere."

She nodded, and looked thoughtful, her face pinched with worry even through whatever shit they'd given her to calm her down.

She was tenacious, I had to give her that.

"You sure you don't want to go in?" I asked one final time, and she shook her head.

"No, let's go. I don't want to disturb them."

"Sure they won't be more disturbed when they find out you ninja'ed right up to the door and didn't say anything?" I asked, wheeling her around.

"Oh, they'll probably be pissed, but it's not their decision," she said and I had to chuckle.

"Alright then," I said, pushing her back down the hall toward the elevators. "Away we go."

"Away we go," she murmured. "Where this hell ride stops, nobody knows."

I snorted, and we went down to the ground floor. I didn't give a fuck, I wheeled her right out and across to the garage, hitting the elevators and going right on up to the floor I'd parked on. She fussed about walking and I was half-tempted to ask, *what, ain't anyone ever take care of you?* Honestly, though, I thought I already had a sneaking suspicion on the answer to that. She had the fierce independence of someone who had only relied on herself and no one else for a while.

I stopped her a pace from my borrowed unmarked cruiser and put the brakes on the chair. She got up quick, and I snapped out an arm for her to grab onto when she swayed.

"Easy, slow down there, Lone Ranger. Let me get the door open."

"I can do it myself," she snapped, and I frowned.

"Yeah, I know, but that's not how this works so just slow your roll for me there, Turbo." I hit the button on the key fob and reached out, hauling open the passenger side door for her.

"Which is it?" she demanded. "Lone Ranger, or Turbo? Both of them are shit nicknames."

"You prefer Princess?" I asked.

"How about just Teresia?" she shot back, getting into the car. "And shouldn't I be in the back?"

"You a criminal mastermind or something else I should know about?"

"No," she said with a snort.

"Then the back is for the skells," I said and shut the door on whatever she planned to say next. I left the chair, a dick move – sure, but taking it back kind of defeated the purpose of being a protective detail if you left your asset to their own devices. You know?

"Shouldn't you put that back?" she asked, staring out her window at the chair.

"No, now buckle up. It's the law," I said, pulling my seatbelt around me.

"Maybe you should put me in the back, then," she said, her tone dripping with sarcasm as she rolled her eyes, but she reached for her belt.

"Don't tempt me," I told her, starting the car. She wouldn't look at me.

"What's your address?" I asked.

"You don't know?" She turned to look at me as I touched the screen on the GPS.

"Would I be asking if I did?"

She let out a gusty sigh. "Some detective you are," she muttered, but she gave me the address and I punched it in.

"Thank you," I said coolly, but she was starting to claw her way up my nerves like a kitten climbing my pants' leg. Sure, it was cute as shit, but goddammit, those claws still pricked.

We drove in silence and as we turned onto her street. She perked up like a meerkat, which again, would have been cute but for the trembling energy of trauma that shuddered through her entire body from the crown of her head down. The movement had taken my eyes off the road and I turned eyes forward and caught sight of what had elicited the response out of her.

Party lights. Red and white, some blue smattered in for good measure. Fire and Police. *Fuck me.*

"No, no, no," she moaned and hugged herself. "My babies!"

"Hold on, just a second," I muttered. "Let's not jump to conclusions."

I steeled myself for whatever it was, knowing it was going to be bad. I pulled up down the line of emergency vehicles and Blaze looked back at me and threw up a hand in a wave, coming toward me in his thick gear. I rolled down the window, and he leaned heavily on the edge with his gloved hands.

"What's going on?" I demanded.

"House is okay," he called past me to Teresia, for her benefit. "Neighbor called it in," he told me. "Said that a person was hanging from the tree out front and they were on fire. We got our asses out here, but it wasn't like the neighbor thought. Somebody strung up a crash test dummy, female, and put a blonde wig on it."

"Shit," I muttered.

"My babies?" she asked. She shook her head as though to clear it and said, "My cats, are they okay?"

"Looks like a brick or a rock went through your front window, ma'am. None of us had cause to go inside. I can't say about your cats."

She let out a little moan of worry and despair and her seatbelt was off in a flash. I hurried my ass up and got out the same time she did, Blaze taking a big step back.

"I don't have my keys!" she cried when we got up to her house.

"Take it easy," I said. "I'll get you in."

I put two fingers into my mouth and blew an ear-splitting whistle. Blaze looked up, and I called down, "Get me a ladder to get in this busted window!"

He waved and jogged over to the truck to get one of the ladders down off of it. He and a couple of the other guys came over and a couple of the patrol guys for Teresia's sector came over.

"That the homeowner, Detective?" one of them called out.

"Yes," Teresia answered before I could.

"Let me. I've got the gear for it," Blaze said grunting, stepping up the ladder to the big broken front window. "Gonna have to knock out some more of this glass to fit. I got your permission?" he asked.

"Yes!" Teresia called, a tinge of desperation in her voice.

He reached down and one of the other fire fighters handed up a metal bar thing and he knocked out more glass.

"Thank God, it didn't break," she said, and I knew what she meant. She figured another Molotov had gone through her front window. I didn't think so.

Blaze climbed through the big picture window and made an annoyed sound as he got over the lip.

He came to the front door and unlocked it.

She was laser focused on finding her cats, calling out to them, while I surveyed the damage.

A big-ass fuckin' rock, wrapped in paper and brown string, sat in the middle of the shattered remnants of her glass coffee table and what was left of the window glass.

"Huginn! Muninn!" she cried, and I reached out, barely snatching her arm as the patrol officers pushed in behind me and past us.

"Let them clear the place," I said, and she looked up at me starkly, her blue eyes too wide and startled. "Stay here with Blaze," I ordered and pulled my service weapon to go do my job.

"Seriously?" she demanded and gave me a flat and unfriendly look.

"Stay here," I demanded.

I went and did my job. Her house was empty, but I did see one of her cats crawl up under her bed.

"I think your cats are in your bedroom," I said, and she went, coming back out and asking, "Are you sure?"

"The one over here." I pointed at another door and she rolled her eyes.

"That's the guest room!"

"Well, whatever," I said with a shrug. "Find them, do whatever, and pack a bag. You can't stay here."

"Well then you better book a hotel that takes cats, because I'm not leaving them here!" she snapped.

I took in a slow deep breath and let it out slowly.

Blaze laughed at me.

"You got your work cut out with that one," he said.

"I already need a break," I said. "Corvallis," I said, calling to one of the beat cops standing by. "Stay with her and make sure she packs for like

41

a week or more. I'm going to go get the scoop on what's going on out there."

"Yes, sir," he said with a nod.

First stop was the living room. I photographed everything as it was and sighed before bending my knees into a squat over all the broken and shattered glass to poke at the rock with my pen.

The note tied to it read *We gon' lynch you, bitch. Just like you did to us letting that bastard off.* Most of the words were misspelled and forget punctuation. Something about it didn't sit quite right but I couldn't put my finger on why. Not yet.

I went out and found Janski, one of Blaze's firehouse mates who had a phone out and had been filming and taking pictures since arriving on the scene.

"What's your number?" he asked me. "I'll send you everything I took since getting here."

"Janski, I could kiss you," I said.

He shrugged. "Got a degree in criminal justice. Wanted to be a cop first."

"How the fuck did you end up in fire?" I demanded.

"Basics of Criminal Justice 101 class. Learned how bogged down, fucked up, and all around corrupted the system is for you guys and it only got worse the more I learned. Decided if I wanted to do some real good, I should go red, not blue. Had a better chance at it."

"I shouldn't have asked," I said sardonically, and held out my phone with its number on the screen.

He copied it into the phone he held and said absently, "Yeah, but you did."

I took a deep breath and let it out slowly.

"What made you think to do all this?" I asked as I watched them lower the smoldering mannequin to the ground, the air rife with the smell of burning rubber and plastic.

"Thought we were rolling up on a homicide scene," he said dully. "Figured if we were, you guys would need it."

"Yeah." I nodded. "I think I've exceeded my quota of fucked-up shit today," I said. "I know *she* has."

"She one of the ones from the bakery downtown?" he asked. "Old city? Where they padlocked the doors?"

"Yeah," I said.

"Somebody wants her dead," he said, blowing out a breath. "You know why?"

I felt my mouth thin down into a grim line.

"Yeah," I muttered, staring at the dummy being laid on her grass.

"Why's that?" he demanded.

"Me," I said, and he looked over at me sharply. "She let me off."

"Oh, shit," he muttered.

Yeah. Oh, shit. The guilt came crashing down, and I was lucky I wasn't pile driven to the neck in the woman's front lawn from it.

7

*T*eresia…

   I found Huginn and Muninn hiding under the bed in the smaller guest room. I sat on the floor and held onto a very scared Muninn who was like, *mom, what the fuck!?* While Huginn bonked me with his dark furry head at my elbow and arm all while purring up a storm.

"It's okay," I said, fighting back tears. "It's okay, Momma's got you."

I sniffed and one of the two uniformed officers brought me their soft-sided carrier out of the hall closet.

"Thank you," I said.

"How does this damn thing work?" he asked, setting it up on the bed and unzipping the top.

"Just click the support bars in place," I told him.

He struggled with the one that didn't always want to latch but eventually, it clicked in place.

I struggled to my feet, and Huginn made life a little easier by jumping up onto the top of the bed and then right into the carrier. He liked boxes, though. I put Muninn in with him and zipped it closed.

"Well, that was easy," I muttered and checked to make sure all the mesh flaps were zipped closed and secure.

"Go get a bag packed for you, miss," the cop said kindly.

"Thank you," I said, and he shouldered the carrier.

One of my cat's yowled, and I stopped.

"I'll have 'em by the front door, ready to go."

"Okay," I said, and I felt awful listening to their pitiful howls go down the hall.

I went to my room and stopped in front of my closet doors. They were full-length mirrors and holy God, I looked awful. Soot streaked and pale eyes wide with shock and blonde hair a bird's nest of tangles and wisps escaping my lank ponytail.

"Holy shit," I whispered at my reflection and was almost shocked that the reflection's lips moved.

Two raps fell at my doorframe and I jumped with a bit of a yelp, clapping both hands over my mouth.

"Pack a bag," Detective Stahl ordered. "Enough for a couple of weeks if you can. Where's your animal's food and their shit box?" he demanded.

"Why?" I asked, confused.

"Divide and conquer. These guys haven't got all day to hang around out there. They're sticking around just long enough for me to get you out."

"Oh, my God... do you think whoever did this is out there watching?" I asked horrified.

"Could be. Never can tell. Your neighbor, Mike, is boarding up your front window."

"Okay." I smoothed my sweating palms over my dirty jeans, trying to process. "Okay."

"Get your shit," he ordered tersely, and I nodded. "Teresia," he said just before he ducked out the door, and the use of my name made me meet his eyes. "Don't fall apart right now. There's time enough for that later. Right now, get some clothes, what's important like documents and shit, and let's get out of here for now."

I nodded carefully, and he left me in my room. I opened the closet and pulled out my big suitcase and heaved it up on the bed.

Bras, socks, underwear, tee shirts, jeans, a nicer business outfit or two in case I had to go to court before I had to come home and I paused… they were some of the same outfits I had *already* worn to court. As a juror for the proceedings against the man who was supposed to look out for me now – the man whose actions had turned my whole life upside down and inside out.

That's not fair, a tiny voice echoed in the back of my mind.

I went into my bathroom and pulled my travel toiletry bag out from under the sink. I started throwing what I could into it – a bunch of it wouldn't fit, of course, so it went haphazardly into one side of my suitcase – makeup too. I was going for speed. Hopefully nothing would explode on me and make a mess.

Shoes, um… what else?

I could hear Detective Stahl's heavy tread on my wood floors in the hall.

Shit! Almost out of time. Um. The office!

"Close that up," I ordered and pushed past him and went across the hall into my home office.

"What are you doing?" he demanded.

"Laptop and insurance paperwork for the house and the bakery," I called back. "The family recipes."

He just grunted and didn't say anything about it. I grabbed the file box's handle that held the insurance and important documents and then turned and grabbed the box that held the recipes. I made quick work of dumping the recipes in with the important documents box and crammed it full but consolidated it as best I could. Less to carry. Next, I snatched my laptop bag out from between the bookshelves and I tore the laptop down and crammed it away.

"You almost done?" he asked, wheeling my suitcase past the doorway.

"Take that," I said, holding out the file box. "And guard it with your absolute life. You lose it or leave it behind, I swear to every god there is, I will hurt you."

He looked amused, but I wasn't joking.

My whole life was in that box.

"Hurry it up," he said.

I slung my laptop bag over my shoulder and stood up from where I'd plonked down on the middle of the area rug on my floor.

He reached down, grabbed my arm, and effortlessly hauled me the rest of the way to my feet.

"Thanks," I muttered. "Let's go."

We went out into the living room just as one of the firefighters, the one who had spoken to us before anyone else, lifted my babies up off the floor.

"This is it," he said. "Your other stuff is already loaded.

"Thanks, Blaze," Stahl said, and he handed me my plastic file box. "Go," he ordered the both of us and Blaze gave a nod and went out front. I followed.

"Teresia!"

"Hi, Mike," I said glumly as I made way down the stairs of my front stoop.

"Don't worry about a thing," he said. "I'll board this up and clean up the glass with Sally when she gets home from work. We've got your house key and we'll lock up."

"Thanks. If I ever get to come home, I'll need you to let me in."

"Sure thing," he said before venturing, "What happened to you?" as he looked me over with concern.

"They burned down the bakery this morning – tried to lock me, Mom, and Gran in while they did it. We barely got out."

"Oh, my God!" His eyes went wide behind his wire-rimmed glasses and he crossed himself.

"We gotta go," Stahl declared.

"Where are you going?" Mike asked.

"Protective custody, I guess," I said unhappily.

"Okay, well… just… keep her safe," he told Stahl.

"That's my job," the detective grated.

"Hey, aren't you—" Mike asked.

"Gotta go!" Stahl gave the back of my shoulder a little shove and I nodded and moved down the steps and to the walkway to the sidewalk through my yard. There were fewer vehicles out here now.

Blaze held out his hands, Huginn and Muninn making a racket from the back seat of the car, the poor things.

I handed him what I carried, and he tucked it into the car. Stahl went around to the other street side of the car and opened the back seat, shoving the big suitcase into it.

"Trunk's full of cat shit and police shit," he declared.

"I didn't ask," I said.

He grunted, and I got into the passenger seat. Blaze closed the door behind me and called through the cracked window, "You're in good hands with Driller. Listen to what he says."

I looked up at him speculatively.

Driller?

Stahl got into the car and turned it on, calling out, "Later, Blaze!"

"Later, man!" Blaze waved as we pulled away from the curb and I stared out the window, my chest tight as my cats howled unhappily.

"Goddammit," Stahl grunted.

"They're scared," I said defensively.

"They're *loud*," he declared as he drove with one hand and manipulated the phone's screen with the other.

"Will you drive!" I demanded as he tucked the phone between his ear and his chin and shot me a dirty look.

"Yeah, Captain, it's Stahl," he said into the phone. Then unhappily said, "It's her cats."

I rolled my eyes, crossed my arms, and wondered to myself silently, *what happens now?*

8

*D*riller...

I didn't even bother with a hotel. I don't know why, but something in the back of my brain told me that one, the hassle of finding a hotel that accepted cats, and two, the hassle of getting the department to fucking pay for it, wasn't worth the effort. She could maybe afford it, but with her business destroyed and her house needing repairs, I didn't know how long that would be sustainable and the insurance companies could and would drag shit out for months.

I pointed the borrowed police cruiser with the silent woman and her howling terrified cats in the direction of home. Everleigh would be delighted with the kitties. Narcos would probably be less than pleased – but I could handle him.

Shit, I mean, if Youngblood could get away with it, why couldn't I?

I had my doubts on that, mostly because Youngblood had known and dated Chrissy before that shit had gone down, but at the same time... Holy God, this woman had just been through it today, in the span of so few hours that it was a miracle that whatever the hospital had put her on was still holding out. That or she was as tough as nails without the benefit of the shot they'd put through her IV.

I was pretty sure that was the case, but it was still hard to tell through the glassy-eyed, medicated stare she had out the windshield. Her eyes vaguely unfocused as I steered us back through the city and out the other side, across the bridge toward my place.

I thought to shoot a text ahead but didn't. I couldn't remember if Narcos was on or off today. Everleigh might be home already from her work as a beekeeper at the city gardens and conservatory. It was getting to be late enough in the afternoon, the sun dipping low enough in the sky overland that I had to put down the visor to shade my eyes.

"Where are we going?" Teresia asked, when we hit the bridge.

"Someplace safe," I said, my hands gripping the wheel and sort of squeaking against the vinyl.

"Well, that's informative," she said, rolling her eyes, her voice thick with sarcasm and derision.

"Someplace no one would ever think to look," I said, and she looked my way.

"You know, that sounds ominous and terrifying, right?"

"Sorry," I muttered. "Not used to dealing with anyone in a protective capacity that automatically hates my guts from the word go. Usually that develops later."

She looked surprised, her eyes going a little wide for a half second, her face pale and turned completely in my direction.

"I don't hate you," she protested.

"Sure got a funny way of showing it," I grated.

She huffed out a harsh sigh and turned her face out the window as we came off the bridge and I made my way over to exit.

"I don't," she insisted, and I had to ask...

"You trying to convince me, or yourself?"

She was silent for a moment and finally muttered, "Touché."

I took the second exit past the bridge, headed down the straightaway with businesses to either side, and finally hooked right into our subdivision and toward the water.

No, we didn't have a water view, but what we did have was magical all the same.

I took the sweeping curves through a neighborhood that honestly looked a lot like Teresia's and finally swept up into the driveway of our house. We'd put in the work over the last year or two and the old place had some modern flare to its front now.

Everleigh was a veritable earth witch or dryad or something and had done wonders with a flowering landscape in the front that was what she called pollinator friendly. That is a happy home for bees. She even had a hive or two out back.

She'd made friends with the neighbor and was working in their yard half the time too, with permission, of course.

Teresia looked at my home through the windshield as I cut the engine to the car and asked, "This is a safe house? On TV they're always dingy inner-city things in a miserable part of town. This is... this is really nice."

"Thanks," I grunted. "We worked hard on it."

I got out, and she stayed seated in the car, only taking her seatbelt off as I rounded the front of it to get her door.

She got out and sort of stood a little zombified as I took her cats out of the back and handed them over to her.

She shouldered the carrier, and I went to the trunk, keyed it open, and pulled the garbage bag with their empty cat box in it, and the bucket of litter out of the back. I closed the trunk lid and made my way past her and said, "Come on, I'll get the rest after I get you settled."

She followed mutely, and I keyed open my front door.

She slipped in after me and I shut the door as she looked around wide eyed.

"Going to put this back here," I said, indicating the way through the kitchen and into the mudroom that contained the washer and dryer.

She followed me, the cats' howling diminished, but not through, and I found a nook under a bench that held a bunch of shoes to put the litter pan. I pulled it out of the trash bag and set it up. She set down the carrier as Everleigh came in the back door, no doubt drawn by the ruckus of distressed cats from outside.

She blinked wide eyed at our guest as she unzipped the carrier, and one of her black cats dashed out into the small room.

"It's okay, Muninn!" Teresia cried and Everleigh practically squealed in delight and waved, her dancing green eyes fixated on the ball of fur trying to get away and hide.

Teresia said, "Hi," rather distractedly, and pulled what had to be Huginn out of the carrier and cradled the terrified thing against her chest.

"It's okay, babies," she crooned and Everleigh cast me a curious look.

"Come on, let's leave them for just a second," I said and waved Everleigh to follow me. Her expression crushed down into a frown at the look on my face and she followed me into the kitchen and then halfway into the living room past the dining space.

"What's wrong? Who is she?" she whispered for my benefit alone when she figured we were out of earshot of... our guest.

"One of the jurors on my trial," I said quietly, and she perked up with a bit of shock, recognition flashing like heat lightning through her eyes.

I tried not to shudder at the echoing sound of blue thunder that was trapped in my head from that night. The night I'd been shot. The night I returned fire on the suspect that'd stopped in that alley during the ensuing adrenaline-fueled pursuit... except he hadn't stopped. He'd kept running and that kid... *fuck*.

Everleigh's slender arms went around my waist and she hugged herself to me tightly, comforting, or at least trying. I put my hands gently to her shoulders and kneaded, but she wouldn't relent until I hugged her back.

She always seemed to just... know.

I sighed, some of the tension leaving me as I breathed in her familiar floral and herbal scent.

"What is she doing in our house?" she asked softly, but without reproach. No, that I would get plenty of out of Narcos. I was sure of it.

I gave Ev the CliffsNotes' version of events and she looked up at me stricken and horrified.

"That poor thing," she murmured, looking past me in the direction of the mud room where things had grown silent.

"I figured you'd understand. She can't afford it and she wouldn't leave the damn cats..." I trailed off as Everleigh looked up at me with dismay.

"I wouldn't either!"

I smiled down at her.

"I know, which is how we wound up here. You might have to help me with Narcos," I said, and she wrinkled her nose with an impish smile.

"Two against one is fairly good odds," she whispered, and I chuckled.

"Glad to know you're on my side with this one, baby."

She looked past me, a troubled look on her face, those green eyes of hers haunted.

"It wasn't so very long ago I was in the same position," she murmured. "I remember."

I gave her a squeeze and said, "You mind introducing yourself while I bring the rest of her stuff in?"

She rolled her eyes up to me and gave me a little frown.

"Practice makes perfect," I said with a one-shouldered shrug. While no longer as bad as she'd been with her not speaking, she still found it difficult to speak around new people. She was getting better, though, and seemed to always have an easier time of it when it was a woman.

She gave a nod in acquiescence and I let her go, taking a step back.

"This is going to be hard," she confessed, and I raised an eyebrow.

"Why?" I asked.

"She's so pretty," Everleigh said with a blush and I smiled a little bigger.

"Best of luck with that," I told her. "I couldn't agree more – but her attitude's been ugly all damn day, so it definitely helps put shit in perspective."

Everleigh sighed and glanced worriedly over her shoulder in the direction of the kitchen. "From everything you've said, she's trau-matized."

I nodded.

"I don't think we'll know for a bit what she's like. Trauma does funny things to people."

"You sound like a therapist," I teased gently.

"That's because you two decided I needed to see one." She frowned stubbornly at me.

"And?" I demanded.

She rolled her eyes beneath the fringe of bangs of her auburn hair and sighed. "And you were both right. It was probably the best thing I could have ever done."

I smiled. Once she'd felt comfortable enough with her doctor to open up, she'd really put an impressive amount of healing on. She was thriving instead of just surviving nowadays and she knew it.

"I'll leave you to it," I said, and she nodded. We parted ways for the time being. We didn't exactly have a guest room in this place – it was too small for that – so, I'd likely be camping with Narcos and Everleigh.

This was going to be interesting…

9

*T*eresia...

Detective Stahl and the woman he apparently lived with came back into the small room that Huginn and Muninn were busy exploring and trying to find a place to hide themselves while I desperately tried to comfort my scared babies.

"Everleigh," he said. "This is Teresia. Teresia this is..." he hesitated, "... one of my housemates, Everleigh."

"Hi," I murmured tiredly and tried to force an awkward smile to my face.

She gave me a bright almost caricature of a smile and an awkward wave. She was strikingly pretty, but the awkwardness of the situation didn't let me notice that much. Or maybe it was the medication. I didn't know.

"I'm about to get dinner started," she murmured. "Please take all the time you need to get comfortable."

I nodded and said, "Thank you. I'm not worried about me, though. Just these guys and my family."

She nodded and her elegant face crumpled into lines of empathy.

"I'm going to bring the rest of your stuff in and get a room ready for you. Let me know when you're ready for the grand tour," Detective Stahl said.

"Thank you, Detective," I murmured.

He gave a one-shouldered shrug and said, "Sam or Driller, and you're welcome."

"I'll just be in the kitchen right here," Everleigh murmured, and she was a quiet woman, both in voice and whispered movement, gliding on bare feet as she slipped past Driller who put a hand to her hip as she passed.

"Your girlfriend is seriously okay with my being here like this?" I asked and he gave me a crooked sort of smile that *almost* reached his eyes.

"She's not my girlfriend. She's my best friend's girlfriend," he said. "I know we have an established history of you judging the shit out of me, but if you could maybe curb that inclination where they're concerned, I would appreciate it."

He scratched his tattooed forearm with his opposite hand and I scraped my bottom lip between my teeth and said, "You can't really judge a book by its cover, can you?" I asked softly, and he barked a laugh.

"You're not *supposed* to," he said. I nodded and bit my lips together but didn't really know what to say to that – or about anything that'd gone on today, really. I was honestly just so tired again.

I turned my attention back to my cats and a little while later I heard the tread of heavy boot on the tile floor of the kitchen and the distinct sound of a couple exchanging a kiss.

"What's happenin'?" a male voice asked. "You look tense."

"We have company," Everleigh responded softly, and I heard the man with the unfamiliar voice scoff.

"Do what now?"

I had Huginn in my lap now and I was massaging the back of his neck. Muninn was scuttling back from the kitchen doorway that he was *just* about to venture through, slinking back in my direction low to the ground and stopping to look up curiously and assess the danger before trying to duck into the carrier.

"Uh, hi..." the man looked down at me from his much greater standing height. "Who are you, now?"

"Narcos," I heard Detective Stahl call and the man looming in the doorway jerked around. Detective Stahl appeared behind him and clapped a hand to the other man's shoulder.

"Teresia, this is my other housemate, Narcos. Narcos, this is Teresia Ehrling. She was on my jury. Some shit's got real, and she's here with us until it gets sorted out. Sorry for the CliffsNotes version but I'll get you up to speed a little later."

Narcos grunted and looked unhappy.

"And who're the furballs?" he demanded.

"Huginn and Muninn, they're my boys. I couldn't leave them," I said and raised my chin a little brazenly.

"I hate cats," Narcos declared.

I said, "Funny, any time I hear that, I have to wonder – most people that don't like cats don't really *not* like them. They don't like the fact that they can't be *controlled*."

Detective Stahl laughed and clapped the other man on the back of the shoulder and said, "Bro, I think she's got you pegged!"

Narcos just scowled and almost growled.

"Cats are assholes," he muttered. "Little fuckers better not piss anywhere they aren't supposed to."

"If they do, it's only because they're scared. They shouldn't, honestly. They just need time to adjust and to mellow out. The poor things didn't ask for any of this and cats are creatures of habit. They don't like change and this was both a wild and abrupt one."

"Come on, Ms. Ehrling, you can't stay in the laundry room forever. Just shut your bedroom door if you don't want 'em in there," he told Narcos offhandedly as I struggled to my feet and set my cat down, running fingers down his glossy black back. Both Huginn and Muninn were raven black and hence why I'd named them after Odin's ravens. Both my boys were rescues, and both had come from the same shelter at the same time, though they were from different litters.

It'd been a hard time eting them, because when they'd shown up in the shelter it had been in October. The shelters didn't always like to let go of black cats in the month of October. The only reason they'd let them go to me was that I'd had a friend who worked for the shelter who had vouched for me.

She and I were no longer friends due to a falling out. A falling out that'd been rather painful to me. I think I'd gone through enough pain today so I closed the vault door in my mind on that one.

I struggled to my feet and Detective Stahl said, "Come on, I'll give you that tour and a chance to clean up before dinner."

I nodded carefully and tried a polite, "It was nice to meet you," and a "Thank you for letting me and my boys stay for tonight," on Narcos.

Narcos was tall, and fearsome looking with his long hair and rough beard. He harrumphed and said, "We'll just see how it goes, huh?"

I nodded and squeezed past him into the kitchen. He was intimidating and didn't really move out of the doorway except to turn sideways to give me a *little* more room to get by.

Detective Stahl gave Narcos a hard look, and a raised eyebrow. Narcos just looked down at my two boys and made a noise of derision at them as I was led out of the kitchen past an apologetically smiling Everleigh.

"Bathroom is here for you," Detective Stahl said, flipping on the light in the first door of the home's hallway. "You're going to be in here," he said, pushing open the door to a room almost directly across from it.

"That one down there," he said, pointing to a closed door, "is where I'll be if you need anything in the middle of the night. If you can't find me down here, you can probably find me up there," he said, pointing at a super tight spiral staircase leading up into the ceiling at the end of the hall.

"Just do us a favor. If you're looking for us up top, make sure to really announce you're coming. Sometimes we have sensitive case file shit up there that no civvy is really meant to see."

"Civvy?" I asked absently.

"Civilian," he said. "That would be you."

"I don't know about that, anymore," I said. "I mean, I don't feel exactly normal after today. I don't know what I've been indoctrinated into but whatever it is, it's a club I'd rather not be a part of."

"Yeah, well, sorry to say, you're in the 'victims of violent crime' club, which reminds me. There's a fund for that, part of the city budget. I'll get you the paperwork to maybe get a grant. Your insurance might not cover everything but this might help fill the gaps, you know?"

I stared up at him as he opened up another door in the hallway, a slim one. He reached inside a hall closet and pulled a couple of towels off the shelf. His voice gentling as he said, "None of that is anything you should think about now, though. You should take a minute for yourself and get yourself cleaned up before dinner."

"I don't understand why you're being so nice to me," I blurted out as he pushed the towels into my arms. "I haven't exactly been... charitable, all day."

"You've been through a lot," he said, swallowing hard. "I maybe know a bit about that."

He turned around and walked away, rather abruptly, actually. All I could do was stare after him for a moment.

I may be the asshole here, I thought to myself and I closed my eyes and swallowed hard.

I drifted across the hallway and found a neatly made bed that looked like it might be a queen. The bedroom furniture was black, boxy, and very modern. The head and footboards a black boxy steel with a satiny finish. The nightstands and dresser across and at the foot of the bed sleek and minimalist in a way that made my Swedish heart happy. I don't think any of it was IKEA furniture; it was too high end and well made for that, but it was definitely styled nicely. The room's walls were a cool blue gray, the sheets a steel gray and the comforter a straight black.

The nightstands held a lamp each. The one closest to the door had an added coaster and a glass of water on it.

The dresser had a television mounted above it, and my suitcase was open on one of those racks you found in hotels. I didn't think I knew anyone that had one of those in their house, let alone in their guest room. I turned and took in the photos on the wall by the bedroom door and drifted over to them.

Various photos of Detective Stahl at the academy, his graduation, and older photographs of men that *had* to be related. His father maybe? His grandfather? I couldn't be sure.

I went over to my suitcase which was open-faced on the rack in front of the closet door and I sighed, running light fingertips over the mishmash of hastily thrown in items. I set the towels on the corner of the dresser top and opened one of the dresser drawers. I had thought to put some of my things away. I mean, I was likely going to stay awhile, but I froze at the sight in the open drawer, finding it loaded with neatly folded tee shirts.

I blinked, long and slow and silently slid it shut as a fission of emotion tightened everything in my chest and I swallowed hard.

Nobody had clothes stored in a guest room dresser... did they?

Was I in his room?

I bit my lips together, breathed in slow through my nose and let it out through my mouth.

I pushed the swirling miasma of thoughts out of my head and gathered some things to wear – a pair of panties, a clean bra, and a set of leggings. I found an off-the-shoulder tee with a red heart on the front and gripped it between shaking hands.

My mother had bought it for me when we'd been shopping at this chic little half-vintage, half-funky finds boutique in the old city.

I swallowed hard and took the pile of clothes and the set of towels across the hall and went back to retrieve my forgotten shampoo and conditioner bottles from the other half of my suitcase where they'd been buried beneath other things. They hadn't leaked, for which I guess thank goodness for small favors. I ended up ferrying the rest of my toiletries across the hall, because why not? I was going to be here a while... certainly.

I showered, lingering a little longer than I probably should have beneath the hot spray. I scrubbed my face twice with my slightly abrasive face wash and scrubbed my hair twice for good measure, amazed at how dark a gray the water from it swirled down the drain. Even the second time I washed; the soot stained the clear water the color of a light smoky quartz.

I got out and dried off, wrapping my hair up in one towel and drying myself completely with the other. I dressed quickly, and felt marginally better for it, slapping a bit of my moisturizer on my face and hands and rubbing it in. I sighed and stared at my face in the foggy mirror before I tumbled the towel off my head and combed through the snakes of my wet hair. I twisted it up and clipped it at the back, out of my face, and sighed.

I took the towels and my clothes that were probably beyond sparring with me, but I might be able to... who knew? The jeans, maybe if not my bakery tee.

"Hi." I smiled at Muninn who was the braver of my two boys and who had come to find his mamma. He was standing on the back of the couch, sniffing the air imperiously, his keen green eyes looking down the hallway where he'd undoubtedly heard me.

"You looking out for your brother or did you leave him to figure it out on his own?"

"What do you think?" Narcos asked, leaning back in his seat at the dining table which seated six but was set for four. He lifted a brown bottle of beer to his lips and took a hard swig. Detective Stahl sat at a ninety-degree angle from him and his dark eyes were wary as they roved me from head to toe.

I cleared my throat, shifting uncomfortably, and said, "They're rescues. Born within a week of each other and rescued from the same shelter. I almost didn't get them, it was October. They don't adopt black kittens or cats out in October. I got lucky."

"They're beautiful," Everleigh said with a smile, coming over to the table with a plate and setting it between the two men. She indicated a chair next to Detective Stahl and said, "Please, sit."

"Um, I was going to ask if I could maybe try to save these and find out what you wanted me to do with the towels."

"Oh, yes. Of course." Everleigh gestured to the laundry room. "Help yourself, and just put the towels on top of the washer for now. I'll do a load later."

"Thank you," I murmured, and with cheeks flaming with the intense scrutiny I was under from both men, I went through the kitchen and into the mud room/laundry room. Huginn was still in there, atop the dryer now, though.

"It's okay, boy," I murmured and petted the top of his little fuzzy head.

"Use whatever you need." Everleigh smiled from the doorway and I nodded.

"Whatever I do, it can't hurt," I said.

She smiled and with a sigh said, "No. You survived the day. Nothing can hurt you now."

I wondered about that. I mean, I didn't even know where to begin to unpack any of this.

"Beer?" she asked me.

I laughed a bit nervously and said, "Uh, yeah. Pretty sure what they gave me for anxiety at the hospital has worn off by now."

She nodded. "Always wears off too fast."

I got the clothes going, and she held out a bottle to me. "Thanks," I said and took it, taking a healthy swallow.

"You're welcome. Dinner will be out of the oven in just a few. Why don't you come sit with the boys."

"The boys?" I asked, quirking an eyebrow. She smiled and raised one of hers.

"Big scary packaging, but you don't know them like I do yet. When things aren't so heavy? They're just big kids at heart. So yeah, the boys."

Interesting.

"Thank you for being so understanding about your housemate just dragging me into your home like some hissing stray cat," I said.

"It's no problem, really."

"You aren't afraid it's going to *become* a problem?" I asked.

"No one knows you're here." I jumped at the sound of Detective Stahl's voice from behind Everleigh. I couldn't see him from here and I hadn't heard his tread through the doorway.

"He's right," Everleigh said. "No one knows you're here. I know it's been a hard day but you can try to relax, if only just a little. You're safe here."

I bit my lips together and nodded, picking up Huginn and leaving the small laundry. My cat seemed alright with me taking him from the small room and I took a seat at the table with my beer and my cat in my lap.

"You're good," Detective Stahl said with a nod and he lifted his glass of what appeared to be iced tea to his lips and took a drink.

"I should call the hospital and check on my family," I said, and he nodded.

"After dinner, I promise."

"You ain't gotta do everything all right now," Narcos said and the way he was eyeing me up was a little different now. Less hostile, I guessed.

"No, you're right... I don't."

I looked down into my lap at my cat digging claws into my knee as he raised his butt into my hands as I scratched at the base of his tail. He was purring, and that made the stricture around my heart ease just that little bit more.

I wanted to, but they were safe in the hospital and likely sleeping still... at least I hoped. I wished I could sleep through this nightmare, too.

10

*D*riller...

"What?" I asked when I stepped out of the hall and caught Narcos giving me that look from his end of the table.

"What d' you mean, 'what?'" he demanded. "Motherfucker, you know what. You got some explaining to do."

I sighed and nodded and went to the table, pulling out a chair. Everleigh brought me a beer without asking and I looked up to her and said, "Thanks."

She leaned down and pressed a kiss to my forehead in that silent soothing and supportive way that she just had. She went back into the kitchen and I breathed deep the smells of good, cooking food.

I loved it when it was her night to cook. She never disappointed.

I caught Narcos up and he grunted occasionally but didn't interrupt. The debriefing was a quick one, and he finally sat in thoughtful silence for a minute or three, taking the occasional drink of his beer and finally giving me a slow nod.

"They're going at her hard," he said judiciously.

"Way hard," I agreed.

"Any of the other jurors?" he asked.

"Fucked if I know," I said. "I haven't gotten any more down the line. I've been a little busy."

"Call in, check things out."

I nodded. "Stand by."

I picked up my phone off the table and called in, and low key got told for basically going off the grid. My captain finally asked, "She secure?"

"Yep."

"This gonna cost me man hours and overtime?"

"Some," I said.

"How much the hotel bill gonna be at the end of this?" he demanded.

"Your budget's gonna be just fine, Cap. She's secure. I'm on a twenty-four-hour clock, and ain't no place safer and nobody gonna find her."

"Not gonna give me any more than that?" he asked.

"No, I'd rather play shit close to the vest for the time being. That was a lot of fuckin' overkill today. Any of the other jurors run into problems?"

"Three," he said. "Three, and one of 'em doesn't look like they're gonna make it."

"Anyone claiming responsibility?" I asked.

He shared what he could which wasn't a whole lot via the phone. There was a grassroots city group, the Equal Justice League, which was on the up and up, organizing peaceful protests and the like and then there was a louder fringe group that liked to call themselves the Colored Guard.

Some videos were posted by the first, denouncing the acts of violence against the jurors that'd acquitted me at trial. The second group was also refuting responsibility, but they were more along the lines of "we didn't do it but we're glad it happened." At least one of their founders was pretty vocal to that effect. The weird part was that there were emails coming into the brass, claiming that the violence was "an eye for an eye" and *was* perpetrated by the Colored Guard and militant anti-fascist groups.

It was confusing, the clashes continuing downtown, and a lot of shit was just getting lost in all the noise. I hated it. Hated that the city was being ripped apart along the dividing line of not just race but poverty. It was turning into class warfare just as much as a race war out there and I couldn't blame anybody for it.

Too much shit was getting gotten away with for too long. I hated that I couldn't turn back the fuckin' clock to that night. To stop myself. To... *shit*... I don't know.

There was no going back, only forward. Once upon a time that path forward was clear but now? Now I felt like a lost babe in the fuckin' woods and I couldn't fucking *stand* it.

I quickly briefed Narcos on the update and he looked at me, shaking his head.

"Something doesn't feel right," he said. I nodded slowly.

"No, it does not," I agreed.

"You say there was a burning effigy hanging from a tree in her front yard?" Everleigh asked, coming to sit in Narcos' lap, twining her arms around his neck. He put a hand to her waist and smoothed his thumb over her hippy dress she wore.

"Yeah, and something's bugging me about that the most," I said.

"Yeah, it seems out of place," Narcos agreed.

"Like, why would a group email in responsibility after posting videos saying, 'I didn't do it, but it's cool that it happened.'"

"Disorganized?" Everleigh asked quietly.

Narcos was staring off into space and raised his eyebrows. He said, "Either the left hand doesn't know what the right is doing, or the videos and emails are clashing with the intent to confuse us."

"Think you can get a hold of some group leaders and have 'em come in for a neutral meet at the 10-13?" I asked.

"If I can't, some of our boys probably can," he said.

"Let's see if we can't make that happen. See what shakes loose."

"Copy that, I'm on board," he said.

"Thanks for not giving me a ration of shit about bringing her here," I said, and he searched my face.

"She let you off," he said.

"They all did," I agreed. "But that was a matter of law. Nothing else. Don't get it twisted."

"Yeah?"

I nodded and looked up the hall, the sound of the shower spray cutting off. I sighed, polished off my beer and got up to get a glass of iced tea and went back and took my seat.

"Hi." I turned in my seat and looked at Teresia scratching her cat who had made himself at home on the back of our couch.

"You looking out for your brother or did you leave him to figure it out on his own?" she asked him.

"What do you think?" Narcos asked, leaning back in his own seat. He took a pull off his bottle of beer.

Teresia cleared her throat, shifting uncomfortably, and said, "They're rescues. Born within a week of each other and rescued from the same shelter. I almost didn't get them, it was October. They don't adopt black kittens or cats out in October. I got lucky."

"They're beautiful," Everleigh said with a smile, coming over to the table with a snack plate with some fancy French name or some shit and set it between me and Narcos. She didn't always make them, but they were damn good when she did – full of fancy meats and cheeses with all sorts of other good shit. She indicated a chair next to me and said, "Please, sit."

"Um, I was going to ask if I could maybe try to save these and find out what you wanted me to do with the towels." Teresia held up the bundle of laundry she had under one arm.

"Oh, yes. Of course." Everleigh gestured to the laundry room. "Help yourself, and just put the towels on top of the washer for now. I'll do a load later."

"Thank you," Teresia murmured and with cheeks flaming and decidedly *not* looking at me and Narcos, she went through the kitchen and into the mud room/laundry room. Her other cat greeted her with a tentative meow from around the corner and I heard her say, "It's okay, boy."

"Use whatever you need." Everleigh smiled from the doorway before drifting back to the stove.

"Whatever I do, it can't hurt," I heard Teresia say.

Everleigh sighed and said, "No. You survived the day. Nothing can hurt you now."

I thought to myself that seemed to be all any of us had been doing for months – just getting through one day to the next.

"Beer?" she asked Teresia, who assented.

I didn't say anything, just stared at the condensation on the outside of my glass and resisted the urge to fidget in my seat.

Teresia got the clothes going, and I heard her say, "Thanks."

"You're welcome. Dinner will be out of the oven in just a few. Why don't you go sit with the boys?"

The girls fell into whispers too quiet to hear and Narcos and I smirked at each other. Didn't take world class detective work to know when we were low key being dragged by his girlfriend, but that shit was all in good fun. We loved, respected, and trusted each other, the three of us. There was no malice or heartbreak between any of us.

Still, I got up anyway and edged up behind Ev just in time to hear Teresia say, "Thank you for being so understanding about your house-mate just dragging me into your home like some hissing stray cat.".

"It's no problem, really," Everleigh was saying.

"You aren't afraid it's going to *become* a problem?" Teresia asked, concern and worry tinging her voice. My respect for her went up a notch. Then again, anyone who cared that much about her cats couldn't possibly be a bad person.

"No one knows you're here," I said and heard Teresia jump with a little noise of surprise she probably didn't even realize she'd made at the sound of my voice.

"He's right," Everleigh said, turning back to her from where she'd looked back at me. "No one knows you're here. I know it's been a hard day but you can try to relax, if only just a little. You're safe here."

Teresia didn't say anything but appeared a half second later with her other black cat in her arms.

"You're good," I told her.

"I should call the hospital and check on my family," she said, and I nodded.

"After dinner, I promise," I told her. I didn't want her getting into a long and involved conversation and her food get cold.

"You ain't gotta do everything all right now," Narcos said, backing me up. The way he was eyeing her up was a little different now. Less hostile, I guessed.

"No, you're right... I don't," she said reluctantly.

"Okay!" Everleigh called from the kitchen after a protracted silence. Narcos and I both got up at the same time and we chuckled at each other.

"After you, sir," he said, dropping back down into his seat.

"Keep an eye out," I told him with a wink.

His hazel eyes crinkled with mirth when he said, "Fuck you, I'm off the clock, and you said she was mean to you."

He gave Teresia a look, but she wasn't looking at anyone. Instead, her eyes were fixed on her cat in her lap as she stared off into space, her finger working through his short fur as he rumbled and purred in her lap, eating up the attention.

"Over her head, man," I said, and she snapped out of it.

"What? I'm sorry?" she said and Narcos declared, "You missed it."

"Knock it off you two," Everleigh chastised as I stepped into the kitchen to help her out, bringing the food to the table. She handed me the salad bowl, and I took it. She handed me a trivet to protect the tabletop and thrust her chin, donning oven mitts on both hands to bring in the stuffed shells she'd cooked up.

One of my favorites.

I gave her a crooked smile and a wink.

"You can be so antagonistic sometimes," she whispered to Narcos, and he looked up at her.

"You know how it goes," he said. She nodded and gave a furtive glance in Teresia's direction.

"Maybe a little grace is in order?" Everleigh asked.

"You know I'm an asshole," Narcos declared.

"Yeah, *my* asshole." Everleigh gave him a grin and leaned down and kissed him. I smiled at them both and settled in my seat, passing the salad to Teresia.

"Thank you," she murmured.

"You're welcome."

We ate dinner in relative silence. Narcos, Everleigh, and I chatted a little about inane things but were careful to avoid anything regarding my day because, well, obvious reasons by way of a small blonde spitfire who was looking a lot less fiery and a lot more like a smoldering ember the more the evening wore on.

As soon as the meal was finished, I got up, handled the back of Teresia's chair, and said, "Come on."

She took the cue, didn't argue, and got to her feet. I jerked my head toward the kitchen and she fell into step behind me. I took her through the mudroom and out onto the back deck overlooking the sloping backyard with Everleigh's she-shed space thing off to the left with its whirly gigs and hippy knickknacks all over it.

"Have a seat," I said, pulling out my phone and unlocking it.

Teresia sank onto one of the four deck chairs surrounding the outdoor firepit and I handed her my phone.

"Call the hospital. I'll give you some privacy. Another beer?" I asked.

"Yes, thank you," she said after hesitating.

I went back in the house and let her make her call, calling back over my shoulder, "I'll be back in a few."

I went inside and shooed Everleigh away from the sink. "You cooked, we clean," I told her as Narcos brought in the dishes from the table.

She nodded and asked, "How is she?"

"Tired, I think," I said and Ev nodded. "Hard not to be after a day like she's had."

"Get a decent read on her yet?" Narcos asked.

I shook my head.

"Nope."

He eyed me funny. "And yet you still brought her here?" he asked.

"Call it a hunch," I said.

He gave me a sort of flat look and opened the dishwasher. I flipped on the water at the sink and rinsed a plate, handing it to him. I rinsed, he loaded, we all talked, Everleigh standing nearby, leaning back against the counter with her arms crossed over her chest.

"You said she was shitty with you by text," Narcos said.

"Jury had to be unanimous in order for this to be over for him," Everleigh gently reminded him.

"It'll never really be over for me, babe," I said gently. "But that's exactly the point that stuck out for me."

Narcos nodded. "I can dig it," he said.

"Trauma makes people do funny things," Everleigh said and Narcos smiled at her with a deep love and pride.

"Also fair," he said with a nod.

"Just give it some time," Everleigh said. "We won't really know what she's like until she's had a little breathing room, you know?"

We cleaned up, changing topics to the things we could control for a time, like what we needed from the grocery store and the like – for now. It was Narcos' turn to cook tomorrow night and as soon as the dishes were through, I retrieved a beer from the fridge. With an intrepid sigh, I went back outside to see how Teresia was faring.

The answer?

Not good.

11

*T*eresia...

I sniffed, set the flat cellphone in my lap and swiped at the tears under my eyes with my middle fingers, hiccupping a bit. The call with my mom had been emotional. She and my gran were so scared for me, but both of them would be alright. They were both being discharged tomorrow.

I'd asked them to go to the Stilton House. It wasn't the actual name of the place, but it was literally a house on stilts somewhere in the Outer Banks. The place my mother, grandmother, brother, and I had vacationed many times after my father's suicide when Toby and I were just kids.

I knew they'd be safe there. I'd asked them to take a couple of weeks, to recharge and refresh while things were settled here, with whatever was going on with whoever wanted to harm me. With the insurance company. With... with all of it.

Of course, I'd cried when my mother and grandmother had cried. How could I not?

I couldn't tell you how much that I hated that I cried, though.

How much I *hated* to be weak like that.

"Yeah, okay." I looked up startled.

"Detective, sorry, you startled me."

"I already told you, Sam, or Driller, and sorry. I didn't mean to, but I'll be right back. I don't think a beer is going to cut it. Wait right there."

I blinked at him stupidly and sat still. It was growing from dim to just plain dark out here and was starting to cool off, *fast*. I could smell the bay, even if I couldn't see it. The breeze coming in from the east that brought that salty scent with it was going to leave me shuddering in my seat soon.

De – Sam came back pretty quickly and handed me a glass with a couple of fingers of what smelled like Brandy in it. It wasn't my grandmother's *Aquavit* but it would do. He unfurled a red-and-black plaid-patterned throw blanket and laid it in my lap. He took a seat in the lounge chair beside mine and picked up the beer he'd brought out from where he'd left it on the arm farthest from me. He tipped the neck to his lips and took a draught off it and I raised an eyebrow.

"Aren't you technically on duty?" I asked.

"Yeah," he said with a shrug. "You know nobody likes a rat, right?"

I took a sip of what was in my glass and it was good. Real good. High-end stuff.

I sniffed and said, "I wouldn't tell."

He scoffed and barked a bitter laugh.

"Ha! You've been busting my balls from the word go," he said. "Gonna have to forgive me for being reluctant to believe you on that."

I took in a deep slow breath, in through my nose and let it out through my mouth.

"I'm sorry," I said. "I don't handle things outside my control very well. I'm very type A."

He turned his head and searched my face, his deep brown eyes lingering on my own.

"Why d'you think that is?" he asked, and I swallowed hard.

I looked away first.

"A lot of reasons," I said. "Emotional damage."

"Wanna talk about it?" he asked.

"No," I answered him shortly.

"Fair enough," he said and took another drink from his bottle.

We sat in silence and it was... it was surprisingly comfortable. I mean, it wasn't super tense. I wouldn't say it was *friendly*, but it was certainly better than it'd been all day.

"I..." I faltered. "I think it's only fair I should tell you that I wanted to convict," I murmured.

"Eh?" He looked up and over and his expression was a curious one. "Why would you say something like that to me?" he asked.

"I mean... um... it seems only fair. I wouldn't feel right living in your house if I wasn't honest about it. Feels, I don't know... disingenuous. Rude."

"Ruder than telling me you wanted to see my ass put in prison?" he asked a little incredulously.

"Yeah," I said and nodded.

"Okay, if you don't mind my asking... *why* did you want to throw my ass in jail, and what stopped you from hanging the jury or whatever?"

"It wasn't the right thing to do. I mean, we were given explicit instructions and with the evidence presented and the testimony and, well, everything, it... things weren't beyond a reasonable doubt and I hated it. For that boy's family, for justice... I don't know. If I had voted my conscience, we wouldn't be here right now," I said, answering his second question but completely ignoring his first one.

He tilted his head way back and stared at the night darkened sky and blew out a breath. I blinked and realized maybe I'd misread him in the courtroom.

"That closes door number two," he said, and I felt my heart sink a bit. "What about door number one?"

I sipped the bourbon in my glass and swallowed hard, feigning innocence. "What's that?"

"Don't try and bullshit me now," he said flatly, and I heaved a sigh.

"You looked *bored*," I answered. "Like the proceedings were a waste of your time and beneath you," I told him. "Like... like that boy didn't matter."

He snorted. "Wow. Okay, then."

He closed his eyes and tilted his head back against the back of the wooden chair.

"That's it?" I asked quietly after several heartbeats.

"What else is there?" he asked. "You sound like you've thoroughly got your mind made up."

Ouch... why did that sting more than a little?

The wheels turned in my head for several minutes on that. *Why did it?*

Maybe because you know by now you harshly misjudged him? I thought to myself.

I mean, he'd not hesitated, nor fought me at all about my babies. He'd brought me here, to his home... which...

"Could you get fired?" I asked. "You know, for having me and my boys here?"

"Yeah," he answered. "At this point, probably."

I felt my brow wrinkle and I asked, "Then why bring me here at all?"

"Hm?" He seemed lost in thought, though as soon as he'd made the questioning noise it was as though what I'd said had caught up to him. Before I could repeat myself, he was answering.

"Seemed like you'd been through enough. I knew you probably couldn't afford an extended stay anywhere – especially not with the cats – and, truth be told, I'm not about to fuck up the first assignment I received after coming back. There ain't no place safer than with me and Narcos in the same house. Plus, it's good to be home. I've spent enough time away from it with undercover work and shit."

"There's an undercover unit with *robbery?*" I asked.

He huffed a laugh. "There's undercover work in just about every subdivision in any given department – but no, not as a general rule. Robbery is where I got rotated after mine and Narcos' stint in the narcotics division."

"Oh," I murmured.

"You're a civilian. Most of what you get about police life you get off of an episode of some Primetime procedural drama. It's okay, I get it."

"You're not wrong," I said a little derisively. "Still, you don't need to sound like such a condescending asshole about it."

"Did I?" he asked, and he looked genuinely surprised and curious.

"That's the way you just came across," I said.

"Didn't mean to," he grunted and took another healthy swill of beer out of the bottle in his big hand.

I huffed a gusty sigh.

We were silent again.

"You getting sleepy yet?" he asked gently a little while later and his voice came out of the dark so suddenly it jolted me. Or maybe I'd been starting to drift. I didn't know. All I knew was I almost spilled the last few drops of bourbon in my glass and that would have been a true crime. I downed the rest and nodded, realized he likely couldn't see it, and sat up and said, "Yeah," for his benefit.

"Okay, come on. Let's get you settled for tonight."

He got up and held a hand down to me and not thinking, I handed him up the glass. He chuckled, and I struggled a little to my feet. I was stiffening up some between the chill out here, the hard seat, and the wild fight for my life earlier in the day.

I put the throw around my shoulders and followed him to the back door.

"You need anything before bed?" he asked.

"Like what?" I asked.

"Fresh glass of water, to pee, any of that type of shit?"

"No," I said, following him into the house. "Well, maybe to pee."

He nodded and clicked out lights as we passed them on the way to the hall.

"You remember which one is the bathroom door?"

"Yeah."

"Okay, I'll see you in the morning sometime," he said.

"Okay." He headed for the door at the end of the hall, before the spiral stairs.

"Sam?" I called and hesitated.

"Yeah?" he asked.

"Thank you," I whispered.

He glanced back over his shoulder and gave a nod.

"You're welcome," he said and opened the door, the blue glow from a television flickering from inside it, casting blue highlights against his black hair. He stepped through and shut it behind him and I went in to do my business.

I was mid-stream when I realized he'd gone into the only other bedroom I'd spotted down here and I wondered…

No…

I frowned slightly to myself and finished up and as I was washing my hands. I had only one conclusion to reach…

Sam Stahl and his housemates were a little bit more than just a pair of best friends cohabitating with said best friend's girlfriend.

Yikes.

I stopped myself at the thought.

Hadn't I been judgy and *mis*judgy enough where Detective Stahl was concerned? Maybe now was the time to keep an open mind.

I went to bed, leaving the bedroom door open for Huginn and Muninn. They came in and slept with their mamma every night, and I didn't want them to be any more freaked out or thrown off their routine any more than they already had been.

I took off my bra and tossed it into the open half of my suitcase and crawled up into the too-big bed in the dark, settling beneath the crisp sheets. I closed my eyes and burrowed into the pillows and breathed in deep the spicy masculine scent I'd caught coming from Sam himself after the close proximity of the car ride with him.

I closed my eyes and one of my boys jumped up on the bed. I reached out, and he came up to sniff my fingers before bonking his head into them. I scratched behind his ears and along his delicate skull. He came up further, turning around and flopping into the curve of my midsection to purr.

My other cat would, at some point, find his way up here, too, when he was done adventuring and exploring the new place. He would settle behind my knees. It was just their way. I sniffed, grateful to have them with me. Sometimes when things were so overwhelming, I just wanted to quit. It was just their little fuzzy asses that kept me going.

I silently cried myself to sleep.

I had to let it out sometime.

Sometimes it sucked being the only strong one, being the only person that you could rely on, but it'd been that way for me for a while now. Didn't look like that was going to change any time soon.

12

*D*riller...

Everleigh got up first, wriggling her way out from between me and Narcos and disappearing out the bedroom door to the bathroom in the hall. When she came back, I reached up and groaned without looking and muttered "Coffee," making a pathetic grabby hand gesture.

Her fingers linking with mine startled me and when I opened one eye to look at her, she had a finger pressed to her lips in a classic sign for *be quiet* and was tugging on my hand.

"Whatsa matter?" Narcos demanded when I shifted the bed getting up.

"Nothing, go back to sleep," Everleigh murmured.

I frowned and immediately asked, "Teresia alright?" I got up and sat on the edge of the bed, dragging my jeans up my legs and standing, pulling them up the rest of the way. Everleigh again made the motion to be quiet, more insistently this time, and I followed her tiptoeing to the bedroom door.

That's when the smells hit me.

Mouthwatering, warm, fragrant, and... comforting. The whole house smelled of sweet baking things and I raised my eyebrows.

Everleigh looked up at me and her expression was worried.

It clicked then, that I should be paying attention. That as a woman she knew something I didn't, and I nodded, picking up what she was putting down. I touched her lightly on the shoulder and tilted my head back the way we came at the bedroom doorway, and she nodded.

She drifted down the hallway and shut herself quietly into her and Narcos' bedroom. I raked a hand back through my hair with a sigh and chewed my bottom lip from the safety of the alcove of the hallway and wondered just how to handle this.

The timer on the stove in the kitchen went off and Teresia struggled to sit up from where she'd been lying on the couch. I took a hurried step back and watched her, curious as she wearily got to her feet and shuffled into the kitchen to shut off the timer and to open the oven. She pulled out a baking sheet of these twisted knot rolls that smelled divine and set them on the stove's burners, lifting another sheet off the counter and sliding them in.

She reset the timer, her expression haggard and I went to her. She looked over at me from the mouth of the kitchen and asked, "I didn't wake any of you up, did I?"

I shook my head. "No, baby. You didn't."

She arched an eyebrow, and it took a second of confusion on my part to realize the overly familiar term of endearment had slipped out.

"Baby?" she asked me.

"Sorry," I said. "Habit."

She frowned then, fully, and asked, "You make it a habit of calling women you don't know 'baby?' That's a little problematic and sexist, don't you think?"

I leaned my butt against the counter and crossed my arms over my chest, chuckling.

"Boy, you sure do love busting my balls, don't 'cha?" I asked and her frown deepened into a scowl. "No, I don't make it a habit of calling women I barely know 'baby.' It is a bad habit of mine to call women I *like* 'baby,' though. Especially strong, spicy women like yourself. In case you hadn't noticed, I can be a bit of an asshole like my partner," I said, jerking my head slightly behind me in the direction of the hallway.

I moved past her and lifted the empty coffee carafe off the coffee maker's base.

"You did all this without the benefit of coffee?" I gave a low whistle.

"Don't change the subject," she said, her glower changing to an expression of confusion.

I flipped on the sink and started filling the empty coffee pot, but didn't say anything, waiting on her.

When she didn't say anything, I said as gently as I could make it, "Well, if you got something to say, say it."

She put her hands over her face and breathed in slowly, scrubbing it with her hands as she turned those wide blue eyes to the ceiling of my kitchen and said, "I'm sorry. I don't mean to be a bitch—"

"How long have you been up?" I asked her quietly, shutting off the tap and filling the back of the coffee maker with the water. I kept at it – filter, grounds, and shutting the lid while she mulled the question over. I flipped the top of the maker shut and hit the button to get some caffeine in my system.

"I don't know," she murmured. "A while."

"Bad dreams?" I asked, returning to leaning against the counter, arms crossed.

She looked upset for a fraction of a second and said quickly, "I don't know. I just woke up and couldn't go back to sleep. Probably because it was around the time I'm used to getting up." She paused and then shaking her head as though to clear it, repeated, "I don't know," angrier this time. Like she thought I was interrogating her or some shit.

"Okay, take it easy there, Tiger," I told her and held up my hands as if to ward her off.

She groaned slightly and put a hand to her forehead.

"Fuck," she muttered. "This is a lot." She sighed. "I'm sorry I just took over your kitchen, but I just wanted to feel better and baking always makes me feel better. Useful. You know?"

I surveyed the disaster of flour on my kitchen counters and the sink full of mixing bowls and such.

"I see you managed to find where everything is, and I don't mind so much. It smells good."

"Thanks," she murmured.

"You look tired," I said. "You think maybe you're ready to go lie back down? You ain't got nothing going on today. Nowhere you have to be, nothing you have to do—"

"I have to call the insurance company and my cell phone provider to see about getting that replaced," she rushed out. I held up my hands again and made a gentle motion as though pushing her anxiety down.

"Yes, you have things to do but you don't *have* to do them… not today. The world isn't going to implode if you don't deal with everything right-fucking-now."

She tipped her head back, shoulders dropping, and took in a slow deep breath in through her nose and out through her mouth, then another.

"How long have you been this anxious?" I asked, recognizing that it was *not* a new thing.

"I don't know what you're talking about," she snapped. "I'm fine."

"I didn't say you weren't," I said mildly, starting to figure her out a little. "You're maintaining like a champ. I get the impression that it's been a while, though. Like maybe you've been through some things long before this whole mess."

"What are you, my psychologist?" she demanded.

"No," I said, shaking my head, my patience starting to fray. "I'm just trying to help."

Her face fell, and she turned away from me, flipping on the water at the sink and leaning up hard against the edge.

I turned off the tap, and she bowed her head.

"Shit, come here," I said when she started to shake. I pulled her into me and hugged her. She shuddered for a moment, stiffened up, and pushed against me. I instantly let her go.

"No, sorry, it's fine," she rushed out. "I'll be fine."

I nodded and said, "I know you will."

She looked up at me sharply at that.

I shrugged and said, "You're a ball-busting badass. Hard for it to come out any other way."

She cracked a smile and a bit of a laugh then, and I smiled back. It finally felt like the ice between us, thick as it was, cracked; the pieces jutting up against each other as we inched, metaphorically speaking, closer together on some common fucking ground. Well, ice floes... I had a hope that we'd find ourselves on common ground, eventually.

She seemed like a woman I would like to get to know.

∼

THE ROLL THINGS she made were good. Not cinnamon rolls, like I'd thought – but some sort of Swedish cardamom knot thing that went well with coffee.

Ev and Narcos had some and our morning routine was changed up as we had our coffee and the rolls at the breakfast table together before Narcos and Ev headed off to their respective day jobs.

It was back to just me and Teresia staring across from each other at the table, listening to Narcos' bike roar off into the distance, the silence backfilled with the rhythmic noise of the dishwasher in the kitchen doing its thing.

"You look tired," I remarked, and she nodded.

"Yeah," she agreed.

"Should go lie back down, try to get some sleep," I told her.

She raised her eyebrows, and I chuckled.

"I'll get your loaf of bread out of the oven when the timer goes off," I said and she finally reluctantly nodded.

She got up and started cleaning up the dining room table and I said, "Stop," as gently as I could. She stopped. "I've got it. There's a rule around here. Whoever cooks the other two clean. Now it's the other *three*, but the rule still stands."

She nodded slowly and said, "That sounds nice, actually."

"Go lie down," I ordered, and she nodded and drifted around the table and up the hall. One of her cats jumped down off the back of the couch and trotted after her.

My dick stirred in my jeans. It was hot that a woman as in control as she was would listen to me.

Real hot.

I liked that she was strong, and feisty, and yet… and yet, I wondered at the deep hurt and the hyper self-reliance she displayed.

Teresia Ehrling was interesting to me.

I didn't think she was half as hard as she fronted, but she wasn't unkind. Honest – maybe blunt or even brutally so in some cases which could complicate things – but I didn't think she was unkind. She even left a list on the back of an empty envelope she'd fished out of the trash of what she'd used up in the kitchen.

"Huh," I muttered and set it down, adding some other things to it that I knew we were going to need.

By the time the bread came out of the oven, I'd picked up the rest of the kitchen and with the bread cooling on the wire rack she'd found somewhere, I headed down the hall for the spiral staircase leading up to the retrofitted attic space Narcos and I had converted into an office.

I paused outside my bedroom door and found Teresia fast asleep, facing the doorway, one cat tucked against her stomach over the blankets and fast asleep, the other with its chin on her knee, hidden behind her legs and blinking at me slowly with judgy yellow eyes.

I gave the cat a nod of respect and he closed his eyes and huffed out a sigh that was audible all the way by the doorway that had me suppressing a laugh. Shoulders shaking, I made for Narcos' and Everleigh's room and the clothes I'd stashed the night before.

I picked them up off the dresser and went and took a shower to finish waking up and to get on with my day. I figured I'd make a few phone calls and the like and see if I could get some folks pointed in the right direction on sniffing out who'd tried to kill the woman in my bed.

Once upstairs, and still thinking about the problem, I leaned back in my seat and sighed, thinking heavily about it. About her.

I couldn't imagine being dragged into a courthouse, being expected to perform her civic duty, performing that duty with the class and respect I'd seen out of her the whole trial, and then to turn around and have her life upended for it.

If ever there was a prime example of *wrong place, wrong time*, this certainly was it.

I felt a particular gravity, a duty to return her life back to her.

After all, even if she hadn't fully agreed with it – isn't that what she'd done for me?

Likewise, I couldn't help but feel an almost need to prove that I wasn't some kind of monster that she maybe thought I was. I mean... holy fuck, am I right?

I picked up the smiling photo of Témaël Etienne off the back corner of my desk where I was forced to look at it every day. It was a little four-by-six, nicely matted in a five-by-seven frame. The kid deserved the respect. Deserved to be remembered. I deserved to face what I'd done every fuckin' day until the day that I died – mistake or not.

It was the mark of a man to *own* his mistakes, which I did. Which I tried to do with as little fanfare as possible. I felt damned if I did and damned if I didn't in this particular case. Before if I'd spoken how sorry I was, it would have been seen as an admission of guilt – which it wasn't. It still wasn't, but to say anything now could possibly be perceived as a slap in the face to his family, to the community as a whole. I didn't want to do that, either.

I was sorry, though. I'd been shot, surging with fucking adrenaline, pissed off – yeah, but most of all? I was a pussy. Scared as shit and running off of training instead of brain cells, maybe? Fuck, I should have just stayed on the ground – but I didn't. I'd gone after the kid who'd shot me and I'd shot an innocent bystander. I would fucking have to live with that for the rest of my fucking life.

And talk about spiraling out of control?

I opened my laptop and turned it on, waiting for it to wake up so I could do some things. First off, I sent off to dispatch for the audio files of Teresia's 9-1-1 call as her bakery started going up in flames.

While I waited for that, I sent off some more emails through the department's secure servers and made a few phone calls and sent a few texts.

My email pinged somewhere in the middle of it all and when I opened it, my request for the audio of the emergency call was waiting as a file attachment.

I picked up my headphones off of my desk and put them over my ears. Steeling myself, I hit play.

I still wasn't exactly ready for the horror that poured into my ears, nor did I expect the iron core of strength the woman downstairs had when it came to the shit-fire she'd been dumped into. She bit the head off the dispatcher's head a number of times and even straight up told them to shut up and let the recording get what she was saying. She had fully expected that she and the other two women with her were going to die, and that if she did? She would be fucked if whoever was doing it was going to get away with it.

She repeated every detail her overworked brain could produce, and she was fucking marvelous at it. I wrote everything down about our suspect and sad to say – it was like the motherfucker had thought of everything. Despite her rockstar recollection and giving us everything she could, it sounded like whoever it'd been had put a lot of thought into covering their tracks should there be any survivors who could potentially ID them.

Fuck.

I was on my second, maybe third loop of going through the audio to pull out anything and everything I could, when I nearly hit the roof at the light touch on my shoulder and the brush against my leg.

"Fucking *Jesus!*" I cried and turned around to a bemused look on Teresia's face.

I looked down and one of her cats looked up at me like, *the fuck's the matter with you, human?*

"Scared the shit out of me!" I cried and swallowed hard. "What'd I say about announcing yourself?"

Her expression cooled off from its amusement pretty damn quick.

"I tried. Several times in fact. You had your headphones on." She set a small plate down on my desk with a clack.

I looked down to a sandwich with a pickle spear and a side of chips. I blinked at it stupidly for a half a second and when I looked up, she was already headed down the spiral staircase, the lower half of her body disappeared to her ribs.

"Hey," I called out, and she looked up. "Thanks. I'm sorry I snapped at you."

She gave a steady, even nod of her head and said, "Hope you don't mind, but I've sort of taken over the known world that was your dining room table."

I shook my head.

"I don't mind. Do what you gotta do."

She nodded, took another step down and then stopped and said, "If you can't hear me come up on you like that, what if...?" She didn't finish her thought out loud but the sorrow and fear in her eyes were telegraphed clearly.

Shit...

"First of all, no one knows that you're here. You're safe here. Second of all, you're right. You're absolutely right. I wasn't entirely thinking that one through. I'm sorry. I'll leave them off."

She nodded again and said, "Thanks," so softly, I felt like she tore a book out of Ev's playbook.

"It's nothing. I should have thought about it," I said. Swallowing hard, she finished her descent.

I looked down to the cat who was still sitting there staring up at me.

"What're you looking at?" I demanded.

He just blinked steady green eyes at me and I shook my head.

I looked at my pages of notes and sighed.

For as much as I'd written down, there still wasn't anything here... *damnit*.

13

*T*eresia...

The days were wearing on me. One, because I still couldn't go home and two, dealing with the insurance company was becoming a massive headache. The adjuster wanted me to set a date to come out and meet him at the bakery and I was growing frustrated, trying for the umpteenth time to explain to him that I couldn't do that. That I was in police protective custody until further notice, and no matter how professional I was trying to be, no matter how calm, cool, and collected, I was about to lose my shit when he said, "Surely that won't last forever. Why can't you just set a date?"

I opened my mouth to respond when the phone was plucked from my hand.

"This is Detective Sam Stahl of the Indigo City Police Department. Who am I speaking with?" he demanded in his most hard-edged and brook-no-argument tone.

I blinked and met his eyes, vaguely annoyed that he'd felt the need to come to my rescue when it'd just been a matter of the dipshit on the other end of the line *not fucking listening to me!*

Ugh!

"Uh-huh," he said. "Well, since apparently listening to this in a woman's voice seems to have you seriously confused on the matter, maybe my baritone could be of service here. Ms. Ehrling is in my custody. Someone is trying to actively kill her for reasons that you don't need to know. Given that someone is actively trying to murder Ms. Ehrling, she is in police protective custody. My custody. And given what I say goes and I say she's not going anywhere, right now or in the foreseeable future, you're just gonna have to think outside the box on this one, Jake from State Farm, and figure something out."

He paused as the adjuster said something on the other end of the line.

"Uh-huh, I know you told me your name... Yes... Oh, yeah no, I know it isn't Jake... Right... Yes, I know you don't work for State Farm either. See, the point that you're missing is that was sarcasm and I don't care... Mm-hm. Now you're going to put your boss on the line."

Sam winked at me and I couldn't help but smile by this point, my hand over my mouth to smother my giggles as he said, "Now, I know your line is probably recorded for quality assurance and Ms. Ehrling and myself have been nothing but polite thus far and we'll continue to be so, so I gotta say, things aren't looking too good for you. They're going to look even worse if you don't put your manager on the line something like yesterday."

Sam's tone had darkened considerably by this point and even I swallowed hard, my mouth going a little dry at the implied threat.

"Thank you, Jake."

He winked at me and we waited. Finally, he said, "Yeah, hi, I'm Detective Sam Stahl with the Indigo City Police Department. Who am I speaking with? I missed your name."

I sat back in my seat.

Sound of Blue Thunder

"Alex? Nice to speak with you Alex. I'm going to hand the phone over to your policy holder, Ms. Teresia Ehrling and see if you can't clear some of this up with her. If you need anything from me, I'll be standing by right here."

He handed me the phone, and I said, "Yeah, hi, Alex?"

"Yes?" A perfectly pleasant woman's voice sounding a little concerned came over the line.

I took a deep breath as Sam wandered off in the direction of the kitchen and began again. Something like forty-five minutes later, I was smiling again, and getting off of the phone with Alex. Things were much better and sorted out. My claim would be handed to another adjuster and I wouldn't be expected to repeat anything else.

I ended the call and blew out an explosive breath, handing Sam's phone back to him as he sat across from me at the paper-strewn tabletop.

"Thanks," I said.

He took a bite out of his apple, saying around a mouthful of the fruit, "Happy to help."

"Ugh, God, I can't wait for my new phone to get here," I said and sighed again, shaking my hands out.

"Me either," he said. "I'm always afraid when you're on mine the department is going to call or something and fuck up your call."

"First world problems, right?" I murmured, actually *disappointed* that it hadn't happened.

I wish.

I wanted to know when I could go home and start *really* putting the shattered pieces of my life back together.

"Hey, they're out there working on it," he said gently, and I turned back and looked, nodding quietly.

It was getting on toward the late morning, early afternoon. I sat back heavily in my seat and heaved a sigh. If I had to choose, the early mornings and the late afternoons and evenings were becoming my favorites in terms of time of day.

In the wee dark hours of the morning, I could bake something. It helped having that time alone, to myself, to do what I loved most. In the late afternoon and early evening, it was because Everleigh was home. She was so full of interesting things, from her beekeeping to her gardening. I enjoyed helping her.

The late nights and middays were the hardest, though.

The late nights because every time I closed my eyes... well... let's just say I didn't stay asleep for very long.

"You look like you could use a nap," he said, and I nodded wearily.

"Yeah," I agreed.

"Go on, I'm pretty sure I can hold down the fort for a few hours," he said with a wink, and I nodded. I got up and sighed, looking at the mess on the table of my laptop and my scattered documents.

"Leave it, it's fine," he said, and I nodded. Rubbing my eyes, I called out to Huginn and Muninn that I was going to bed. Both of them were curled on the couch in a kitty snuggle pile and neither of them could be bothered.

"Guess you're on your own," Sam remarked, and I agreed.

I went in to lie down. Truth was, I slept better when I knew he was awake and moving around downstairs.

I woke up sometime later to the sound of the television in the living room. When I ventured out, unable to go back to sleep for now, I found Narcos out on the couch.

"Sup sleeping beauty?" he asked.

"You're home early," I remarked mildly.

"Yeah, came to relieve Driller."

"He's not here?" I asked, surprised, then raised an eyebrow at him. Huginn was up against the burly bearded man's hip and Muninn was sprawled in his lap.

"Nah, he'll be back, though," Narcos answered, his hand buried in Huginn's fur as he absently rubbed the cat's back.

"Furry little traitors," I muttered with affection, dropping onto the other end of the curved sectional.

"Yeah," Narcos said with a gusty sigh.

"So much for not liking cats," I smirked, and he smiled, but he wasn't looking at me. He was looking at Huginn who was just eating it up, rolling on his back and rubbing the top of his fuzzy little head up and down the side of Narcos' thigh, just being a ham.

"You know, I read a cat's purr has actual fuckin' healing properties?"

"I did know that, actually," I said with a small laugh.

"Yeah, these guys ain't half bad," he declared, thumping my boy on his flank affectionately.

I sighed and said, "They're the best."

"So, what's for dinner?" he asked casually and I chuckled.

"Swedish meatballs, of course," I said and pushed to my feet.

I'd insisted on being added to the kitchen duty rotation for dinners. It seemed the least I could do. I just needed them to go out and do the shopping, which Narcos and Everleigh had done the night before for me.

I pushed to my feet and went to the dining table and began clearing up my mess. Narcos continued watching whatever space laser shoot 'em up cartoon thing he was watching while I got dinner started.

When Everleigh came home, she kissed her man then came into the kitchen and gave me an affectionate side hug while I stirred things at the stove. I laughed, and she asked, "What can I do to help?"

"Um, just set the table, I guess," I said.

"You got it," she said cheerfully.

I sighed, actually quite content. I hadn't realized how lonely living alone had gotten in the last three years and I was sort of surprised at how easy it was around these three. How they gave me my space and included me without really expecting anything from me.

It was a strange sort of little family they had, and it was unique to watch. I had questions, but I mostly kept them to myself. A few I had quietly asked of Everleigh when she and I lounged on the back deck around the firepit one evening with a glass of wine each, the men leaving us to it but still just right inside if we needed anything, Sam coming out to check on us.

I'd grown comfortable thinking of him as Sam rather than Detective Stahl the last few days, although I still didn't understand the whole nickname thing of Narcos and Driller. When I'd asked at the dinner table if they meant anything, Narcos had responded he was in narcotics, which was easy enough but when it came to Driller, all three of them had chorused, "don't ask" in perfect unison.

We'd shared a laugh over that, and Sam had said, "Seriously, you don't want to know," and I'd let it go.

When he returned, it was to the sound of a motorcycle. He came in the front door in a jacket and a colorfully patched vest with a helmet in his hand and called out, "How's it going?" as he hung up his keys by the door.

"Alright," I said.

"How was the ride?" Narcos asked as Sam hung up his helmet.

"Too short," he answered. "It's a good day for it."

"I hear that," Narcos declared with a gusty sigh.

"We should go after dinner," Everleigh suggested. "Poor Teresia needs to get out."

"Um, what?" I asked at the sound of my name.

"Not a bad idea, babe. I can dig it," Narcos declared.

"Do what now?" I asked a little wide eyed.

"Go for a ride, after dinner. I don't think that would be a bad idea. Get you out of the house for a little bit," Sam declared, hanging his jacket and the vest over it on his chair at the table.

"Um, okay," I said reluctantly. "I mean, do you think that it's safe?"

Narcos snorted. "He rides like a grandma – ain't no one safer to take your first ride with if you haven't before."

"I haven't," I said. "But I'm also not talking about that part."

"It's been a few days. I'm pretty damn sure no one knows where you are, and as far as anyone is concerned out there, you've just disappeared. Plus, if it makes you feel better, we can stay out of the city – that's no problem."

I scraped my bottom lip thoughtfully as I finished up dinner and held out my hand for the first plate on the pile waiting nearby. Everleigh handed it to me and handed a bowl of salad to Sam, jutting her chin at the table behind him.

He smiled at her and gave her a wink and did what she asked and returned for the plate that I held out, calling, "Narcos."

We got ourselves organized and settled at the table before continuing the conversation which pretty much got immediately derailed by Narcos saying, "Holy shit, that's good!" after taking his first bite.

I smiled and said, "It's my *mormor's* recipe," I said.

"That your grandma?" Sam asked astutely.

I nodded.

"Good deal. This shit's fuckin' great."

"It's sort of a comfort food for me," I murmured.

"I can see why," Everleigh said, and she smiled at me sweetly and wrinkled her nose, turning the grin adorably impish.

I chuckled and asked, "So where would we go?"

"Dessert?" Everleigh asked.

"Ooo, ice cream," Sam said.

I perked up a bit at that.

"Ice cream?"

"Yeah, the good shit out at that family dairy – what's it called?" Narcos asked. "The country one that's not too bad of a ride from here."

"Don't know the name of it, don't care. That was some bomb-ass shit and I'm in," Sam declared and I laughed a little.

"Mm, the praise is real. They use real strawberries and no artificial colors or flavorings. It's so good," Everleigh chimed in.

"Alright," I said. "I'm sold."

So that's what we did. We finished eating, and I was asked to swap my leggings for jeans, told to put on the sturdiest shoes I owned and when I came back out, Everleigh was standing by with a heavy leather jacket with embroidered roses and hummingbirds on it while she wore one embossed with skulls and roses on the sleeves.

"Oh, that's beautiful," I said of the jacket she held open for me.

"Safer than anything you got going on, which is what I care about," Sam said.

I shrugged into it and turned to smile at her.

"Looks good on you," she said.

She may have been much taller than me, but she was willowy and we wore the same size, so it seemed.

"C'mon, c'mon, c'mon. I want to goooo," Narcos said and bounced in his heavy boots, already in his own jacket with its vest.

"Ah! Safety first," Sam declared, winking at me as he led us all out the door.

I wasn't really all that intimidated by the idea of going for a ride until I saw the bike. Then it was a little more daunting but I would be damned if I would show any weakness to that effect.

He went through his safety spiel and it all seemed pretty straightforward and then it was time to go. I jumped when he fired it up. I didn't know why, or what I expected but I guess for some reason I hadn't expected it to be that *loud*.

"Loud pipes save lives!" Narcos shouted as Everleigh got onto his bike behind him. I watched what she did and emulated it, settling onto the bike behind Sam.

"Scoot up a bit," he ordered, and I did. *Yikes*, I hadn't realized just how compromising or intimate this would be! He gave my leg a squeeze as I twined my arms around his waist and took a deep breath.

"You ready?" he called back to me.

I simply nodded, the helmet feeling strange on my head, a borrowed pair of sunglasses over my eyes.

"Okay, here we go!"

He led, gliding us down the driveway and turning us smoothly onto the street, Narcos and Everleigh falling in behind us. Butterflies exploded in my stomach at the sensation of the big machine beneath me and the sensation of Sam's hard body between my thighs. I tried not to think on the latter too much.

I didn't really have the chance as we picked up speed, the pavement rushing beneath the tires as we rode out of their subdivision. Any thoughts about anything but the speed and the feel of the bike beneath me was ripped away by the rushing wind which was nothing short of cleansing for the soul. I mean, there was something completely therapeutic and *alive* about this, unlike anything I had ever experienced before. I mean, not even the few brief minutes of a roller coaster ride compared.

It was like... like the universe breathed a collective sigh of relief and my brain was like, *alright, okay, we're good now – no more need for thinking, no more need for worrying. We really* are *okay.*

I relaxed at some point, my body losing the tension borne of fear of the unknown and as soon as I did, Sam reached back, letting his hand drop from one side of the handlebars to smooth up and down my jeans-clad shin. An almost silent 'atta girl' that suffused me with – well I don't know exactly, but whatever it was, it wasn't *bad*.

We rode about a half an hour or so, and honestly the way they'd made this creamery sound, I thought we were going further, like out to the country or something. Instead, we ended up in this charming little town with one of those old-school central-touristy streets. We cruised down that street to a lot at the end and he turned us around. We cruised back up and found free parking on the street, pulling up. Following Everleigh's cue, the both of us hopped off of the bikes to step up onto the curb while the men backed the bikes against it.

"So, what you think?" Everleigh asked in her quiet way, in the vacuum of silence left behind by the bikes once they'd been shut off.

I let my stupidly wide grin do the talking for me. Everleigh was so happy because of my happy she did an excited little dance which made me laugh.

Sam came over and undid my helmet and put it with the bike. I took off the sunglasses and hung them by the arm on the front of my tee.

Everleigh hugged Narcos' arm and Sam put a gentle hand to my back and steered me lightly in the direction up the sidewalk that we needed to go.

"It's crowded," I said nervously as we moved through the throngs on the sidewalk.

"It's Friday night," Narcos observed ahead of us.

"A beautiful summer Friday night? Can't say I'm surprised that it's a crowd, but you're safe. Narcos ain't gonna let anything happen and I damn sure ain't gonna let anything happen. Try to relax. We've got you," Sam said near my ear and his proximity was so close, the way his lips brushed the shell of my ear, well... I'm afraid I couldn't help but shudder.

"No, I know," I said, and I was all shaken up for a very different reason, now.

We slipped in the door of the creamery and stood in line at the counter.

"My treat," Sam said behind me. "Whatever you want."

I rolled my eyes at him and smirked when I said, "Considering my purse is melted to the desk in the back room of my bakery..."

He gave me a wry grin and nodded. "Guess that just means I'll be buying for a while."

"Hey, I've got all my cards and such ordered from my bank. I've got my passport for ID for now, and my driver's license should be coming in the mail. Yay for technology!"

"Right, it's nice they've got that shit in the system. Can mail you out a new one at the press of a few buttons."

I sighed. "The contents of my purse were pretty much the easiest things to replace."

"Still worried your phone won't be as easy as all that?" he asked.

"Oh, I guarantee it," I said. "I've *never* had a phone replacement go that easy. I've always had to take it in to a branch or whatever."

"We'll cross that bridge when we come to it," he said, and I nodded.

We were next and ordered our ice cream.

We found ourselves back out front of the ice cream shop, the counter man had told us there was a way down the alley beside it to a sort of patio square courtyard for the building. That sounded good to us, so we sauntered down the alley strung back and forth with lights, plants climbing down the walls until we spilled out into a surprisingly spacious hidden courtyard.

There were barrels set around the outer edge with tall seats, and tables made of giant industrial wooden spools that sat four to six people. We snagged one of these tables, a charming classic stone fountain burbling in the center with plenty of space to show the alternating red and regular gray-black flagstone checker-patterned floor of the courtyard.

Flowering baskets bursting with blooms hung in intervals and likewise a planter at the center of the top of the fountain dribbled with white, purple, and pink blossoms.

Everleigh looked delighted, and I found it soothing back here. It was cooler with the lowering of the sun. The musicians set up in one corner, taking the small triangular stage.

One of the men tapped the mic, a fancy guitar over his shoulders, a young woman standing back and with her own guitar behind him.

He introduced the small band and thanked everyone for coming out. They began to play this wonderfully bluegrass folk music, and the combined effect of setting and sounds, sights and the cool sweet treats we held and the warm and sultry summer night – it was difficult to be anything other than delighted, the weight of the week which had rested heavy on my heart lifting like a stone weight off a stack of papers.

That stack of papers a jumble of emotions that I finally felt free to thumb through and to sort as I listened and watched and enjoyed my ice cream.

Soon, Narcos was sweeping Everleigh onto her feet and onto the open space around the fountain to dance.

I sat with my hands around my knees, legs crossed and leaning back on the stool that was another, smaller industrial spool that'd been retrofitted with some batting, cloth, and the handy use of a staple gun.

"So," Sam said, and I turned to give him my attention.

"Ever married?" he asked.

I nodded slowly. "Once, you?"

He shook his head.

"Nah," he said.

"How come?" I asked.

He gave a shrug, "Never found the right one. What about you? Divorced... or?"

"Divorced." I nodded. "But we're still good friends."

"How's that work?" he asked.

I laughed a little.

"We were young when we got married," I said. "Still in college. Um, he was into computers and I was in culinary. When all was said and done, we had the house and we were comfortable and then... then he got a job offer on the west coast."

"Yeah?" Sam looked at me curiously.

"Yeah. I couldn't leave my mom and my grandma. The bakery was going really well. I just didn't want to move... and he did. We realized we were really great friends, but that was all we were and that staying married just didn't make sense. We were together ten years and divorced three years ago. He moved, got remarried just a few months ago. She's really wonderful."

Sam grunted and looked me over. "Guy didn't know what he had," he said, and I felt my eyes widen as I barked a laugh.

"You think so?" I asked a bit incredulously.

"I know so," he said, rising. He held down his hand and without really thinking about it, I took it. He hauled me up to my feet and before I knew it, he was taking me around the dance floor.

I couldn't help but smile, tickled pink, and delighted as we passed Everleigh and Narcos. Everleigh was laughing and looking wild and free and sometimes... sometimes I wished I could let go like that for just a minute. As with all things, though, and any time I had ever tried to be that free, the reality that things needed my attention, and that I must be ever vigilant, always the responsible adult – just my *whole world* would come crashing in; and so, I remained reserved, ever watchful and waiting for the next wild or crazy thing that would need me to step in to take responsibility over and to tame.

It didn't mean I couldn't have a good time. It didn't mean I wasn't having a wonderful time now, because I was. It just meant that I couldn't be as loosened up as the next person and sometimes I wished I could.

So, when Sam spun me, laughing, and brought me back in, and then brought his mouth down to mine and he kissed me? I threw caution to the wind when he did and I kissed him back, leaning into his hard lean body, and parting my lips to the flick of his tongue against my bottom one.

I jumped when the smattering of applause came and blushed a bright carmine red when I thought, at first, the applause was for *us*. Sam laughed and clapped too. Awkwardly, I clapped too when it finally had caught up to me that the song had ended and the applause was for the band.

I guessed it was safe to say that Samuel Stahl had quite the effect. *Holy shit.*

While the number that had just been played hadn't exactly been super lively, the slow number they launched into next sent my nerves to jangling with its call for an even closer and more intimate embrace. We settled into the circle of each other's arms and stepped slowly. I still felt slightly hot in the face with my embarrassment, which was silly. I didn't think a single person, Sam included, had known or guessed what I'd been thinking or had noticed my confusion.

"You alright?" Sam asked evenly.

"Yeah," I rushed out, a bit breathless.

"I didn't upset you, did I?" he asked.

"No," I replied much more evenly.

"I don't know why I did that," he said after a slightly uncomfortable laugh.

"Liar," I said with a lighthearted one.

He laughed and shook his head. "Look at you calling me out on my bullshit."

I smirked and said, "You like it."

His expression turned to something... different. Something heated, and primal, something that if it were a physical thing, it felt as though it brushed against the inside of my skull with sable soft fur in the dark. One of those motions that left you turning to look, to see what'd just touched you as it stared at you and stalked you in the night from the nearby trees.

I felt my mouth go a bit dry even as I resisted the urge to squeeze my thighs together.

I don't think I had ever had a man look at me quite like that. I certainly had never responded in such a way just by way of a man giving me a look.

I was breathless as he leaned even closer and lips barely brushing the shell of my ear, breath hot, voice deep, he practically growled, "I *do* like it."

Oh... shit... check and mate, I thought as we moved around the fountain on the checker-patterned patio stones of the courtyard. This queen had just laid down her arms, and the king smiled down at me as though he knew he'd just won the prize.

We stayed until the music picked up pace again and for some reason, none of the four of us were feeling the livelier tunes.

The sun was almost set, the stars coming out overhead, even though the sun still hung onto the horizon by its fingertips.

We made our way back to the motorcycles and then made our way home.

The ride grew crisp at the end, there, but still pleasant enough, the temperature outdoors warming some once we were still.

"I could use a beer by the fire. What say you, man?" Narcos asked Sam.

"Nah, I'm good, bro."

"Suit yourself. Ev? Teresia?"

"No thank you," I murmured. "I'm exhausted."

"I'm down," Everleigh murmured.

Narcos winked at his girlfriend.

"Set to disturb the peace. I like it."

I handed Sam the helmet in the foyer and he took it. Everleigh took back her jacket and the sunglasses I'd borrowed from her.

"Thank you," I murmured.

"You're welcome!" she said cheerfully.

We parted ways at the hallway, me going down it ahead of Sam. Narcos and Everleigh headed for the kitchen and the back door.

Sam's hand fell lightly at my lower back and he stopped outside his bedroom door with me.

"Well, this is you," he said with an almost sad smile. I smiled back a little wistfully myself and looked up at him.

"This is me," I agreed and his smile grew. He leaned down slowly, giving me ample time to turn my head or to turn away, and he kissed me once again – a soft, chaste press of lips against my own, my small whimper running into the backs of my teeth. I wouldn't let it escape.

He straightened just as slowly and murmured, "Get some good sleep."

I nodded mutely, not trusting my voice, and then he was gone, disappearing into Narcos and Everleigh's room and shutting the door, and me and the cats out.

I heaved a sigh and went to bed, alone – which didn't bother me – and lonely, which did.

14

*D*riller...

I woke up to the pitch black and silent dark of deepest night. I turned and found Everleigh snug in Narcos' arms and both of them sound asleep. I frowned, not knowing what'd jarred me awake, but now that I was with it in the here and now? I had the urge to take a leak awful enough there would be no going back to sleep without doing something about it.

I got up with a grunt, body creaking with my growing age and just general abuse of it, and once on my feet, I had to give it a second before opening the bedroom door in silence and slipping out into the hall, shutting it behind me as quietly as possible.

I didn't want the cats getting into the room. Narcos was still steadfast on that one, which I low key thought was ridiculous. I didn't envision they'd abandon their mama even if the door was open and it was a new space for them to explore. Still, my buddy wanted the door shut, so it stayed shut.

I went to the bathroom, tapped a kidney, and with the urgent need to go behind me, I flipped out the light and opened up the bathroom door, freezing in place.

I'd heard it, but it still didn't register where it'd come from right away with my still-sleep-addled brain.

There was a thump from across the hall and I tensed, ready, but it was just the black shadow of one of Teresia's cats.

I held still and swallowed hard, tense, wondering what was up, every hair standing on end and palm itching for the butt of my gun in it. I cursed myself silently for leaving it in the bedside table of Narcos' room.

A low, guttural, fearful whine emanated from my bedroom doorway and another thump as Teresia's other cat left the bed for the floor and slunk out the doorway.

He stopped, low to the ground and perked up when he saw me, then scurried down the hallway toward the living room, his belly swinging comically back and forth underneath him. I fought not to laugh at the poor thing and shoved a hand back through my still too-short hair. Tense muscles relaxed as I went to my door and shoved it open the rest of the way.

Teresia thrashed slightly and made another guttural gasping noise.

I wondered briefly, as I moved to wake her, if she'd been dreaming like this a lot. If she'd been keeping mum about it – which of course that was the case. She was the type of strong, borne of some sort of past necessity. Even though it wasn't necessary anymore, when you've been that type of strong for so long, you find it impossible to let it down for even just a minute. Too many people around you taking it for granted that you would and could always be the rock… and that so wasn't fair.

I got up onto the bed and eased up next to her, sliding my arms carefully around her, fully expecting to get popped in the face or the chest should she wake up badly, but she didn't. She gasped and still fully asleep, went limp against me, sagging with relief. Her breathing was awkward for a few breaths, before deepening and evening out once more. I simply held her close and kissed the top of her hair.

I closed my eyes and sighed out as she relaxed in my embrace and I could feel it in every fiber of her – the her that her subconscious had the wheel, the real her without any waking anxiety or front brain thoughts and second-guesses getting in the way.

She needed someone else to be strong for a minute. She needed the relief, and she melted into it without those second thoughts to get in the way.

I held onto her and closed my eyes and felt like, for right now, I had a true north-pointing purpose again.

I'd lost that sense of purpose for a long time when I'd pulled the trigger on Témaël Etienne, believing wholeheartedly he'd been the one to shoot me. And even though I would never say it out loud to a single soul, I couldn't lie to myself. When I'd shot him, I'd been angry; angry as fuck that I'd taken one in the vest. Angry, knowing that if his aim had been just a little higher, I would have taken it in the throat, or the face. Angry that I wouldn't have ever seen my brothers, or Everleigh, or any of the people who I had loved the most ever again.

In that moment, I wasn't thinking like the cop I should have been thinking like. I'd been thinking like a frightened animal, and I would live with the guilt of that loss of control for the rest of my life.

A different sort of insidious guilt threaded its way through the center of my chest, jabbing me in the heart and causing a visceral reaction that made me tighten my hold on the woman in my arms.

So much was my fault, including her nightmares. The total destruction of her life and business... all because I couldn't maintain control in that one instant. To stop and realize that the kid I was shooting at, that had turned on me, wasn't the right kid, and that there was absolutely nothing I could do about any of it now.

Nothing at all.

I lay on my back in the dark, on my bed, this beautiful, competent, and wonderful woman who'd weighed the facts and had let me go, riding me. I honestly didn't feel like I deserved her mercy now and look at what she'd gotten for it?

The ripples washing out from that night were so damn far reaching. I didn't know where it would all end up. I just knew that not a damn thing good had come out of it thus far and as I looked at the smoldering wreckage all around us from it, I wondered heartily if it was even worth being a cop anymore.

I glanced up and over to the photos on the wall of my dad and my pop-pop, and I wished I could ask 'em. But my pop-pop was long gone and my dad too, shot by some skell in the dark like I'd been shot. Only he hadn't been so lucky and the guy that'd shot him had better aim. I'd still been a rookie.

My mom had died of cancer a few years later.

I took a deep breath and let it out slow. I wondered what my dad would say if he were here now. How he would feel if he were in my place, because to be honest, I felt like I'd been sold out – by the brass, mostly. But I didn't fucking know what else to do. Being a cop was in my blood. I was a third-generation ICPD blue blood and I couldn't imagine being anything else, but fuck if it wasn't *hard*.

Felt like every day the criminals gained more ground and the brass that was supposed to back us up receded just that little bit more in the face of it. We were still facing forward, boots on the ground, facing down the threat and when we finally did manage to look – we were just out there, hung out to dry, no backup.

This?

This though?

Teresia tucked against my side, head on my shoulder, warm breath blushing out over my chest in deep and even draughts as she slept. The mere fact that my presence stilled her dreaming and kept the nightmares at bay?

That meant something. I didn't know what, but it felt good. Like I had a modicum of control after spiraling out of control – free falling with nothing to stabilize me, for so long.

Keeping her safe, letting the boys that I knew I could trust, do their job, find the answers, bring this case to a close – that I could do. That felt right. Felt normal in the sea of chaos and discord that'd erupted around all of us.

It let me ignore the guilt for a little while and was a drop in the bucket for all I needed to do to make up for something that I could *never* make up for, no matter how much good I did, no matter how much decency I put out into the world.

Nothing would ever make up for taking Témaël Etienne out of this world.

Nothing would make up for me taking myself out of it either, though I'd thought about it a time or two…

No, I needed to face what I'd done and live with it. I was just grateful that I could stay out here and do *something* right and that I wasn't rotting in prison right now.

Still, so much was my fault, and it was a mess bigger than I could ever imagine.

"Mm?" Her voice was light, a lilting little questioning sound as she jerked against me, awake.

I held very still while she came back to herself and thickly asked, "What are you doing?"

I chuckled and kissed the top of her head and told her the truth.

"I was up to take a leak and I heard you makin' noise. You were having a nightmare, so I came in here to – I don't know. You didn't wake up though, and here we are."

"Oh," she whispered.

"Sleep," I told her. "No getting up at the ass crack of dawn today. I don't know the last time you slept in, but me being here seems to have done some sort of trick. So get some rest, baby."

"What about you?" she asked.

"I'll get back to sleep eventually," I murmured in a consoling tone.

"Mm…" She was already starting to drift, snuggling closer, and I felt a tension in me ease slightly.

It was nice to be needed again.

Wanted.

Even just a little bit.

15

*T*eresia...

I closed my eyes and relished his warmth. I'd forgotten how much I loved being held and how much I missed it. I was so very tired, after days of not sleeping well, and with his hands where it was appropriate, and his gently whispered permission of "sleep," I did. I cuddled in a little closer, let myself enjoy the guilty pleasure of it, and I went back to sleep. I thought I slept *hard*.

When I woke it was to sun streaming through the curtains, the sound of birds outside the window, and I honestly couldn't remember the last time I was up well after the sun.

I pushed up into a sitting position and found myself alone. I figured Sam had gone back to the other bedroom, but I would be wrong. No, he nudged the door to the bedroom open, Huginn and Muninn both trotting in, licking their chops.

"Furry little bastards weren't about to give up on the absolute state of misery their food bowls were in."

"Oh?" I asked amused.

"Not a scrap of wet food in sight," he affirmed, and I pushed myself up into a sitting position as he set a tray with two coffees with all the fixings for said coffees, and a pair of muffins onto my lap.

He got up onto the bed beside me as my two cats twined and milled, eyeing the tray in my lap to see if they would be getting anything good off of it.

"It was a good thing you were able to save the day," I murmured, and he chuckled, propping his head up on his hand and lying on his side. He picked up the mug nearest him and sipped his coffee black.

"Ugh," I remarked, adding cream. "I use cream and sugar because I like myself."

"Hey, I like myself just fine," he said. "Most days."

Something about the way he said it gave me pause.

"Why wouldn't you have a reason to?" I asked curiously, and he gave me a flat look. I gave a long slow blink.

"What?" he asked.

"I just... I guess I never really thought about how much it affected you," I said, embarrassed.

"I mean, how could it not?" he asked me.

"All through the trial you just... I don't know. You looked unflappable, I guess."

"News to me," he said, taking another sip. "I was freaking out the entire time on the inside."

"Yeah?" I asked softly, stirring in the cream and sugar before taking up my mug to sip.

"Hell yeah, that has to be a cop's second worse nightmare," he said. "Being sent to prison with all those fuckers you put in there for something – well, not that you didn't do it in my case but... for an accident." What he said ended on almost a whisper and I sighed some, trying to keep it silent.

"You really didn't know it wasn't the man who'd shot you?" I asked. "I mean, it's over now. Double jeopardy and all of that... just..."

"Please tell you that you didn't get it wrong by letting me walk?" he asked and his eyes weren't unkind, but they *were* somewhat guarded.

"Yeah," I said softly.

"My dad died when I was a rookie. He got shot by some fuckin' sovereign meth head. I mean, I knew that I'd just been shot. I don't think it quite computed at the time that I was alive or going to live, though. Everything was happening so fast. I didn't know that I'd took it full in the plate and that I'd be fine and all. I gotta tell ya, getting hit in the plate like that? That shit hurts! It's way worse than a punch in the gut like on TV and shit. Worst pain I've ever felt."

"I saw the bruises," I murmured, and he nodded. The photographs and x-rays had been presented as part of his defense.

"All I kept thinking – fuck, I *wasn't* thinking. I was just pissed. Pissed at the fucker who'd shot my dad and pissed I'd been shot and almost been taken away from the people who love me. That *I still might be.* I didn't honestly know how bad I was, if I was bleeding or not, or whatever. I shot first when that kid turned on me and asked questions later. I didn't want to get shot again, and I didn't want him shooting anyone else. I maybe should have slowed down. I don't know... I-I fucked up," he said and swallowed hard. "And the more and more I think about it, the more and more I go over it in my head, the more and more guilty I feel, and I sometimes... sometimes, *no,* I don't feel like I deserve a second chance. I'll spend the rest of my life trying to make up for shooting that kid, but I know I never can."

The look in his eyes was something *painfully* raw and honest and I found my throat tight with some nameless emotion. I brought the coffee mug to my lips, clearing my throat and taking a sip.

"I'm sorry," I said finally, not knowing what else to say.

"There's no scenario more perfect for the label of 'it is what it is' than this one," he said with a shrug. I could watch his walls start to go up and I realized that what he'd just told me was something... something sacred. Something he hadn't told anyone else, and it was something he'd sorely needed to unburden himself of.

"Thank you for telling me," I murmured, feeling a little guilty now, at having asked for my own peace of mind when clearly... clearly there were parts of Sam Stahl that would never know peace again. Not after something like that.

"It's no problem," he murmured, and I cocked my head and regarded him.

Like this, shirtless and personable, as relaxed as he could be in his own space, there was something less hard about him. Something... something painfully handsome and beautifully primal. Like glimpsing a wolf staring back at you through the trees of its natural habitat – wild and yet at ease.

"So, what happens now?" I asked quietly.

"So tonight, I have a buddy of mine on the force coming to house sit you and Everleigh, while Narcos and I go have a chat with some of the community leaders, and we try to figure out some of this mess going on around you and some of the other jurors."

I nodded slowly.

"I wouldn't be able to wait to get rid of me either," I attempted to joke lightly, but it fell flat on its face. He rested a hand on my knee, letting it ride up atop my thigh over the blankets and giving my leg a squeeze.

"I'm not in the habit of kissing anyone I'm eager to let go," he said.

I bit my lips together and nodded slowly.

"I don't get it," he said.

I asked, "Get what?"

"How are you single?" he asked.

I turned and looked at the window, at the shadows dipping and wavering on the other side of the curtains from the birds landing on the bushes outside it and taking off in flight.

"I don't know," I said honestly. "I guess I didn't much see the point in trying after David."

"David?" he asked.

"My ex-husband," I said.

"I thought you said you guys were on good terms," he said, his brow wrinkling in confusion.

"No, yeah, we are," I said with a bit of a forced laugh.

"But?" he asked.

"But it was still really hard, you know?" I asked.

He looked me over and nodded slowly and I felt like... I felt like he really did know. That he got it somehow. It clicked like it just sort of never had for me with any other person and my mouth was suddenly dry for a very different reason.

"So, what did you and Ev have planned for today?" he asked.

"Um, some gardening, why?"

"Thought I might take you for a ride." At the surprised expression on my face, he laughed and amended, "*On the bike.*"

"Oh! Oh, shit." I blushed furiously and he laughed, and I mean *really* laughed. It was a sound that made me smile. I mean, I couldn't help it when someone laughed like that. It really was infectious.

"Okay, eat your breakfast," he said, getting up and picking up his muffin. "I'll be up in my office if you need me."

I nodded. "Okay," I murmured, and he winked at me and left the bedroom. I drank my coffee and ate my muffin which was big and still warm, and very, very good – but my thoughts were on Sam Stahl and the shift in things – the change between us.

I had to say, I liked it. It felt good.

∾

LATER IN THE DAY, I found myself in an equally deep and somewhat philosophical conversation with Everleigh as we kneeled by one of her flower beds, weeding together under the hot summer sun.

She too asked me about whether I was single, and what my last relationship was like. I, being comfortable enough, talked about David and our split, but she had a bit of a different take on things and asked me *why* I thought it hurt as much as it did.

"I don't know what you mean," I said.

She cocked her head and regarded me with her lovely green eyes under the shade of her broad-brimmed straw hat held on by a floral scarf and I immediately felt slightly *guilty* of all things, like she was somehow catching me in a lie. It was when she said, "Tell me about how you grew up," that I realized I may or may not be a liar but not to her... but rather myself.

"Um, pretty typical. My mom, my dad, my older brother and me..." I hedged.

"You talk about your mom and grandma but what about your dad and brother?" she asked.

I sighed then and sat back on my haunches and said, "My dad committed suicide when I was eight, my brother was eleven. I didn't know it, at least not really, but my dad had a hard time with some mental illness. When my brother went off to college, his problems started. He, um, he's homeless somewhere. We don't know anymore.

He's schizophrenic and doesn't want to admit he has a problem. I mean, he *knows*, takes his medication for a good long while, starts to feel better and then... then decides he doesn't need it and goes off it. Rinse and repeat."

"Oh, I'm sorry to hear that," she murmured.

"Yeah." I nodded. "Me too."

We worked in silence for a little while and finally she said, "If you don't mind me saying, I think I get the whole picture now."

"Oh, yeah?" I asked with a bit of a scoffing giggle and she smiled and it was a little... I don't know. Shy? Pained?

"It hurt so much when David left because he didn't choose you, and that was an echo of when your dad left because he didn't choose you either," she murmured and it was like a punch in the gut.

"I'm sorry," she said, stopping when I came to a full stop with what I was doing. "I shouldn't have said anything," she said, and I shook my head.

"No, no... I think you might be right. Um, I just didn't think about it like that is all. I mean, I-I guess I don't really deal with anything. I just put my head down and keep going."

She sighed and said, "I don't think your mom was very supportive."

I laughed a little, shook my head and said, "No, but that's alright. I mean, her husband died and then her son... I needed to be there for her, not the other way around," I countered and she frowned slightly.

"You were eight," she said.

"No, I know," I replied and my voice faltered some as my foundation sort of just shifted. "My grandmother always said I was the strongest little girl she knew." I smiled brightly and frowned slightly at Everleigh's expression of dismay.

"You were *eight*," she reminded me.

I gave a long and slow blink.

"I just want to hug your inner child tight," she said, and I laughed, again with some sort of nervousness.

"I'm okay, really," I said. She opened her mouth to say something but was cut off by Sam and Narcos, a third man with them, coming across the grass from the back door of the house. Everleigh got to her feet, dusting off the knees of her flowy hippy skirt before throwing her arms around her man and getting a long slow kiss.

I smiled and held a bit of envy in my heart. I looked up to Sam with his mirrored sunglasses covering his eyes and waited for the introduction I knew had to be forthcoming.

"Teresia, this is Poe."

"Hi." I smiled pleasantly at the young man behind Sam, in a pair of jeans and a tee, a gun riding on his belt just tucked behind one hip.

"Hi, Teresia," he said.

"Hey, Poe," Everleigh murmured with familiarity.

"Hey, Ev."

"I take it this means you're leaving?" I asked.

"For a few hours," Narcos declared. "I'll get him home before he turns into a rat or a mouse, or some fuckin' thing."

"I think you're thinking about a pumpkin," I said, and Everleigh giggled.

"Nah, the bike turns into the pumpkin, the cages and shit. The driver and valets and shit turned back into mice or whatever."

I snorted.

"I expect a fuckin' cheese tray," Sam said and Everleigh shot him a little salute.

"Aye, aye, Captain," she said.

I saw Sam's eyebrows go up behind the impenetrable mirrored aviators and I shook my head a little.

He dropped to his knees near me, a fist in the grass and said, "Poe's another Knight. A beat cop and a good man. You'll be just as good as if Narcos or I were here, okay?"

I nodded and smiled. "Okay," I murmured.

"Good deal," he said and leaned forward and smacked a kiss to my forehead. I giggled and shook my head, turning back to the patch of flowerbed that still needed weeding.

"Alright, back in a bit," he said, his voice a bit strained as he heaved himself to his booted feet.

"Anything I can do to help you ladies?" Poe asked.

"Yeah, grab a seat up there and mind your business before Everleigh gets you doing all her heavy lifting."

"Ah!" Everleigh scoffed and lightly backhanded Narcos' arm in a swat. He laughed and walked back calling, "I love you, baby."

"I love you too," she said with great affection and my own heart sighed at the exchange with happiness for them. I loved to see it.

"Okay, off we fuck," Sam declared, and he pecked Everleigh on the lips and turned to depart too.

I thought about that, and I was surprised to find while there was a fine stirring of jealousy, I had to ask myself, *why?*

Seriously. Why? There was no need. It wasn't like Sam was pretending there was nothing going on there. I mean, clearly there was, but he'd also said that Everleigh was Narcos' girlfriend and, well, they were all consenting adults.

Poe shook his head slightly and trailed the boys up to the deck and dropped into one of the deckchairs a polite distance from me and Everleigh.

I watched them go and then turned back to Everleigh watching me with great interest.

"What?" I asked.

"I just watched a kaleidoscope of things crash into each other and swirl behind your eyes."

"What, like thoughts or feelings?" I asked with a laugh.

"Both, like literally *all* the things," she said.

I sighed. "I'm not sure I can handle much more introspection today," I said honestly. "I don't have just *food* for thought, I have an entire *feast*."

She chuckled and shook her head.

"That's fair," she said and with a gusty sigh, she got back into digging through her flower bed.

"I do have questions, though," I murmured.

She smiled, chuckled and said, "I thought you might."

"I don't even know where to begin," I said and blushed.

"Well," she said. "Those two were a sort of unit well before I came along."

"Oh, yeah? And just how did you and Narcos meet?" I asked.

She turned, a twinkle in her eye, and said, "Now *that's* a whole-ass story."

"I'm all ears," I said, rooting through the dirt and adding to my pile of weeds.

"Well, it all started when Narcos nailed me to a tree – and I know what you're thinking," she said at my laugh. "But to borrow one of his turns of phrase, that ain't it."

I sobered immediately and said, "Wait, *what?*"

"Mm-hm." She nodded.

I blinked and slid onto my ass, giving her my full attention now.

"It's why no one, not even Driller's captain, knows you're here. When I was under protection, there was a leak in the department. Narcos had to take me to the cabin – which oh! We should take you to the cabin! You would love it there!"

"I'm sorry, hold on, wait. Can we please go back to the part where you're telling me Narcos nailed you to a tree? Like with nails?"

She pulled off her gloves, held out her hand and pointed out the tiniest of scars on her palm and a matching one on the back of each hand. My mind was blown.

"He had to," she said somberly. "Or we would both be dead."

I shook my head slowly and said, "I may need something to drink for this."

"Time to make that lemonade?" she asked.

"I think so," I said, and she smiled. With a nod, she got to her feet and reached down to help me up. I let her.

"Well, the good news is, you already know this story has a happy ending."

I laughed a little at that and secretly, I sure hoped so, because holy shit.

16

*D*riller...

    We rode to the 10-13, and I felt like I could breathe for a minute. Not that watching over Teresia was suffocating or over-whelming – no, as I'd said before – she was giving me purpose and life and a way forward out of the madness.

Speaking of madness, it was fuckin' sobering, rolling up on the 10-13 and it's boarded-up windows, Muller St. littered with trash and broken glass.

"Shit," I said when we'd stopped the bikes and parked 'em in the alley off the street. "I knew it was bad but had zero clue it was *this* bad."

"I can't figure this one out," Narcos said, balancing his helmet on his hip.

"What, that the jurors are getting doxed left, right, and center, but our place has remained untouched?" I asked.

"Exactly that. If it *was* the blacktivist groups, why haven't they come for you? You're the man that pulled the trigger."

"Maybe we shouldn't quite be putting that shit out in the air," I said, leaning this way and that, looking around.

Narcos grunted. "Maybe, just maybe, it's because they know you *have* pulled the trigger and you ain't afraid of doing it again," he said.

"That I'm perfectly okay with you putting that out into the ether, because it's true... I would, but I wouldn't like it. Didn't like doing it the first time." I sighed and got off my bike.

"I know that," he said with a grunt. "We all know that," he said, and it was all much quieter this time.

"I know you know, my man. I know you know."

"You seem to be taking a liking to Teresia," he said as we skipped the front door to the 10-13 and went to the kitchen door here in the alley.

"Talk later on that?" I asked.

He nodded.

I rapped out the predetermined code on the kitchen door and Reflash opened it up and stuck his head out, looking this way and that. Narcos and I laughed.

"Shut it, you two Mooks, and get in here," he ordered. We went inside and it hit me hard. This was the first time I'd ever seen his kitchen dark and dormant, like some great sleeping stainless-steel beast.

"How bad has it been through here?" Narcos demanded.

"Bad enough," he said. "One broken window was enough for us. We boarded up and ain't been open the last three days."

"Shit," I said with feeling.

"Not your fault, man," Reflash said, reading my mind.

We followed him on through to the fishbowl.

Skids, Oz, Golden, Youngblood, Angel, and Yale were inside. In addition, we had guests... a young, light-skinned black woman with cheekbones that could cut, her hair long and braided and up in a high ponytail, almond eyes keen and as sharp as the rest of her features. I'd seen her on the news along with the dark-skinned black man next to her. Oz was talking to them, and a third and fourth kid were in some of the office chairs around the table. The Hispanic kid was probably college age, and was leaned back in his seat, lookin' like a regular kingpin from every bad movie about cartel life – button-down shirt, striped and crisp in black-and-brown stripes, gold chain at his neck and pressed chinos with expensive looking designer loafers with no socks.

I hated to fucking stereotype, but that kid was wearing some straight *money* and with the years Narcos and I spent in the narcotics division undercover? Well, he and I traded one look, and we were on the same fuckin' page.

There was something dark about him, but like a lot of outlaw types – they rode on the right side of the law in some things too. The cartels were popular in parts of Latin America for a reason. That reason being that they sometimes did more, supplied more food and housing and you name it to the people than their fuckin' governments did. Made it hard to pull a war on drugs when you bought the support of the people with basic survival needs.

The last kid wore bright colors, a baggy hooded jacket and his slanted eyes were quick. A representative from the city's Asian community, though I couldn't tell you if he was Chinese, Japanese, Korean, or what. Not that it mattered. He was here, and representing, and that was good.

Narcos dragged open the door to the fishbowl and Reflash went in ahead of me and man, if looks could kill. I was *cookin'* from the hostility coming off the Black and brown people in the room – except my fellow Knights, obviously. I had to say, though, as much as I didn't like it, I understood it.

I steeled myself, ready to step away if shit wasn't going to work and things got heated.

It wasn't what you would call an extremely productive meeting. A lot of shouting ensued, a lot of anger – righteous, furious, and earned – bounced around the inside of the glass. But in the end, the only lead we got on the open case of the threats, attempts, and yeah, even murders of a couple of the jurors on my case, was the fervent promises of the community leaders in the room that it *wasn't their people*.

"Fuck," I muttered when Skids returned after letting them out onto the street through the front door and locking up behind them.

"I got a sinking feeling," Youngblood declared.

"You on this?" Oz demanded.

Youngblood nodded. "Pulled Marcus Dreslin's murder," he said. "Juror number twenty-three."

"Shit," I muttered. "How did he go?"

"Drive by," Youngblood declared. "His kid is still at Trinity Gen fighting for his life. He's only fourteen."

"Fuck," I muttered.

"What's this sinking feeling you got, Youngblood?" Skids asked, dragging us back on point.

"I don't know, yet," he answered, chewing his bottom lip and shaking his head.

I looked at Narcos and Narcos looked at me. "You thinkin' our place may be compromised?" I asked.

"I'm thinkin' it might not be a bad idea y'all head on up to that cabin of yours for the time being," Youngblood said.

"You want I should bait a trap first?" I asked.

Youngblood perked up and asked, "How's that?"

Narcos and I traded looks again and Narcos cleared his throat.

"After Everleigh a few years back, Driller decided to play shit closer to the vest than usual."

"How's that?" Oz demanded, crossing his arms over his chest.

"Ain't nobody in the department knows where Teresia is *except* the Knights," I said. "Not my captain, not nobody. Now, my captain is a pretty stand-up dude." I dropped into a Texas accent and said, "He don't rightly care about where the fuck I get her at as long as it ain't comin' out of his budget."

"Ah." Golden nodded knowingly.

"I might be dumb as fuck because I ain't pickin' up what you're puttin' down," Oz said.

"Back when it was me and Ev on the run for our protection, we were sold out from *inside* the department."

"Oh, what the fuck?" Oz demanded. "I must have missed that part."

I nodded. "Yeah, so this time around, I didn't want to take any chances. You know how many good 'ol boy legit racist pieces of shit we got floating around the bowl that just won't fucking flush."

Oz blew out a somewhat disgusted breath. "Too many," he said. "ICPD is lookin' like a public toilet. Afraid to sit down without like five ass gaskets between you and the bowl."

We were all soberly silent for a moment.

"Too much of this shit is aping what these white supremacist fucks would do. Burning effigies in the yard ain't exactly anti-fascist style. They had just stuck to the Molotovs, we'd still be scratching our heads but yeah, rolling up on that particular scene? The dummy hanging from her tree like that, the brick through the window? That's hillbilly shit."

"Good point." Youngblood was nodding, like a bloodhound I'd put on a scent.

"What are we gonna do about the cats?" Narcos asked thoughtfully.

"Cats?" Skids asked, and I smirked.

"Teresia's got two cats, Huginn and Muninn. She wouldn't leave them at her house. That's how we ended up at our place."

"You? Worried about some cats?" Oz started laughing.

"Shut up," Narcos grumbled.

"Gonna pull your man card," Golden teased, and I shook my head.

"Not the point. He's got a point there – she won't leave without her cats."

"So have the girls take a cage, you two ride," Skids said, rolling his eyes.

I laughed a little and said, "Give us a day or two to warm her up to the idea of a long car ride. Those cats are her kids, and she's a strong one."

The guys all glanced at each other.

"Yeah, don't say it," I said. "She's growing on me."

"What, like mold or fungus?" Golden asked.

"More like a flowering vine," Narcos declared, and he smirked at me and winked.

"I don't hear you complaining," I said, and he gave me a shit-eating grin.

"Nah, Ev and I would hit that," he said.

"You fuckers are weird," Oz declared.

"Don't be a judgy fuck," Narcos said defensively.

"Nah, it's just me an' Ellie. Nobody else," he said with a flat look.

"All he's sayin' is don't yuck somebody else's yum," Reflash told him. "For fuck's sake, it ain't hurtin' you and they don't want in your bedroom. C'mon!"

"I ain't say nothin'!" Oz said defensively, but Reflash was full-on cursing his ass out and we were all laughing.

"I need this city to get its shit together and everybody start treating everybody else right so I can get his ass back in his kitchen," Skids said under Reflash's dressing down – which Oz wasn't taking personally. He was laughing just as much as the rest of us.

"You guys go on home," Youngblood declared. "I'll be in touch in the next day or two and we'll set and spring this trap."

"Sounds good," I said, nodding.

"I sure wish we had some better leads and insight." Narcos sighed.

"Like you really gonna bitch about a trip up to the cabin," I said.

"No," he said, shaking his head. "No, I am not."

I clapped him on the back and we said our goodbyes and headed out.

"Let's take the long way home," I said. "I want to survey the damage a little and need some time to think."

He eyed me. "Why you need to 'survey the damage?'" he demanded. "Sounds to me like it's less idle curiosity but another excuse to self-flagellate, my dude. You want a beating, I'm more than happy to square up with you in a ring somewhere. Better yet, put you up against one of the hose boys. See how you do." He grinned savagely at me with the last.

I sighed and shook my head and his face fell.

"Hey, you good?" he demanded.

I shook my head.

"No, man. I keep thinkin' what would my pops think if he were still alive to see this? To see how the brass did me dirty and all?"

He looked sobered by that.

"You thinking about quitting the force?" he asked.

"I don't know," I answered him honestly. "Honest to God, it really feels like the force quit me with this one."

He sighed, nodded, and said, "Doesn't matter where you go for work, what you do, you know? You'll always be my brother and I'll always be grateful Teresia and the rest of 'em saw some fuckin' sense. You know?"

I nodded and looked over after hefting my helmet onto my head.

"I know," I told him and pulled the bike up under me, straightening her out and starting her up.

"Still want to take the long way home?" he demanded.

"Yeah," I said. "Yeah, I do."

"Psht! Suit yourself, man. You go, I go. Let's do it."

"Let's do it," I said under my breath and let it be drowned out by the pipes.

As good as his word, I led and he followed and, man, our city was a sorry sight to see.

Fuck.

～

IT WAS good to cut the motors on the bikes out front of the house to peals of girlish laughter drifting over the roof along the stars in the sky.

I traded a look with Narcos and both of us instantly had smiles painted on our faces from the sound.

"It's good to be home," Narcos uttered.

I nodded tiredly saying, "I couldn't agree more. I think I'm going to give my own bed a try tonight."

"Rock on, my dude. Hopefully you score something better than just a good night's sleep."

"That all depends on *her*," I declared. "I'm not about to push it."

"You sound so serious," he said, backing to the front door, a six-pack of our favorite craft beer in each hand. I got into my saddlebag for the two six-packs I'd picked up. Still cold, thankfully, but Lord were they likely shook up from the vibrations of the bike.

I caught a whiff of smoke as I followed my best friend in the front door of the house and smiled.

Fuck yeah, I could handle a bonfire and some beers tonight. Sounded like a good way to end the evening.

Everleigh caught us in the kitchen, kissing first Narcos and then me.

"Go play host for a minute," she told Narcos with a solemn look.

"Uh-oh, what do you want to talk to me for?" I asked.

"I found some things out today," she said, and her mane of auburn hair was wild, her green eyes glassy.

I asked her, "Why, Everleigh Tate, are you drunk?"

"Goddamn right I am, and she's a little buzzed too, but it's for a good cause." She toddled up to me and looked up at me, poking me in the chest.

"Samuel Stahl," she said. "I like this one."

I felt my eyebrows go up in amusement at the use of my citizen name.

"Oh, yeah?" I asked softly.

She nodded sloppily and it was adorable. I put my hands on her hips to steady her and she whispered only loud enough for me to hear it, "She's been hurt, a lot. No one from her family to her husband has ever chosen her. Don't you dare do anything unless you do, mmkay? Her inner child is just screaming to be loved. So don't you play with her and abandon her like e'rybody else."

I cupped Everleigh's cheek with my hand and smoothed my thumb along her soft skin. "You really *do* like her, don't you?" I asked, smiling faintly.

"She's a soul sister. Her vibes resonate with me, so don't you... Don't you fuck it up!"

I laughed a little and squeezed her in a hug.

"I'll try not to," I declared, and she nodded once, turned, and a little unsteady on her feet, went out to drop into Narcos' lap. I looked out the kitchen window and watched Everleigh go. I caught Teresia's icy blue eyes watching us, her pale face illuminated by the fire.

I smiled at her and that neutral look she'd been giving me transformed, thawed into something soft and beautiful.

I brought out a couple of beers and handed one to her and kept one for myself. Narcos had taken care of Poe.

We chatted, sitting around the fire, and Poe asked how things went. Narcos and I got a little quiet then and that set Teresia on high alert. She perked up and demanded, "What? What is it?"

"Thinkin' about heading up to the cabin for a few days," Narcos said and took a drink off his beer.

"What does that mean?" Teresia demanded.

"Just what it sounds like," I said. "Just getting out of the city, away from the mess for a little while."

"So, there's been no progress whatsoever then?" she asked, deflating in her seat.

"I wouldn't say that," Narcos said.

"Far from it," I supplied. "Plenty of leads have been chased down – just to no real avail."

"Shit," she swore and sighed. "No offense to any of you, you've been wonderful hosts, but I would very much so like to pick up the broken pieces of my life and find a way to start over."

I looked up from the bottle between my hands at that.

Teresia locked eyes with me and said, "There's no sense in pretending there is any sort of going *back*. Not to the way things were before. This has irrevocably changed a lot of things."

I nodded.

"Yeah," I agreed.

"All depends on how you look at it," Poe said. "I know plenty of victims of violent crimes who took it and made it into a net positive."

"I'm not a pessimist," Teresia said. "Nor would I call myself an optimist, either. I'm more of a realist. I won't know what things look like until I can start working on them. I can't start working on anything while someone is out there trying to kill me."

"Not gonna happen," I said and her gaze flicked to mine. I raised an eyebrow, and it made her smile.

"I appreciate your enthusiasm for keeping me alive," she murmured, and Narcos chuckled.

"Happy to do it," I said. When our eyes met this time, something passed between us.

"What about my babies?" she asked, and I sighed.

"That's one of the things we'll have to figure out," I said.

"Well, I'm going to say thanks for the beer and say goodnight. I want to get back to Saylor," Poe said, getting up.

"Alright, man, thanks for hooking us up," I said, and he gave a nod as he set his bottle aside on the table out here.

"Anytime," he said. "It was a pleasure," he said to Ev and Teresia, who both smiled affectionately at him.

"Thank you," Teresia said, and he gave her a nod.

"No, don't get up, man. You just got home," he said, waving me down, and I sank back into my seat.

"Alright, see you around," I said and he let himself out through the house, careful to corral the cats who were trying to get out here with their mom.

Teresia let out a long sigh, and I turned back to catch her staring wearily into the flickering flames in the firepit.

"I take it things are getting worse instead of better?" she asked tiredly, and I smiled. I knew it held a little sadness.

"No, just stalled," I told her. "We're heading up to the cabin, shuffling some information around, and letting the boys back here see what shakes loose."

She looked up sharply and raised an eyebrow.

"How much did my girl here tell you about how we met?" Narcos asked quietly.

"The CliffsNotes," Everleigh replied softly and a soft smile of pride touched my lips. She'd found her voice since back then in a big way, and both Narcos and I couldn't be any prouder if we'd wanted to be.

"I would say a fair bit more than that," Teresia said with a laugh, and I cocked my head at the apparent blush even with the firelight interfering.

"We'll touch on *that* later, but what he's talking about is the nuts and bolts of the investigation and trial side of things…" I kept my eyes on her, letting my words trail off.

"Oh, not much about that," Everleigh said, sighing and cuddling into Narcos.

"I figured," I said.

"Why?" Teresia asked.

"Part of the shitshow that was Everleigh's case was that her location at the hotel was leaked," Narcos said.

"Leaked?" Teresia asked. "By whom?"

"Some shitgibbons in the department," I answered.

Her chin rose slightly and her eyes widened, showing a bit too much white.

"Which is why Driller here played shit close to the vest from the word 'go' when it came to you," Narcos explained.

"What do you mean?" Teresia asked.

"This might sound bad, but nobody knows that you're here," I said. "Not even my captain. I said I'd take care of you and I took care of you."

"Most of the department knows about what went down with us when it came to Ev," Narcos said.

"Word got out and went around after the fact. It gave us a bit of play in either direction. My captain's a good guy, on the verge of retirement. He knows me, and when I say I've got it handled, that's all he needs to know."

143

"We can trust him, and the rest of the boys in the Knights," Narcos said.

"Which has been great at keeping you locked down and safe so far," I cut in.

"But the investigation's stalled out. We've got no forward momentum and the way things have played with some of the other jurors and the fact that nobody's taken a crack at Driller himself here?" Narcos grunted. Finishing each other's thoughts like this was pretty par for the course with the two of us. It always entertained me when someone new to it was listening and when one of us stopped, how their eyes automatically bounced to the other for the rest. Like Teresia's true-blue eyes did now, coming to rest back on me.

"It leads us to believe we've got another dirty cop or cops involved, leaking information to whoever's behind all this."

"Why?" she asked.

"Because they knew your bakery, and your home address – all easy enough to find out, mind you – but as soon as Driller had you in protective custody? Nothing—"

"What about the other jurors?" she asked. "Any of them hurt or...?"

"Got a few killed," I said. "One of the Knights in homicide is on the case." I told her the truth. She paled.

"Do you know who?" she asked, anxiety written all over her face.

I sighed and let her know and she visibly deflated in her seat. She looked thoughtful for a time and finally sighing she asked, "My mother and grandmother going to be okay where they are?"

"No one knows where they are, and being out of state, they should be fine. They aren't after your family, just you."

"The community activists from the Black, Indigenous, and other People of Color backgrounds, swear up and down it's not any of their people," I said. "We just met with them tonight and while it was tense because of obvious reasons, my being there and all, we believe them when they say none of them or theirs are involved in this."

"So, who do you think is involved?" she asked uneasily.

"Who would benefit the most at having the majority of the population angry with the people who are just fighting for their right to live and let live?" Everleigh asked, her green eyes glittering in the firelight. She'd caught on a few steps back, but then again, she was with me and Narcos. She knew how a pair of cops thought and so the puzzle pieces fit quicker than for an ordinary citizen like Teresia.

"What, like the KKK?" Teresia asked.

"Or any other white supremacist group. Pick your flavor with those yahoos," Narcos said.

"They're really crazy enough to do all this?" she asked.

"Sure," I said. "They're crazy and bold enough to go marching through the streets with their fuckin' tiki torches, spewing their bullshit out loud."

"Crazy enough to get into their cars and mow down peaceful marchers and kill that woman," Everleigh added. "Trust me, they're violent enough and crazy enough, and really do think they're better than everyone else just by virtue of having white skin. Which I'm here to tell you, we all bleed red. Of course, these dumbasses skipped that part of biology class."

"Shit, ain't most of 'em passed the third grade," Narcos declared.

"It's the ones that made it all the way through the educational system that scare me," Teresia said with a sniff.

"Me too," I agreed. "And those are the ones we've gotta let the boys focus on. It's driving me crazy that I can't be in two places at once."

"I can only imagine," Teresia said and it held sympathy.

We talked more, the fire burning down. We didn't add any wood. It was getting late enough now, we wanted the fire to go out. Teresia was the one to break first and with a yawn, clambered to her feet with a groan.

"What's wrong?" I asked, sensing it was more than your average groan of just not wanting to get up after being comfortable.

"Probably sore from all the weeding," Everleigh said with a slight laugh.

"Bingo," Teresia said dryly.

I grunted and got up myself. "Come on," I said. "Put you in a hot shower and give you a rub down before bed."

"What?" she asked, sounding a bit taken aback as she preceded me through the back door into the house.

"You heard me," I said.

"I did. I just didn't think I heard you right," she said dryly, and I chuckled.

"Gonna get all shy on me?" I asked.

"No," she said quickly and defensively.

"Alright then."

"I have to feed the babies their dry food or they'll drive us nuts all night," she said.

"Have at it," I said, going past her into the kitchen. "I'll see you back there."

"Alright," she said, and I went to be as good as my word, getting a hot shower running for her.

I heard her cats kibble hit their bowls as I turned into the hallway.

Shower running, I ran into her in the hallway outside the bathroom door.

"Towels are out for you," I said. "Let the hot water beat on what's sore and meet me in my bedroom. I'll do what I can."

She blushed and had a hard time meeting my eyes which made me smile.

"Don't go gettin' all brand new on me," I said, stealing one of Oz's lines.

She laughed a little, the ice breaking, and slipped past me into the bathroom, shutting the door behind her.

I went across the hall into my room and changed into a pair of pajama pants – black, cotton, and breathable – and listened to the water hit the shower floor irregularly. I pictured her standing amidst the rising steam, water sluicing down her enticing soft skin and it was an instant boner.

"Fuck." I hung my head, my cock tenting my pajama pants in a too damn obvious way, but how was a dumb fuck like me supposed to stop that? I took some deep breaths and tried to think of anything and everything to get it to go down.

Honestly, it didn't take much. Just thought back to how I got my road name and honestly, that did it.

It was just in the nick of time, too – the water cut off. I was somewhere between glad to get her under my hands and miffed that she didn't take longer when the bathroom door opened.

I was lighting the scented jar candle on my dresser when Teresia came in. Everleigh had made the candle last winter with some of her bee's wax, some kind of soy, and a bunch of smelly shit. She'd done it in some kind of combination that'd turned into this pleasant masculine and musky scent with just a hint of spice. She, Aly and Aly's BFF Dawnie had had a ball doing it, and the candles were up for sale in Aly and Dawnie's shop downtown. It'd become quite the side hustle for the girls, and they were having a hard time keeping them on the shelves, no matter what price they'd jacked them up to.

They called this one "Midnight Autumn Walk" and it was my favorite. It packed a lot of damn punch for such a little candle, and if you kept the wick trimmed right according to their directions, the little bastard burned forever.

"Smells nice," Teresia said, standing there wrapped in nothing but a towel as she closed the bedroom door.

"Cats are gonna be pissed," I mused, and she smiled and blushed slightly.

She said, "Narcos and Everleigh haven't gone to bed. The cats will live."

I went to her and settled my hands on her waist, smoothing my hands over the rough absorbent material of the towel.

"You ain't got a single reason to be shy around them," I said. "You're beautiful, and we all admire you daily."

Her eyes were wide and so blue, I fell right into them. Shit, she had no idea how she had me wrapped around her little finger if she so wanted it. All I could think about was kissing that smart mouth of hers – the feel of her lips against mine, the way she melted into me when I'd done it in that plaza next to that fountain.

"I-I'm afraid I'm not very good at this," she stammered, a bit flustered, and I smiled.

"At what? Taking compliments?"

She laughed nervously and said, "No, this," and waffled her hands between her and I. "And... and whatever you, um—" I put a fingertip to her lips and it hushed her mouth.

"You're thinking too much," I told her. "Just stop. It's just you and me and nothing else right this moment. Nobody else."

She clutched her towel around her, over her chest and swallowed hard.

"What are we doing?" she asked softly, her voice barely a squeak. I didn't know why all of a sudden, things were so difficult for her when she'd always been so in control. It was curious, and I flashed back onto what Everleigh had said in the kitchen, about nobody ever choosing her and how fucking sad that was. I mean, not just a damn fucking shame, but a true fucking tragedy.

"You're lying down on the bed on your stomach and I'm going to work whatever knots and sore spots you got out with a massage."

She swallowed hard, her blush turning her nose and cheeks a beautiful and sexy pink.

"A massage is never *just* a massage," she murmured, and I cocked my head and gave her a slow grin.

"This ride stops whenever you say it does," I whispered slowly, drawing nearer. Her lips were soft, and the tension left her body so beautifully as she swooned into me.

"Go lie down," I whispered against her mouth, and she reluctantly pushed off of me and went to the bed, getting up on it.

I didn't feel the need to hide my arousal for her. In fact, I had a feeling she needed to understand just how desirable she was. Still, I meant what I said. If she wanted this to stop, it stopped. All she had to do was say the word.

She lay on her stomach, pulling the towel out from under her, but keeping it draped across her. I could respect that, even if I thought it was stupid. It wasn't about me and what I wanted. It was about her. It needed to be about her.

To be honest, it was refreshing for it not to be all about me for a fucking minute.

I was so damned tired of having the spotlight on me. Burned the fuck out.

"I'm going to move this down around your hips, alright?" I asked gently.

"Yes," she said and her voice shook slightly.

"You nervous?" I asked, a smile in my voice.

"Yes," she replied.

"Why?" I asked, and she laughed ever so slightly, a nervous giggle.

"I don't even know if I know how to do this anymore," she said.

"Just try to relax," I told her. "You ain't gotta do nothing but that." I grabbed the bottle of massage oil I kept in my bedside table – when it was just me and Everleigh and Narcos was out on assignment – and gave it a flip. I caught it before I hopped up on the bed and eased myself over her, settling over the backs of her thighs.

I warmed some of the oil in the palm of my hand before spilling it across her smooth skin. I eased my hands over her back and she sighed out when I pressed firmly enough to sus out the tight spots.

She held a lot of tension in her back, especially in her upper back between her shoulder blades.

"Where's it hurt, baby?" I asked her and she sighed out.

"My lower back is tight," she confessed, finally.

"Okay," I murmured and eased myself down her body a little further to give myself some better leverage.

I worked on her lower back, easing the towel down just enough to get to everything at the top of her butt, digging thumbs into what I knew was the sweet spot. I'd always had a natural talent for massages. An intuitive touch, the one massage therapist chick I'd banged for a hot minute had called it.

"Oh!" she cried out, and it was in that deep, sexy, sultry way that had everything to do with just how damn good she thought that felt.

I smiled, watching the dim firelight from the candle I'd lit flicker off of her oiled skin.

She was flawless, perfect, and I would have given a hell of a lot more than just a penny for her thoughts.

17

*T*eresia...

His hands were magic, and I was *melting*. The weight of him on my thighs, pressing me into his comfortable bed had the tension leaving my body faster than anything, but then *his hands* – the way he pressed into my body and slid along my skin – he turned me into the dough I worked with every morning like it was *nothing*. I vaguely wondered just how much practice he had at this.

"Just relax," he murmured, and the tension that'd instantly started to come back once I'd started to think started to dissolve at his gentle reminder.

"I told you, it's been a while," I whispered.

"Yeah?" he asked. "How long, baby?"

"Since David—"

"Not a single boyfriend since then?" he asked.

"A few dates, never past the first or second one," I confessed, and the confession came too easy.

"How come?" he asked after a few moments of silence.

"I don't know," I murmured.

He chuckled. "Oh, come on," he chided.

I sighed out, thought about it and finally said, "Truth?"

"Always," he said.

"They didn't want me," I said. "Just my body and it was apparent and felt really gross."

"Hmm," he hummed thoughtfully. "I like sex," he said. "I would love nothing more than to move this towel and to slip inside you and blow your mind."

I swallowed hard and turned my head, taking my chin from the backs of my hands and replacing it with my cheek, closing my eyes so I didn't have to see him – not yet. I think I was a little afraid of what I would see.

"But if that's the wrong thing to do, I would like to know it," he said. "Because you're worth more than just me getting my rocks off and one night of passion. I don't want that to be what this is."

I swallowed hard, his words an almost siren's song, but I'd heard lines similar before just not... not with such a sincerity to them. I don't know, there was something different about this. About Sam Stahl.

I could freely admit to myself that I'd misjudged the man, but if it was one thing that'd been made absolutely apparent by now, it was that I should have zero regrets about ruling him "not guilty" in that court-room. I felt almost blessed about that, about having been given the opportunity to know him, and to learn about him to reach that conclusion. However, I held a deep pain and regret over the ensuing situation. About the jurors who had been targeted who hadn't made it, like me. About my mother and grandmother having to hide and yes, even for my poor cats being ripped away from their home and thrust into this alien environment for them.

My thoughts wandered back to Sam.

The first clue that I had about him being vastly different from what I'd assumed about him had been the way Everleigh spoke about him. The thing that had honestly clinched it for me?

The photograph of the boy he'd killed sitting on his desk.

Of the way he'd been looking at it when I'd accidentally snuck up on him that one day when he'd not been able to hear me.

You couldn't fake the look on his face as he'd stared at that photo and had listened to whatever it was that he'd been listening to. You just couldn't. And the look he'd had on his face? I think that would haunt me for some time to come, maybe even more than the fear and violence that'd played out in my bake shop.

"You're awfully quiet," he murmured. "Do I need to stop?" he asked and his voice held uncertainty.

"No," I said quickly. "Please don't stop. You feel so good."

I heard him smile, his breath... that sound... it was unmistakable.

"I'm glad," he said finally, and I felt my lips quirk into a smile as I sank into a place of comfort, a state somewhere between dreaming and awake. You knew the one. The one where everything felt good, and safe, and warm... where you felt like you could confess all of your sins and be forgiven, where you could admit all of your fears and you would be taken care of. Looked after. Safe.

Not that I was crazy enough or stupid enough to ever think that counted for *me*. It was a nice little illusion, though.

"Still with me?" he asked.

"Mm-hm," I murmured drowsily.

"Okay, good," he whispered.

"Why?" I asked drowsily.

"Because I would hate for you to be asleep and miss this part," he said. He leaned way over me and placed his lips so sweetly, so tenderly on the back of my neck, just below my hairline.

The sensation of his lips on my skin caused me to suck in a sharp breath even as a pleasurable shock went through my entire system, galvanizing me into the here and now. Like he had magically flipped a switch, and I went from practically asleep and putty in his hands to completely aware and cognizant of every touch, every breath easing out across my skin and every ripple of his fingerprints as they rested against my skin at my flanks.

His lips lifted from the back of my neck, warm breath blushing out across my skin and damn near making me shudder if I wasn't so damned frozen in place and taken aback.

"Want me to stop?" he asked.

"No, that's so nice," I replied quickly – surprised I had the breath with which to speak it.

"Yeah?" he asked, and his lips barely hovered above my skin as he said it; the little eddies of his breath against my flesh making me want to shudder, but my body locked in this frozen state, breath held, waiting and wanting him to do more.

His lips met my skin in a light kiss of a butterfly's wings slightly lower than where he'd pressed the first one.

"Oh," I moaned and my hands slid out from beneath my cheek and gripped the covers to hold on. Even though I was going nowhere, I couldn't help the deeply internalized sensation of falling.

"Yeah?" he asked, his tone so very serious and yet teasing at the same time as he knowingly and slowly drove me mad for him.

"Yeah," I echoed in a forced whisper.

"Hm."

He sounded so pleased with that one little syllable that meant everything and nothing at all.

"Mm-hm." I couldn't help but both acquiesce and encourage him with that.

"You are so sexy," he breathed against my spine, somewhere between the nape of my neck and just above where between my shoulder blades began, before pressing his lips there as well.

"Oh, please," I begged. "More of that."

He chuckled darkly then but obliged me, moving down a few more inches and kissing me lightly.

I gripped the covers, and he growled lightly against my back. "You make it very hard to maintain my self-control when you beg me so beautifully like that."

I shifted slightly beneath him, well aware he trapped me fast between his hard body and his firm yet somehow soft bed.

I felt myself grow hot and slick at the apex of my thighs, but with the way he sat atop them, pinning my legs together with his own muscular legs, I didn't think there was any way I would get any relief from the dull erotic ache settling into my sex.

"God, fuck, you're turning me on," I whispered.

"Am I?" he asked, mock-innocently.

"Yes," I breathed, sucking in a sharp breath between my own teeth even as he gently set his into the back of my shoulder.

"Good," he whispered into my ear and it was so *deliciously dirty* that I couldn't help but *writhe* beneath him.

"Mm," he grunted and then shifted above me, pressing his erection into the crack of my ass, nothing but a towel and I presumed just his lounge pants, between us.

"You feel what you do to me?" he demanded in my ear, the warm weight of his hard body pressing me into the bed, his chest against my back feeling so damn good.

"Yes," I said.

"You like what you do to me?" he demanded.

"Yes," I told him.

"Oh, that's a very good girl," he murmured and kissed the edge of my ear.

"Mm," I moaned again, and he sucked in a sharp breath, grinding his hard length into me.

"You want me to fuck you?" he demanded.

"Mm-mm," I murmured, because no, I didn't. I didn't want something so impersonal as that.

"You want me to stop?" he asked, confusion tinging his voice slightly.

"Mm-mm, no!" I declared.

"You want me inside you?" he asked.

"Yes," I told him.

"Hmm," he hummed thoughtfully. "So, you want me inside you but you don't want to fuck?" he asked, and his voice held a little playfulness as he continued, for all intents and purposes, to slowly dry hump me through my towel and his clothes.

"Yes, that's right," I gasped.

"So, you want me inside you slow and easy is that it?"

"To start." I gasped as he reared up and whisked the towel off me before pressing against me again, this time through just the thin, soft cotton of his pajama bottoms.

"Well, I'm not going to take you like this," he whispered in my ear. "No, if I'm going to take you slow and easy and make you feel good, you're going to have to look me in the eyes while I do it."

I shuddered beneath him and found that I was all too happy to comply, but that notion also made me incredibly nervous.

"Alright," I murmured.

"Alright?" he asked and his voice was steady, low, and intense.

"Yes, alright," I repeated a bit louder.

He chuckled deeply and said, "That's my good girl..." and I swear to God, if I had been wearing panties, they would have spontaneously combusted right there on the spot.

He pressed his hands into my back, down low by my hips and leveraged himself up. The pressure gave my body a delicious stretch that was made even more decadent when he allowed his hands to smooth up my oil-slicked skin to either side of my spine all the way up to my shoulders.

I felt my back pop in a couple of places and the tension that rode there blessedly loosened for the moment and I sighed with relief.

"This needs to go," he said, tugging at the towel at my low back. I lifted my hips to allow him to take it as he braced himself against the bed by my ear to leverage himself up off of it as well.

As soon as it was gone, he laid his body over the top of mine and the skin-on-skin contact of his chest against my back, his warmth in the air-conditioned hush of his house... oh, God, I was struck by how much I *missed* this. How much I'd silently craved with a pleading heart just to be... well, I know it was far too early to say *loved* like this, but to simply be cared about, cared for, was enough. Like a comfortable home, cozy by a fire while the tempest raged outside.

He buried his nose in my hair behind my ear and hummed in appreciation as he breathed me in, and it was something beyond words in its perfect magnificence. His arms delved beneath me, bands of steel around my body and he held me tight as though he himself were holding on to something precious that was trying to get away, something fleeting, something he desperately didn't want to lose. That desperation telegraphed finely through his body and trembled through mine; a signal along a fine filament of web to the spider of my heart, waiting lonely and patiently for just such a signal that her loneliness could end.

I couldn't help it. My heart opened to him at that silent trembling emotion, that physical sensation of both of us in this time and in this space, sharing mutual vulnerabilities silently, each of us desperate for a connection and to heal broken things about ourselves that until this moment we may not have even realized they were broken... and it was beautiful.

"What's happening?" I whispered, a little scared and unsure.

"I don't know," he whispered back. "But I like it."

Despite my uncertainty, I did too. I struggled in his grasp for barely a moment and he relented, almost mournfully, at the break in contact. But that reluctance eased into something like joy when he realized I wasn't trying to get away from him. Just the opposite; I was trying to turn onto my back, winding my arms around his broad shoulders to drag his mouth to mine.

He smiled against my mouth, arms going around me, holding me as tightly with them at my back as he'd held me around my stomach and chest. It felt a little strange having him still straddling me this way, like our positions were all wrong; opposite.

He remedied that for us by planting his knee between mine. His movements strong and sure, and I gladly *let go* and parted my knees for him, wrapping my legs around his waist as he walked forward on his knees to lock us against each other. He was hard, hot, long, and thick through his pajama bottoms, and his kiss even more fervent than just the moment before.

I slipped my tongue past his lips and teeth and stroked the inside of his mouth with it, exploring and tasting him. I relished his touch, his kiss, his hard body pressed tight against mine and lost myself to the sensation of him against me.

He groaned into my mouth, his body moving against mine as we rocked together on the covers, making out and dry humping like teens who were nervous to go all the way, rather than the grown adults we were both supposed to be.

I realized we were both being so careful with each other and for me, at least part of that, was a deep fear of *would this be it? Would I face rejection yet again?* I didn't know. I didn't think my heart could take it, but I needed this so badly, to just be connected... no matter how much it hurt on the other side.

"Condom?" he asked.

"I'm sterilized," I murmured and yeah, I knew it wasn't going to protect me from anything else but after *living* with Sam for the last several days, I could glean he, Narcos, and Everleigh were careful people.

"You're sure?" I loved that he double-checked with me, but...

"Yes, damnit. I need you inside of me," I said breathless with lust and passion, and he didn't disappoint – crushing his mouth over my own and kissing me until I forgot how to breathe altogether.

He kept his mouth locked to mine like he couldn't stop kissing me, as his hands pushed himself up just enough to shove the waistband of what he was wearing out of our way.

He collapsed over me again, groaning into my mouth as he slicked the head of his cock hot and rigid against my pussy lips and *oh yes, oh, God,* I don't think I'd ever needed to be with someone as much as I wanted to be with him in that moment.

He bowed over me and captured my mouth with his once more as he slid inside of me, swallowing my "Mm!" of triumph at finally having him there.

He felt so good, and I couldn't tell you how desperate I was for this feeling of fullness and connection with another human being.

I just prayed that it wouldn't end up hurting me any deeper than I already hurt in the end.

18

*D*riller...

The words "I'm sterilized..." fell from her lips and the way they fell almost reminded me of tears. The silent kind that to witness them deeply affected you. I didn't want her to be any kind of sad. I didn't want her to hurt. I thought we'd both done quite enough of that in our lifetimes to date and honestly, right now, all I wanted in the most desperate way possible, was to make her feel good.

She was so beautiful beneath me, her blue eyes heavy lidded with passion and lust, her body which she usually carried so ridged and tense relaxing beneath me. I loved how her legs went around me, how she buried her hands in my hair and dragged my mouth to hers. Her deep throated "Mm!" of satisfaction as I slid into her hot and waiting wetness damn near had me nut right then and there, like this was my first fuckin' time.

I didn't want to rush this. I wanted to take things slow, and I wanted to make her feel loved. I think she needed that, desperately. More than anything, I think she needed that connection. I know I did. I felt like I'd just gone through this absolute fucking gauntlet with the trial and all the bullshit and the pageantry of it all. Even though I knew it wasn't fair to feel like I'd gone through it alone when I'd had my boys and their women to support me – I mean, their support could only go so far and I *had* gone through it alone for the most part.

The burden of the consequences of that night fell solely on my shoulders and it weighed heavy on me. As in it *still* weighed heavy on my heart and on my mind, and with everything… it felt like Teresia was the only one who truly understood. You know?

She held on to me as I held on to her, cradling her in my arms so gently, as sweetly as I could manage, the weight of me settled over the top of her cocooning her in my embrace and moving inside of her slowly and deliberately. I didn't hold back, let the emotion show, as I gazed into her eyes and found them clear and judgment free – which was both nice and a little ironic now, considering our strange little origin story that was almost too much for even television.

"Oh, yeah!" Her eyes slid shut and her head fell back as everything about her concentration faltered and shifted to what I was doing to her.

I made a mental note that this was the spot, which was hard as fuck to do with how magnetic her pull was, but as I said before, I was determined to make this last as long as possible.

"That's it, baby," I murmured, and she practically yowled her pleasure, her nails biting into my forearms, and yet she was *still* careful not to dig too deep.

I grunted as she tightened up around me and shit, I wasn't going to be able to hold back. Who was I kidding? I didn't get a choice, not with how sexy she was, not with how tight and hot and wet she was for me.

I came, starbursts going off behind my eyelids which were squeezed shut, and miracle of miracles, I didn't let her down, because she was coming with me – her pussy gripping rhythmically in time with my cock jumping and pulsing inside of her.

"Oh, *fuck!*" I groaned and buried my face in the side of her neck, breathing her in, lowering myself down over the top of her, arms and quads trembling with fatigue from holding them in check.

I'd wanted desperately to pound her into the mattress, and the restraint I'd had to have to keep it slow and sweet had been real – but it hadn't been about what I'd wanted. It'd been about what we both needed in the moment and the moment had called for something light and gentle. A connection which was forged in fire, but now? Shit, I wanted to temper that connection and make it *strong*. Cool it too hard and too fast, that shit would become brittle and snap rather than bend and flex with whatever decided to come at us next.

She held on to me, nuzzling my shoulder, pressing lips against it in the odd and intermittent chaste kiss, nipping playfully at one point and making me gasp – my cock stirring enough to let me know it was contemplating seconds.

I flexed my pelvic muscles to make it twitch, and she gasped. Turn-about was fair play, though. She tightened up and the sensations that pulled through me due to my over sensitivity was *wild*.

"Okay, okay!" I cried, laughing between deep breaths. "You win," I said, and she giggled a sweet sound that belied her serious nature.

Hmm, looks like I got her loosened up, I thought, but then I was gritting my teeth and dragging myself out of her and off of her to collapse beside her.

I opened my arms immediately as she rolled in my direction to cuddle into my side.

I kissed her forehead, and she sighed in contentment, putting her leg over mine and cuddling close. I held her fast and trailed my fingertips over the soft skin of her back.

"Thank you," she murmured after a time and I had to chuckle.

"For what?" I asked.

She paused, thoughtful for a moment, then two, before she quietly replied, "I haven't felt this good in a long time."

"You don't mind me asking, how long has it been?" I asked.

"A year, year and a half maybe," she said.

"Yeah?" I asked.

"Mm, David and I sort of... I don't know, a post breakup moment of weakness, I guess."

"Yeah?" I asked again, letting my surprise color my tone. She didn't strike me as the type. She was pretty damn straitlaced. A what was done was done type; no looking back kind of a girl.

She giggled sort of derisively at herself and looked up at me. "What? Didn't think I was the type?" she asked.

I scoffed and said, "Pretty much. You seem pretty damn straitlaced to me."

"Yeah," she murmured, and there was no question mark on the end of it – just a somberness, a sadness to her tone.

"Hey." I jostled her a little, and she looked up at me. I met her eyes and told her, "There ain't nothing wrong with that."

"I don't know about that," she murmured. "I think it rather denotes a lack of courage."

"What, on your part?" I asked.

"Yeah," she said.

I snorted. "Baby, I listened to the recordings with dispatch. It's what I was doing upstairs – God, was that only a few days ago now?"

She smiled and said, "I suppose it *was* only a few days ago. I figured that was what you were doing but why bring it up now?"

I rolled my eyes. "You don't give yourself enough credit. What I heard in those audio files was a type of bravery most grown-ass men don't even possess. Some of your ancestors must have been one of those Viking women or something."

"Shield Maidens," she said softly. "Vikings weren't even Vikings – Viking is a verb not a noun. The people we refer to as Vikings today were Norsemen and the Danes."

"Interesting," I said, and she slapped me on the chest lightly. I protested, "No, no! I mean it. I didn't know all that."

She settled down and rested her cheek on my chest and sighed out.

"Where and when did you learn about it?" I asked.

"God, something like fifteen or twenty years ago for a school history project, and a little more after I did one of those online DNA break-down kits."

She cuddled a little closer, shifting against me.

"Yeah? You learn a lot from it?" I asked.

"I-I did it for the medical history and markers portion," she confessed and I gave her a little squeeze and smoothed a hand up and down her back. "The history and ancestry part were just a bonus."

"What were you looking for? You mind me asking?" I asked.

"No, I don't mind. I wanted to see if there was anything genetic to explain the crazy running in my family and the odds of me passing it on – plus any other hereditary time bombs I might have going on."

"Ah…" I trailed off. We were silent for a moment and I asked gently, "You find what you were looking for?"

"What? Answers? No, no I did not."

"Oh," I said, surprised.

"Why?" she asked.

"You said you were sterilized," I said. "I thought maybe something came up."

"No, I wanted to do it regardless of what came up. I was just hoping something would to strengthen my case with the doctors and the like. It's not easy getting sterilized when you don't already have whatever requisite 2.4 children or whatever arbitrary number they came up with to deny us our choice."

I gave her a squeeze and kissed the top of her head again and said, "See, fierce."

She looked up at me, pushing herself up and kissed me, her mouth warm and soft against mine – so sweet, yet with a hidden edge in there somewhere.

"Mm," I hummed in satisfaction and kissed her back, my hand coming up to bury in the thick strands of her blonde hair at the back of her neck, holding it back from our faces.

She leaned into me, and my cock was like, *Alright! Round two!* and I had no complaints. Not when her breathing deepened, certainly not when her hands found my chest and she pushed herself up, breaking our kiss, and absolutely no complaints whatsoever when she straddled me before bringing her mouth back down to mine.

She writhed against me, her soft skin all up against mine and it brought my arousal to a fever pitch.

I braced my hands on her hips, kneading them gently and urging her silently to slick her pussy against my shaft. I wanted inside of her something fierce, but I was alright with letting her drive. Still, it was in my nature to be in control, and I couldn't fucking help myself on that front.

She responded to my hands, riding my body and writhing her hips *just so*, sliding her warm wet velvet soft pussy lips over me, up and down my cock, pinning it between us, driving me crazy with the sensation of her body against mine, the scent of our arousal mingling with our prior deliciously dirty bad acts and making me want inside of her all the more.

I had this primal urge to hold her in place above me, to grip her hips with bruising force and press my way inside her. I wanted to slam up inside her with a level of aggression and possession that was out of pocket for this evening, and so I put those urges back in their pen, back a way back in the dark part of my soul and I held her to me and kissed her deep instead.

When she was good and ready, as aroused as me and then some, she reached between us and lifted my cock of my stomach, slipping me inside her, and *Jesus God!* It was my new very favorite place to fucking be!

She sank down carefully over the top of me. I held her to me and made out with her until she pressed hands against my ribs in a way that said she wanted up to ride me, at which point, I gladly let her go to do her thing.

She was a goddess above me, wreathed in the glow from the candle's light, cast in shadow, a dark and formidable thing. Beautiful, ethereal, and I wished to worship at her altar and give sacrifice; proper tribute as it were.

Nothing of her power, her grace, was diminished as she bowed to kiss me again, as she worked me inside her with her hips. If anything, I felt blessed. Bestowed upon by that kiss, and I was grateful. Grateful that she'd given me a shot, and that she was here with me now. Grateful that she trusted me to take care of her with everything going on… and I would. It was what came after all of that that I was concerned about, because this one taste would *never* be enough.

"WHAT ARE you doing up here, bro?" I looked up and over from my computer monitor and rubbed my eyes, resting my chin on my folded hands, elbows firmly planted on my desktop.

"Sorry, man, I wake you up?" I asked. I had dropped a binder I'd reached for off the shelf and I could only imagine the resounding thump on the carpeted floor up here had still managed to reverberate through the ceiling above Narcos and Everleigh's bedroom.

"Yeah," he grunted and spun his desk chair out to face me and dropped into it with a yawn. "What're you doing?" he demanded again.

"I don't fuckin' know," I said with a sigh. "Tryin' to figure this shit out with too many missing pieces."

"Well knock it off," he said. "The boys'll handle it."

I grunted and turned back to the screen and the downloaded video footage from inside Teresia's bakery. The alarm company had caught it all off-sight and had it backed up. The shit was terrifying.

"That the video footage?" he asked, leaning forward.

"Yeah, forgot to silence my phone. Notification woke me up and when I saw what it was—"

"Couldn't leave well enough alone 'til morning?" he asked gruffly.

"If it was Ev, even back then at the start, would you?" I asked.

He gave a bit of a groan and said, "No. No, I wouldn't." He sighed and rolled across the plastic mat over the carpet then scooched his desk chair off it and made his way through the thick pile at me.

"You got it that bad?" he asked.

I grunted non-committedly in response and rolled the footage back to the start. Sighing, not really wanting to go through it again, I hit the triangle icon to run through it again real-time.

Narcos stuck it out with me in grim silence. We switched between camera views, going through each one that'd captured things from start to finish.

"Fuck, man, no wonder she's having nightmares."

An "Mm" of agreement was all I could really muster at this point.

"Why are you watching this?" he asked.

"Was about to run through some notables, see if I could figure out the perp from build, find someone with a predilection for fire and whites-fuckin'-only and hand it to the boys to run down."

"Bro, that's... that's some insanity-inducing bullshit. You'd have a better chance at finding a needle in a haystack."

"It's driving me crazy. I feel like I need to be doing something – anything, to help."

"What'd you tell me when it was me and Ev out there?" Narcos asked, leaning back in his chair.

"Shit," I muttered, knowing my words were about to get used against me and I hated that shit – as one does when it happens to them.

"Huh?" He leaned forward, his elbows braced on the arms of his office chair, raising his eyebrows and staring at me expectantly.

"Alright, alright," I said, leaning back in my seat, conceding his point without taking a bigger hit to my pride.

I'd told him he was helping by keeping Ev out of the mix while we all did our jobs to bring 'em home.

"Never thought I'd be in the same position," I muttered.

"Turnabout is fair play or some shit like that," he said breezily. I nodded but my mind was already on the next problem.

"You know she ain't gonna want to go anywhere without those cats," I said. "Especially if there's a chance they could be in trouble or whatever."

"I already solved that one for you," he said and I looked up at him and let the curiosity of my expression speak for itself.

"It's getting delivered today. Just worry about getting some damn sleep and convincing your girl to pack up and be willing to go."

"Might need Ev's help a little with that," I said and Narcos nodded.

"Easy enough."

"Mm," I yawned.

"Go back to bed," he ordered, and I nodded.

"Yeah," I said and reached over and switched out the light.

19

*T*eresia...

"It'll be fine, I promise," Sam assured me.

"They're gonna love the cabin and turn into real adventure kitties," Everleigh declared, shouldering the big bubble backpack with Muninn in it. Muninn, my ever-adventurous boy, was looking through the window, sniffing with curiosity. By comparison, Huginn, who was on my back, was just *howling* with fear and indignation.

"He'll calm down," Narcos said, and I bit my bottom lip. "Either that, or you just won't hear him over the wind and the bike."

"Not helpful, dude," Sam shot back at him over his shoulder. "I promise, it'll be fine. We'll get to the cabin and get them situated and they'll be okay. They got situated pretty quick here – this'll be no different."

I nodded. I mean, he was right. I wouldn't leave them behind with no one to watch them and the thought of a riverside cabin, no internet, news, phones blowing up, and just being as far away as possible from the chaos of the city... I got on the back of his bike and cinched the straps on my cat backpack and felt poor Huginn move around inside.

I looked over at Narcos who fired up his bike first as Sam settled onto the saddle of his before me.

He had been the one to bring the packs, harness and leashes for my boys to me. He had picked them out and ordered them online and they'd been delivered today... as the men had spent time loading the bikes with things for our stay and waited rather anxiously for the delivery truck to arrive.

"It's gonna be a beautiful ride!" Sam called back to me, and he gave my leg a squeeze. I sure hoped so. I was still so nervous about my poor babies. I didn't want to traumatize them. But a little way down the road, when Narcos and Everleigh pulled ahead, Muninn's little face staring up through his bubbled window at the sky or whatever his little kitty brain could grab onto had put me at ease.

I didn't feel Huginn's panicked shifting at my back anymore so I think he had settled down, too.

The afternoon sun was pretty hot, but the backpacks were well vented along the sides with plenty of airflow, so I wasn't overly worried about the boys overheating. Besides, the guys promised we would stop every hour or so to check on them and give them water and a bit of time out of the packs on the leashes that'd been bought.

They hadn't taken kindly to the harnesses at first, lying prone on the floor, looking at me like, *mooooom, what is it?* Their little eyes wide and a bit mournful.

They'd both started slinking around within the hour, however, which had only encouraged me that this was going to work.

The ride was going to be a long one, and we were supposed to arrive at the cabin sometime late – super late, the more stops we made.

We stopped at a nicer-than-average restaurant along the way that was in this old Victorian-era house. Narcos went in first to ask if we could keep Huginn and Muninn in their backpacks under the table. Soon, we were five adults standing in the gravel lot of the place as a woman joined us to look at the cats through the little bubble portals on their backpacks.

"Oh, my! How precious!" She practically squealed with delight. "Y'all come on in now and let's get you settled. I own the place and if anyone has a problem, they can come deal with me."

So that's how we all four crowded into a booth in the place, with my two cats tucked up under the table on our feet as we tiredly perused the menu of down-home southern fare.

"We found this place by accident," Sam said. "Everleigh picked up a book on history and this place was mentioned in it. It used to be some kind of plantation or other and was turned into a restaurant in the early two-thousands."

"We decided to try it and we make it a point to stop in every time we head for the cabin. It's sorta becoming tradition for us," Narcos added.

"Food looks good," I said.

We ordered, and I asked, "How much further do we have to go?"

"This is almost the perfect halfway point," Everleigh murmured, and I noticed she tended to be quieter out in public like this – pointing to the menu rather than speaking what she wanted, and nervously looking around some before she did speak to make sure she wasn't overheard – or likely that no one would take her speaking as an invitation to come talk to her. I knew a bit about that last one. I think every woman did.

The food was good, we even had dessert, and then it was back to the bikes. I groaned a little inwardly, looking at the machine with its bulk of strapped-on things at the back and its stuffed saddlebags.

"Just a couple more hours, baby," Sam promised.

"Oh, is that all?" I asked mildly, and he chuckled.

"Can't tell if you were being sarcastic or not," he said, sitting astride the big beast of a bike that was more beast of burden in the hour or so post twilight. It was dark with only a glimmer of the last vestiges of sun over the horizon and I was honestly ready to be done with today.

I got on behind him and made sure the straps to my carrier were secure. Everleigh and I had switched cats so that I could see how well my other baby was doing.

He was yowling again and looked freaked out, but no more than his usual not wanting to be in a carrier. I was grateful things were cooling off with the coming night for them. I didn't want to think about them overheating in the full light of day.

We stopped one more time at what was the last rest stop before the cabin, so the guys said, and let the kitties out to slink around in the grass and explore a picnic table.

"Tired?" Sam asked me, and I nodded.

"Pretty sure I'm going to ache all over tomorrow," I complained. He chuckled.

"Got a case of monkey butt?" he asked.

"A case of what?" I laughed at him.

"Monkey butt," Narcos called back from where he was crouched down and petting Muninn.

"What is *that?*" I demanded.

"Chafing," Everleigh said, grinning.

"Oh, no, it's not that. At least, I don't think," I said. "Just muscle sore."

"We're almost there," Sam reiterated. "I promise."

I nodded, watching Narcos and Everleigh with my fur babies and secretly grateful I didn't have to corral my furry little toddlers right now.

By the time we were back on the road, it really was only a few more exits before we were off the major freeway and then it was scenic highways or byways – or it would have been if it hadn't become pitch black. There were no such things as streetlights out here, and at first, I thought I was so tired I was beginning to hallucinate when I started to see glimmers and sparkles at the edges of the road, like twinkling Christmas lights in among the trees.

It took a while to register that what I was seeing were the flitting lights of fireflies.

It was full dark, the tall treetops blotting out any moon or starlight from the sky above and making the corridor of road just that much more ominous. I held a little tighter to Sam and all of a sudden, we were turning, and then crunching over gravel. In a spill of blue-white light, we were in a clearing, with a cabin, the sky opening up in a strip behind the building as Sam heeled down the kickstand on his bike. With a couple taps to my knee, he urged me to get up and get off.

I did, groaning, the silence left by the bikes motors when they were cut deafening, backfilling with insect and frog song into a soothing cadence that allowed just an absolute bone weariness to take hold.

"You doing okay?" Narcos asked, and I jumped as his big hand lightly touched my lower back.

"Mm, yes, just tired."

"If you can take him," Everleigh said, shrugging out of her cat back-pack, "it won't take but twenty minutes to get things set up."

I took my other boy from her and felt him shift around inside his pack.

"Sounds good," I said.

I waited for Sam with my burden of my two boys who were restless. I think they sensed the journey was at its end, and they were eager to leave the confines of their carriers. I know I was eager to shed my borrowed leather jacket and long pants for something lightweight and cooler.

If I had thought the outdoors was bad – both in terms of heat and mugginess – well let's just say I was not prepared when it came to the inside of the cabin.

While a lot drier in terms of humidity – it was *stuffy*. A hotbox thanks to what had looked like a metal roof and all the windows and doors having been closed up tight.

Everleigh and Narcos were opening windows and doors. She turned to me and Sam as we entered with the boys and some of the bags and things that had taken up the saddlebags and had been strapped to the bike.

"You want to get the power turned on?" Everleigh asked Sam.

"I've got it," Narcos declared, heading for the back screen door that looked like it led out onto a wraparound porch.

"What can I do?" I asked.

"Head on up to the loft," she said. "Pull the dust covers off of things?"

"Sure."

"Got a box and some litter downstairs. We use it to soak up oil, usually. We can get something set up for the boys on the back porch." I felt myself relax with relief that there was an ability to get the boys a potty box but it was short lived after his words about putting their box on the back porch registered. There hadn't been room on the bikes to bring a box and litter with us.

At the somewhat stricken look on my face, Narcos chuckled and assured me about the back porch thing. "Relax. It's screened in. They can't get out into the woods. I'll even double-check before we let 'em out there. I don't want to lose either of the furry little bastards, either."

"Be right back, baby. You and Ev sit tight up here," Sam said, and I nodded.

The two men departed and Everleigh said, "Let 'em out up in the loft. It'll take 'em a while to figure out how to get down – if they even can. We might need to figure that out."

I nodded and turned around to the sturdy ladder built into the wall away from the entry we'd just come through.

"Okay," I agreed and set one of my boys down so I could climb – the other firmly still on my back. When I got to the top, Everleigh called, "Here." I turned and reached down, pulling my other boy up behind us while she held him aloft, carrier and all from down below.

"Thanks," I said.

It was really dark up here, but I had the vague impression of a day bed against one wall, and a couple of nightstands made from old, stacked apple crates to either side of it.

"Do you want me to open the window up here?" I asked.

"Absolutely!" Everleigh called.

I shrugged out of the carrier on my back and set it next to the other at the edge of the bed – on the floor of course. I didn't want anyone falling off the bed and getting hurt within the confines of the backpack.

It was surprisingly wonderful and sweet how quickly everyone came together in opening up the cabin. When the power flickered on, I had to smile. There was a central weak bulb that looked like it had been there a hundred years that illuminated both up here in the loft and down below with its dim golden glow. The glow was warm and cheery, and I was pleased to see that every window was, indeed screened, and that every screen was in good repair.

"We'd be eaten alive if they weren't," Everleigh said laughingly when I remarked on it.

I pulled the dust sheet off of the bed and folded it neatly, finding that was the only one up here.

I let the boys out next to explore the loft.

"You guys are up there. Narcos and I will stay down here," Everleigh called.

"Alright," I called back, smiling at the country quilt on the bed and the dried flowers and herbs hanging from the rails along the loft.

I watched the babies and took the things Sam handed up to me while I heard Narcos pour litter and food down below.

The boys got excited by the sound of their food hitting their bowls, thundering up to the edge of the loft, looking for a way down.

"Guys, wouldn't it be cute to find some rough natural wood chunks and nail them in like steps and whatnot here, here, and maybe here?" Everleigh asked.

Narcos looked thoughtful. "That would be good. You good with it?" he asked Sam. Sam looked at the wall and ladder and nodded slowly.

"We got some of that rough live-edge downstairs. We can work something out tomorrow," he said.

"Oh, you don't have to go to all that trouble," I said even as Huginn looked like he was about to jump, which made me cry out, "Oh, God!" and go for him. I snatched him up and set him back to where he would be safe and took first the little stand, then one and the other of their bowls from Narcos as he stood patient, handing me one thing at a time.

"I'll get their water while you get that set up," he said.

We worked on finishing everything up for my boys and by the time all was said and done, I think *I* was just done.

Sam climbed up into the loft and said, "That should do for them for now." I raised an eyebrow and peered over the edge.

Muninn was already through the bars of the railing and jumping down onto the top of the bookshelf they'd brought from the wall beside the shabby two-seater loveseat. The one that'd been between it and the bathroom door.

"Not perfect," he said as my cat jumped from the shelf to the floor with a little kitty grunt.

I winced and said, "As long as they can get to food, water, and their cat box, it's all good."

"We'll get this place hooked up into a kitty play palace in no time tomorrow," Narcos declared.

"I don't like cats," Everleigh said, rolling her eyes and her voice heavy with sarcasm.

"I don't like *most* cats," Narcos declared. "These ones are alright."

I stifled a giggle and Sam touched my back. I looked up at him and he said, "C'mon, sweet girl. Let's get you to bed."

I nodded, not quite sure what to expect, but he simply led me back under the pitched roof of the loft and away from the railing and any prying eyes before he grasped the hem of my shirt.

I raised my arms, and he pulled it off for me, over my head.

He was so gentle and so sweet, undressing me a piece at a time, his rough fingertips grazing my skin in such a whisper of a touch it made me shiver. I relaxed under that touch. I mean, how could I help myself?

I heard a gasp and a feminine moan from down below and froze under Sam's touch.

"Relax, baby," he murmured close to my ear, licking the edge, nipping my earlobe and making me weak in the knees. I leaned back against him and his arms circled my waist.

"We're all out here just to have a good time," he whispered. "Nobody watching, nobody to care. Just whispers and cries in the dark," he murmured and kissed the side of my neck, devilishly seductive, causing me to gasp and tense up for an altogether different reason.

His hands smoothed over my skin as he set about unclasping and removing clothing from my body, one bit at a time.

By the time he turned me around to kneel in front of me and sweep my jeans off of me, my hands found themselves buried in his hair, clutching that mouth of his to my skin as my head fell back and he wrenched a throaty moan of my own from me.

God, what those lips and teeth did to me!

I arched into him and gasped, myself, a throaty inarticulate cry emanating from my lips without me even realizing, at first, that I'd made it.

He made a sound of pride and satisfaction, grasping the back of his tee and pulling it over his head before immediately putting his arms around my thighs, his hands to my ass, and plunging his tongue between the folds at the apex of my thighs.

Again, with that throaty sultry gasp, only this time Narcos chuckled darkly from down below and I tensed again.

"Easy, baby," Sam murmured against my stomach, and the way he looked up at me in the dim light... I felt worshiped, as though I were a goddess stepped out of some other plane of existence, specifically to meet this man for his attentions.

He grasped me to him and lifted one of my legs over his shoulder, grunting when I squirmed at first and growling out, "I've got you, *relax.*"

I believed him, despite his gruff delivery, maybe *because* of his gruff delivery – regardless, I shivered in the too-warm space and then his hot mouth was on me more fully. All I could do was whimper and whine and tangle my fingers in his hair more tightly as he laved my pussy with his tongue, getting it wet, tickling my inner thigh with a ghost of a touch as he held my leg over his shoulder with one arm, and ran fingertips over my sensitive skin with the other.

"Oh, God!" I cried as he plunged his tongue past my clit and his fingers up inside of me. I wobbled imbalanced on my feet and his arms tightened around my thigh as he grunted against me, holding on and true to his word – he had me. Apparently, right where he wanted me – and who was I to argue?

He worked me up into a gasping, chest heaving frenzy; keeping me right on the edge without letting me tip over into that wondrous freefall and it was nothing short of *maddening*.

He knew what he was doing, too, chuckling any time that I sounded even remotely triumphant that I was *there*, switching his tactic, stopping what he was doing altogether, in some cases, to look up at me with this *devilish* sparkle in his dark eyes that honestly made me want to scream in frustration.

"What, do you want me to beg?" I demanded softly to the rhythmic slapping and thrust-punctuated cries coming from Everleigh and Narcos down below. I felt high spots of color on my cheeks, and I was grateful for the dark that – hopefully – hid it from Sam's hungry gaze.

His response was to stop, withdrawing his mouth from the front of my pussy, his stretching fingers giving me that tingling sense of fullness out of my drenched hole. I bit my bottom lip, regretting my words almost immediately.

"You ain't got to beg for a fucking thing from me," he said, rising to his feet and pulling me against him.

I let my hands smooth over his hard body, all warm skin, surprisingly soft and smooth. I worked at his belt and listened to the leather give a little sigh of release as I undid it.

He watched me intently, sliding his hands into my hair and caressing my face. I captured his thumb with my mouth, sucking on it, and watched him suck in a sharp breath, his eyes growing somehow darker still without changing color so much as the intent and emotion shifting behind them.

His hips rocked as I reached into his jeans and gripped him, stroking him, all velvet and smooth, hot and rock hard. His desire for me couldn't be disguised if he wanted to and I was just... wow.

I don't think anyone had ever looked at me with such intensity.

He took his hands from me and I nipped the pad of his thumb as he withdrew it from my mouth. Still our eyes were locked, neither willing to look away, even as he struggled to get his jeans off the rest of the way, stepping on the cuffs and pulling his legs free.

I yipped a high sound of surprise that built and burst into a peal of laughter as he picked me up, bodily off of the floor, wrapping my legs around him, careful not to bash my head into the ceiling of the pitched roof. I bent, capturing his face between my hands and bowing my head to kiss him as he turned and drifted over to the bed.

The power in his touch, in the way his body moved, reminded me of the sleek power of a great cat. Stalking away, its prey in its grasp, to find someplace more private, more secure, to devour it in peace. Only I was his next meal, and I couldn't wait, which you would think odd but definitely not in this context.

I expected him to lay me down, to slide inside of me and to ravage me against the country quilt, but he had other ideas.

Instead, tongues twining and almost blind, he turned, hitching me up a little higher, his cock brushing against my sex and making things tighten up with anticipation low in my body, as he sat himself down, me straddling him.

"Fuck me," he growled against my mouth and he definitely wasn't asking.

I wasn't about to tease him with the desperate fever pitch he'd worked me into. Instead, I rose on my knees and reached down between us, lifting his cock, and trying to get the right angle, which was harder than it sounded with the position we held.

He held me, an arm around my waist, hand on my bottom, urging me to tilt my hips just so. I followed his lead, leaning back, one hand grasping the back of his neck to hold myself up, as he pushed himself down and then *oh, God, yes!*

He slipped inside of me like a fucking *dream*, my body open and welcoming, his cock so hot, so pure, pressing out against my walls and stimulating me gently, and driving me just fucking *crazy*.

"Oh, yeah," he moaned, and his voice held a sort of abandon to it that made my heart soar. I felt lighter than air as I moved my hips, grinding against him, holding on to him with one hand, his hands on my hips, guiding me, helping me grind, as my other hand drifted down my body.

The way his eyes followed the drift of that hand, against my throat, between the valley of my breasts, the lower it went, the more heated his gaze, the more intent, as I dipped my fingertips between us and rubbed an experimental lazy circle against my clit.

"Oh, shit that's good, that's so good, baby. Like that, just like that," he encouraged, and I held on to him, tipping my head back. "That's it, take your pleasure. I want to watch you. Fuck me. Use me to get yourself off, honey. I wanna see."

I panted, writhing against him, his cock buried as deep as it could go and tickling my walls, my fingertips waking up the nerves along, what felt like, my *entire body* with every barely controlled swish of my fingertips.

When I got off, it was more like I went off like a firework. I was vaguely aware of his arms tightening around me, of being swept up into the sky, leaving the atmosphere altogether for one of those heart-beats that felt like an eternity. A whole moment, a whole new world, held in a fragment of time that was smaller than a grain of sand that was somehow suspended for an eon – an eon in which I forgot to breathe as I left my body behind for the pure sensation and pleasure that was Sam Stahl inside of me.

I twined around that man, and he held me fast as I crashed back into my skin like a meteor to earth and the pleasure tore through me, my body rebelling my orders and the signals between neurons scrambled. I was left a jerking and twitching mess in his arms as he held me tight and kept me from sliding off and breaking my ass.

When I came back to myself, I realized that by some miracle, and a miracle alone, not only was I still straddling his powerful thighs, somehow, someway, he remained inside of me. How did I figure that out? When with a darkling, decadent little chuckle, he twitched his cock inside me, wrenching a gasp and sending pleasure out from my core like little lightning shocks through my veins.

"Mmm, good girl," he growled in my ear, holding me tight and lying back, clutching me tightly to him. I rested against his chest, and he kissed my ear, my temple, anything he could reach with his lips as the sweat dewed our skins and a slight cross breeze made it through the open windows to wander over our bodies.

I twitched at the sound he made and gasped anew when he rolled us both to one side and suddenly as I had just been above, I was below. He was driving sharply into me, all the way to the hilt, eliciting another sharp, throaty, lustful cry from me.

"You didn't come?" I whispered, and I didn't know why my mind grabbed onto that.

"Mm-mm," he muttered, nuzzling the side of my neck. "Ride's just starting," he whispered in my ear, and God – oh God, I didn't know if I was ready. Not yet, not – *oh...*

Sam didn't care, because ready or not? He wasn't going to stop until he came.

20

*D*riller...

"That was hot last night," Narcos declared as he looked up and down a rough board in the garage. I was sorting through some of the woodpile we had down here for the firepit, looking for chunks that once sanded, would work for the kitty cat obstacle course he'd envisioned for my girl's boys.

Everleigh and Teresia were both upstairs, Everleigh doing whatever her little hippy dippy and beautiful heart desired and Teresia kneading some dough for whatever rustic bread she'd decided to make to go with sandwiches for lunch.

"Oh, yeah?" I asked casually.

"Shit yeah. Listening to you guys while balls deep in my girl was *fantastic*."

I chuckled and tossed the piece I was examining into the "keep" pile for the project we were working on.

"I think these'll do it," he declared, and I looked up and over, nodding at the boards he had in his gloved hands.

"Need to rip 'em down, any?" I asked.

He cocked his head and said, "No, sanding for sure, but I like 'em thick like this, sturdy for Huginn, the chonker."

I laughed and nodded. "He's just a big boy, like you."

"Motherfucker, you better not be calling me fat. I work fuckin' hard on this girlish figure. You're fixin' to give me an eating disorder or some shit."

I laughed at him harder and said, "The way you eat sometimes *is* an eating disorder – especially when you're pounding that many fuckin' eggs."

In true juvenile dude-bro fashion, he raised a leg and ripped a fart.

"You can be so disgusting." I shook my head.

"Yeah, well, so can you," he shot back, and I grinned. He wasn't wrong.

We sawed some raw, live edged boards in half, sanded them down smooth, and worked in the shadow of the garage, out of the hot sun. Still, it was hot today – in or out of it – the air smelling green, of rich earth and growing things, the air soupy and sticking to our skins. There were supposed to be thunderstorms late in the day, pushing on toward the evening, so said the wind-up radio we had going down here, anyway.

When we got upstairs, things weren't much better, not with the oven going. The smell of fresh bread baking definitely made up for it, though.

"Look at you all rugged and handy," Teresia said with a wink, Huginn in her lap, raising his butt into her scratches at the base of his tail.

"One kitty cat superhighway coming right up," Narcos declared and Everleigh rolled her eyes from the kitchen sink, turning back around to wash out some Mason jars.

"What're your big plans now?" I asked.

"Gonna go out in a bit and forage," Everleigh said. "Probably stop by the swimming hole to cool off."

"Shit yeah. Meet you out there after we're done with this," Narcos said and I looked to Teresia.

She smiled at me and I told her, "You'll like it out there. Boys are safe enough in here and on the porch. We got the screens secured and put that latch on the door out there so you don't have to worry.

"Thank you," she murmured and her smile grew.

"Any time," I told her.

The timer went off before we started hammering things up and into place and the bread came out of the oven to cool on a sideboard.

The girls took a bit to use sunscreen and Teresia used the bug spray that Everleigh had made out of natural oils and whatever. I mean, it wasn't to the standard of store brand shit but it worked pretty okay and it was all natural, so there was that.

Teresia came by and kissed me before they left, and I could tell she was a little nervous and a little reluctant to leave.

"God, you picked good, man. She's hot," Narcos declared.

I chuckled and told him, "Not sure she's into all the extras, might take some time to warm up to the idea. Might be a 'what happened at the cabin stays at the cabin' sort of scenario – I don't know."

Narcos lifted a shoulder in a shrug. "You know I'm good with whatever," he said.

"Yeah, I know, man. Still, I mean, I would like it," I said. "You know, the four of us."

He nodded.

"I know, man. Might be too much with everything going down right now."

"Yeah," I agreed, holding a board in place while he lined up and marked out the "L" brackets we'd found downstairs amidst the junk, to magic make this work.

"Still, last night... Mm." That "mm" was of pure satisfaction and yeah, I had to agree. The sounds filling the cabin, the love and lust and the smell of sex perfuming the air – it'd been a hedonistic paradise.

"She ask any questions?" he asked.

"Some. I think she's curious," I answered.

He grunted and nodded then helped me bring the board down.

"I really hope you don't mind me saying, but I would love to help you rock her world."

"You know I don't mind you saying – you also know I don't mind sharing, but you know the rules."

"Yeah, no, abso-fucking-lutely. Her choice, man. Nothing's changed there and it never will."

I nodded. While I could appreciate my brother's enthusiasm for Teresia, and while I was starting to feel deep for her, I still couldn't be sure that she – I don't know how to say it delicately, so I won't – I don't know if she was going to fit the lifestyle we led. I mean, she was fire under that stone-and-placid demeanor but those stone walls contained her spark for a reason. She'd built herself up from nothing and had done it despite all the people in her life, taking from her, borrowing her strength without asking and counting on her without ever giving her anyone to count on in return... or so I'd gathered.

I understood this, now, as an age of selfishness in a way, for her. That she might just want this to be for her and sharing might not necessarily be on her radar.

I didn't want her to step outside her comfort zone if she wasn't comfortable taking the steps. I didn't want her to do anything for *me*. I wanted her to do it for her and see if it was to her liking.

I guessed I wanted her to feel safe to explore and that might take time. This was all so fucking new and propelled by a giant fucking boulder, made up of chaos and disaster that'd unstoppably had come off a cliff and rolled through her life, smashing it to smithereens.

I didn't want to be one of the smaller rocks tumbling after it, blowing more holes in things. I was tired of blowing holes in things. I said as much to Narcos, my brother, my partner, my best friend, and I did it a little reluctantly because I didn't want a fuckin' pep talk. I wanted for him to hear me.

He stopped what he was doing, lowering his board and looking at me like he finally fucking got it and was *hearing* me.

"You thinking about leaving the force?" he asked, and he sounded a little lost.

I nodded. "Man, maybe it's time," I said and I know it was in my voice, just how lost I felt. "I don't know, I mean, I always thought they would have my back, you know? And I don't feel that way anymore."

He walked over and did something uncharacteristic right then and he hugged me tight, a great big bear hug that nearly cracked my ribs and did crack my back in a couple of places, releasing tension I didn't know rode me.

"It's not just a phase, is it?" he asked.

I said, "No, man. It's not."

"Fuck, I would hate it, but... fuck me, man." His voice was full of emotion. "What would you do?"

I swallowed hard and pulled back just a bit and said, "I have no idea."

He searched my face and nodded slowly. He said, "I can't picture you in the private sector. You've got civil servant encoded into your fucking DNA, bro."

I nodded and said, "I couldn't do private corporate bullshit either. That's the problem. That's what the fucking department has become – corporate."

He nodded slowly and asked, "Fire? Medic?"

I nodded slowly and said, "Maybe. A little old to make the jump to fire, ain't I?"

He shrugged. "Talk to Backdraft? Maybe Blaze? You may have years but you're in great fuckin' shape and could pass their shit on endurance easy. I mean, fuck, you took two to your chest plate, cracked two ribs, got right back up and kept right on fuckin' going like you were Superman or some shit."

"That was all adrenaline," I said.

He gave me a wry grin and made a scoffing "Ch!" sound.

"Like the hose boys aren't on one big, long adrenaline kick?"

I thought about that. "Yeah, well, in the *moment*," I said. "Not like, all the time and during training and shit."

Narcos shook his head.

"Bro, I am like a thousand percent sure that if you put your mind to it, you can fuckin' do it. You want outta the department – literally out of the frying pan and into the fuckin' fire?" He laughed. "You'll do it. No doubt." His belief in me was a little astounding, but if he were in my place? I would probably be saying the same fuckin' thing.

"You get where I'm coming from?" I asked.

He nodded and didn't look happy about it.

"Yeah, I do, and it kills me," he admitted. "Not that you want to make the jump, believe me, I really do get that part – it's the fact that you even feel like you have to in the first place. This particular case? What happened with you and that kid—"

"Témaël," I stopped him. "I love you brother but say his name... Témaël Etienne."

He sighed, looked away, but nodded.

"What happened with you and Témaël Etienne, it was a bona fide accident. You didn't mean to shoot him. You really did legitimately think you were shooting his cousin, the one that shot you."

I nodded.

"You know, I've gone over it countless times, guessed and second-guessed myself and I probably will for an eternity more. I've asked myself more times than I can count – am I a racist piece of shit? Like, really. Down in the dirtiest parts of my heart and soul – am I just like every other white cop?"

Narcos looked sad then and shook his head.

"No, man. I think just by you asking yourself that – the fact that I can see by the look on your face that you've been torturing yourself over it? I think the ones that are don't question that kind of shit. Good people will torture themselves like you are now. The bad ones just don't give a shit."

"We've encountered plenty of the bad ones, for sure," I said and nodded, and he sighed.

"You know, maybe you should talk to someone qualified about this," he said. "Outside the department, for sure – because fuck the brass. You don't want to hand them any more shit and honestly, the more I think about it and the more I get used to the idea, yeah. You *should* walk. This department doesn't fuckin' deserve you, bro."

"That's the hard part, bro. If I walk away, aren't I just still part of the big fucking problem?" I warred with myself on this – constantly. Unsure how, if I really was a good cop like every one of the boys was saying, how my walking away was going to fucking be any kind of solution to anything.

I knew the problem was systemic. Fuck, every one of us knew the problem was systemic – Narcos interrupted my thoughts by pulling what I was thinking right out of my head and speaking it to the universe or whatever.

"The system is fucking broken, bro. We're just but tiny cogs in a machine that's gotten too fuckin' big for us to drive. Do I think walking away is going to break shit further? I don't know. What I do know is it's not about the machine anymore. It's about *you*, and I'm fuckin' worried about you. You got me worried on more than one occasion that you were thinkin' about suck-starting your fuckin' .45 and I can't have that. If you leaving breaks the machine so fuckin' be it, because you're miserable grinding away as one of its gears, and the machine's already proven it doesn't give a fuck about you, or me, or any of the Témaël Etienne's of the street."

He sighed.

"I don't know where this hell ride is going to stop. All I care about is you, and Ev, and me, and yeah… maybe even Teresia and these furry little shits right here," he said, bending down and picking up one of Teresia's cats, holding it like a baby. The cat reached up and pawed the air and Narcos kissed the top of its head, which the cat looked indignant about. I chuckled at the sight. I couldn't help it.

Pretty sure every cat on the planet had a right to be indignant about the fact that God made 'em this perfect little killing machine with their murder mittens and ridiculous reflexes… only to put them in a compact, adorable, eight-pound body that humans insisted on picking up and kissing and naming them after fuckin' food items like Tofu.

"I don't know where this ends," he said uneasily, and I knew he reverted to the situation regarding me and the force and what have you. "I honestly don't care," he said. "As long as you, me, the girls, the rest of the boys, and these two furry little shits wind up healthy, and as close to happy as we can all carve out."

"Swear to God, it feels like the whole fuckin' country is falling the fuck apart." I sighed.

"Yeah, it does," he said sadly.

I shook my head at his tone.

"Maybe you ought to think about making the leap with me," I said.

He shook his head.

"Somebody's got to keep an eye on things from the inside," he declared. I took a deep breath in through the nose, letting it out through my mouth slowly while I thought about that and finally, I had to nod.

"A little paranoid, don't you think?" I asked.

"Motherfucker, you're the one that taught me to always keep an eye on my back."

I nodded, disappointed that I wasn't wrong.

"Yeah. Yeah, I did," I agreed.

"I ain't happy about it, either," he said. "I know we got the rest of the boys to watch our six but… but I'll stay vigilant just the same for now if it's all the same to you."

I nodded.

"Let's finish this up," I said, diverting our attention back to the cat run that was going from a few odd, nailed shelves to give the cats a way up and down into the loft to something – well, I don't exactly know what. That was all Narcos and his fuckin' vision.

21

*T*eresia...

Everleigh and I foraged, and it was highly entertaining. For a woman who seemed so young at heart, she was surprisingly knowledgeable. We collected ramps, a garlic-like plant, and she stopped at a tree in the heart of the woods with a big crevice down the middle.

"Stay back here," she urged and curiously, I did what she asked as she set down her basket of ramps and mushrooms, picking up a jar from the depths of it.

"What are you doing?" I asked, and she put a finger to her lips in the motion for 'shh' and with a wink set out across the leaf-littered clearing in the direction of the tree, climbing up on its gnarled roots and dragging herself closer to the hollowed-out portion of the trunk.

I made to step forward when the buzzing caught my ears and rose around her, the cloud of bees quite the sight.

"Yeah, they aren't happy this time!" she called out, and I worried for her.

"Are they stinging you?" I called.

"Not yet! But I would back off. They might come for me."

I backed off toward the river and shortly thereafter, Everleigh came out of the woods with a jar of golden honey with some comb still attached.

"You, okay?" I asked warily.

"Took a couple stings, but I'm alright," she said.

"Doesn't that hurt?" I asked.

"A little but no need to mess with it and spread the venom," she said.

"You're not allergic, are you?" I asked, and she laughed and inspected the underside of her wrist.

"No. Not at all."

"Well, that's good."

She crouched by the river and sealed the jar with a lid and ring from the basket, rinsing it in the running water and soaking her wrist in the cold runoff for some relief.

I hesitated, trying to figure out the best way to broach the subject. I wasn't exactly used to asking questions about, well, *you know...* but I needed to figure some things out before I let myself get too deep with Sam.

"So, um, how long have you, Sam and Narcos been... like... um..."

She chuckled lightly and looked up at me through her long lashes. I was once again reminded just how *green* her eyes were.

"We're not a throuple if that's what you're asking," she said. "It's a bit more amorphous than that."

"Explain," I said, my mouth a bit dry. I didn't know if I liked the sound of that but rather than misunderstanding, I just wanted to hear what she had to say first and go from there.

197

"Narcos and I are a couple, hands down. We all just like to do what feels good and we're comfortable, you know, ah... sharing, I guess. I mean, at least the boys are. They don't really get involved with each other so much. They're straight."

I swallowed and forced the awkward question out, "They're straight but... you're not?"

She laughed lightly. "I wouldn't exactly say I'm bi, more just a little heteroflexible." She raised her eyebrows and looked me over. I felt myself color to the roots of my hair.

"I don't understand what that means," I muttered and her smile grew.

"You need to lighten up," she said and her laugh was light and pixie-like.

"Sorry, all of this um, *openness* is new to me."

"We're a pack of hedonists more than anything," she said with a one-shouldered shrug.

"Okay, explain it to me like I'm five," I said, making to sit down on a nearby rock.

"Come on," she said standing. "I'll explain on the walk to the swimming hole."

"Okay." I nodded and rose.

"Where would you like me to start?" she asked.

"Heteroflexible?" I squeaked.

"Sure, I think there's a bit more nuance to that one anyhow."

"Okay," I said, and I hated that I probably sounded like I was taking notes.

"For some women, it means they'll make out with someone presenting as their same sex but that's as far as it goes. For me, it's got more of a demi-sexual connotation, I guess."

Sound of Blue Thunder

"Elaborate please?" I asked.

"Okay, so you know what a demi-sexual is, right?"

"Mm, nope."

She grinned. "Okay, well, a demi-sexual is usually someone that isn't or can't be sexually attracted to someone until they get to know that person. Like they have to make an emotional connection for sexual attraction or desire to be there."

"Okay." I nodded.

"So, for me, I can just be attracted to Narcos or men in general, but for me to be attracted to a woman, I have to get to know her. There has to be more than just *'damn she looks fine,'* for me to be able to get there."

"Okay." I nodded. "That makes sense." I was a little relieved that there was a name or a designation for how I may or may not be feeling or how attraction, I guess, *worked* for me. I'd found the odd woman attractive before, but never like I'd found *men* attractive. I mean, I could look at a man and be like *hot* and want to ride that ride so to speak, but women? I mean, I'd felt attraction before, with just how beautiful I could find some to be – but it took a lot more than just that for me to even think about what it would be like to kiss her or to have her touch me.

Also, regarding women versus men, there was a lot more awkward feeling like a teen with an unattainable crush where women were concerned. I said as much, comfortable to an extent with talking to Everleigh and she laughed high and bright.

"Oh, I know, right?" she asked. "It's like being thirteen with your very first lady boner all over again and having absolutely no idea how sex was even supposed to work – just knowing that oh my God, yes, I want that!"

"Yes!" I crowed. "It's exactly like that," I said, following her with the basket over my arm, leaping from rock to rock until we got up to a jam of them and sort of had to start to climb-ish.

She led the way, and still in her long hippy skirts, while I struggled along in my cute and markedly more comfortable and functional overalls that ended in shorts rather than long pants. It was a good thing I had on a sturdy pair of ankle boots. While not precisely designed for hiking, they were a lot better than Everleigh's sandals. They didn't seem to be slowing her down any which was just baffling to me.

I handed the basket of our finds up to her and managed to scramble up after her taller frame with the use of both of my hands to aide me.

"Oh, wow!" I said as I stood up, dusting myself off at the edge of a naturally made rock pool that was, I would say, the size of a ten- or twelve-person hot tub.

"Right? This is what we call the swimming hole. It's no more than six feet deep in the very center and off to that side," she said, pointing. "So be careful about that, but otherwise, it's just like a hot tub and even has a few rocks that jut out like seating over on the shallow side."

"Oh, my God, get out of my head," I said giggling. "I just thought this was about the size of a hot tub for a dozen."

"Yeah, well, it's definitely not a hot tub, but this is going to feel so good after those stings and all this heat," she declared, setting down her basket to one side and reaching for the leather belt artfully draped on her hips over her skirts.

I sat down on the edge and worked off my boots and socks, dipping my feet up to the knees in the crisp and refreshingly cool water. I sighed, tipping my head back and leaning back on my hands, the dappled light through the canopy of the surrounding trees on my face, making shifting patterns in the red through my eyelids.

"Oh!" I tipped my head back down and looked as a nude Everleigh went from waist height in the water to up to her chin.

I blinked and swallowed hard.

I don't know why, but I guess I had expected her to keep her bra and panties on.

Hedonists, Teresia. Of course, nudity isn't a problem, I internally reminded myself.

She swam over to me, like a siren, and I felt my mouth go dry and swallowed hard. She ducked under the cool waters of the pool and came up, resting her hands on my knees, her green eyes vivid over the line of water just beneath them. She came up a little more for air and said, "Come on. There's no one but just us girls out here and even if the boys do show up later, you're beautiful. You should be seen."

Something about the way she said it, something in her eyes, I couldn't help it. I choked up.

That was all I had ever wanted... was to be seen. I mean, really seen. I'd just never felt that before. Seen. Like, really seen heart and soul until Sam had looked at me in the hallway of their house before sending me into his room to rest.

I think that was the first time anyone had looked at me and I felt had really seen what I was and who I was, the core of me all vulnerable and soft... and hadn't tried to exploit it for their own ends.

Sam had just let me be, let me breathe, when I had been so hard on him.

I felt something similar from Everleigh just now, but different. I don't know, it was like a-a-a schism was happening. Like I had been split down the middle and if I undressed and slipped into that pool, I would leave the chrysalis of who I'd been for something so new, so enticing, so-so-so freeing. I was just here, in the idyllic woods that were calling to my soul to leave what I'd been behind and to step into this unnamed *power* that I think had been inside of me all along, but the path was... obscured somehow.

What was once unseen could now be seen, and it felt like it was right there if only... if only I were brave enough to take it.

The question I had for myself was *did I want it bad enough?*

I sat with that for a moment, watching Everleigh move beneath the crystal-clear waters of the pool, dappled by sunlight and patches of shifting shadow by the leaves shifting in the light breeze.

She twisted in the water, elegant, like a mermaid or something else equally of myth and ethereal legend, and I low key ached with how beautiful it was.

Decision made, I reached for the latch over one shoulder of my short-alls, unclasping it.

"There you go!" Everleigh crowed, pleased.

She gave me room to breathe and turned around so I could finish quickly undressing. She didn't turn back around until I was up to my chin in the water and said, "Okay."

She spun lithe and graceful in the water and wound up on her back, playfully splashing in my direction. I giggled and ducked under and came up, tilting my head back so that it would slick back my hair.

"Whoa, hey. Looks like you girls started the party without us." I jumped and spun in the water, Everleigh giggling and wrapping her arms around me from behind and hugging me. My skin tingled from the contact as Narcos and Sam emerged from the rocks and clambered down to the edge of the pool.

"You bring anything good with you?" Everleigh called and Narcos held up a six-pack of something that he dropped into the pool to cool off, both of us flinching away and laughing at the splash, the cans in their plastic rings bobbing around in the pool.

"You girls find anything good?" Sam asked, poking around in the basket in the shade.

"Yep, yep!" Everleigh cried.

I sort of huddled back into her a bit, but neither man was projecting any excessive lascivious attention in my direction and there was a certain comfort in that.

Narcos cleared his throat, and I glanced back in his direction. He winked at me, and dropped his shirt to the ground, well away from the pool, and went for the cut-off army pants slung low on his hips, dropping trow so to speak.

I blushed and quickly averted my gaze so I wouldn't be caught staring. I mean, he had a very nice physique and all, the tattoos vivid under his skin – but I was captivated by Sam who was dropping his shirt and a set of towels over the basket of our foraged finds to help shade them. The shifting sun was going to draw things out from under the shade of the trees sooner rather than later, so he was thinking ahead, like he always seemed to do. It was something I could appreciate about him.

Growing up the way that I had, in a household with mental illness and unexpected outbursts, never knowing what was coming next? I appreciated Sam's steadiness and ability to plan ahead. I needed it, I thought. I was pretty sure it was one of the reasons I felt so safe with him – his grave steadiness and sharp outlook.

I was struck dumb, breathless with want, and had all but forgotten Everleigh's lithe arms around me as I bobbed in the pool, watching Sam undress out of his thin black tee faded to an almost charcoal and slip out his equally threadbare and comfortable-looking tan cargo shorts.

He got into the water and pushed off the rock, siding up to me and pulling me to him. I wrapped my arms around his shoulders and my legs around his lean hips. Our mouths locked, and it was one of those perfect little moments of a newly budding... wait, was this a relationship in bloom? I didn't know. I mean, we hadn't talked about it and—

My slightly panicked thinking about the labels that should apply to us went out the window the moment his tongue touched mine and a sort of sorrow settled into my heart – a sinking feeling as I wondered if I was making a terrible mistake in getting involved with him. I couldn't help it, a whimper escaped me, and while I think it was one that could have passed for one of desire to Sam or even Narcos, it wasn't lost on Everleigh, another woman.

"Oh, honey," she moaned in sympathy, and she drew herself up to my back and kissed my shoulder.

Sam broke the kiss and looked down at me sharply.

"What's wrong?" he demanded.

"Um, nothing," I said quickly, attempting to mask and hide my true feelings quickly.

"Uh-uh." Narcos drifted up, and I was suddenly surrounded on three sides by warmth and skin and my troubled mind tried valiantly not to completely short-circuit. "Not how it works, baby. Something just tripped your trigger and communication is key. It's alright if you don't want to talk about it but denying things isn't gonna fly."

"We can't talk it out and help you heal if we don't know what it is. But we get it if things are still new and you don't trust us, yet. Believe me," Everleigh echoed.

I was lost in the depths of Sam's eyes though, as he stared deep into mine steadily, on an even keel – a silent sentinel just watching and waiting with a seemingly endless amount of patience.

"I guess I'm... um... I'm not quite used to all this attention," I finally squeaked. "I don't know what I'm doing."

"Is it that you don't know what you're doing or is it more that you don't know what's expected?" Sam asked gently, and I swallowed hard.

"Both," I whispered and his lips curled into what I could only describe as a secret little Mona Lisa smile.

"No one expects anything out of you except to have a good time," Narcos declared, and I dragged my eyes off of Sam and looked over at him.

"Relax," Everleigh whispered. "You're safe with us and we've got you."

"Guys, give us some space," Sam murmured. "She's not into it."

"No," I said quickly. "I, um, like the idea, it's just... I don't know, too much too soon, maybe?"

Narcos leaned in and pressed his lips to my temple, and I closed my eyes, even as Everleigh's arms tightened around me.

"Can we just stay like this for a minute?" I asked, my voice small.

Everyone just sort of crowded around me and held me tight. A well-spring of emotion opened up and I fought tears... but I couldn't say why.

I didn't know why.

All I knew was that it was like a weight I hadn't known I'd been carrying just sort of shifted, and it felt like it slid somewhat off my shoulders.

Curious.

"We can stay like this for all the time that you need," Sam murmured somewhere above my head and I trembled slightly.

"Okay," I whispered, and I tried to relax; to just soak it in.

22

*D*riller...

"You ready to talk about it now?" I asked her. She shifted against my chest, where she was staring into the fire hissing and spitting in the firepit in front of us.

Narcos had Everleigh over his shoulder and she was squealing with mad laughter as the screen door leading into the cabin slammed shut and bounced in its frame behind them.

"Talk about what?" Teresia asked cautiously, her blue eyes glittering in the dark, her blonde hair cast in a halo around her face, the firelight dancing through the strands, making her achingly beautiful.

"Back at the swimming hole, earlier today," I said steadily, reminding her of what I knew she already knew without any reproach. Something had rocked her to her core, had her wildin' out and shifted sideways from her usual calm-and-collected baseline.

"I just..." she shifted her gaze off of my face to one side, a classic tell that she was about to lie to me, but I couldn't do anything about it until the lie slipped free. So I waited, patiently. She closed her eyes and her shoulders slumped. When she opened them, I could see the truth shining there.

"I'm scared," she admitted.

"Scared of what, baby?" I asked her, petting all that shining blonde hair, a touch meant to be soothing as I cradled the back of her head gently.

"Of... of loving you," she said. "Of being loved, I guess, by you, by all of you. I'm afraid I won't... fit."

I cocked my head and considered what she was saying.

"It's just you and me right now, babe, and I want you to hear what I'm saying, okay?"

"Okay," she murmured and I could tell she was listening.

"I don't give a fuck about sharing. If you want me all to yourself, that's cool—"

"I'm not saying that," she interjected quickly. "I'm not saying that at all," she said.

"Okay," I said slowly, and I waited her out, her face adorable as it screwed up in concentration, as she sought the words.

"I think it's the way I was raised," she said finally. "I think... I think I'm afraid of disappointing my mother and my grandmother, you know... if they knew. I don't think they would understand. That being said, what you're offering, I find very much appealing. I guess I'm just a little..."

"Stuck?" I asked her, holding very still beneath her, my fingers buried in her flaxen hair as I massaged the base of her skull through it, in that little knot where her head joined her neck and where all the tension liked to reside.

"Frozen," she said. "I don't want to make a wrong move or hurt anyone's feelings or... do the wrong thing."

I chuckled slightly and gave her a squeeze, pressing her against my chest.

Everleigh made an "oh!" from up above and behind us and Teresia and I locked eyes. I loved how hers glittered with a mischievous glee.

"Everything is at your pace, baby. We walk at the speed of the slowest member of the pack. That's just the way we've always been. I like you. A lot. I don't expect anything from you, at all. That's not why I'm doing any of this with you. If you want to explore, that's all fine and good and I'm all for it," I told her. "But expectations? There are none here. I get the feeling you've been striving for and living up to expectations your whole life to this point. Correct me if I'm wrong, but it doesn't seem to have done much for your spirit, has it?"

She turned back to the fire and laid her head back down on me, cuddling closer – if it were even possible laid out over the top of me like she was.

"No," she said, and it sounded very much so like she was agreeing with me despite the negative connotation of the word.

"No, it hasn't. I did my part. Held it together when none of the adults in the room could and I was praised for it. I thought... I thought that was what was expected of me and yet I feel like all it did was render me invisible."

She choked at the end of her confession, and I wrapped my arms around her tight and held on.

I hadn't realized we were tapping into some really deep shit – but now I knew, I wasn't about to let her wade through it by herself. Sounded like that's what she'd been doing for an awfully long time, and nobody should have to do that.

"Well, you're not invisible now, sweetheart. We see you."

"I believe you," she said and her voice wavered slightly. I held her tight, cuddling her close, as her shoulders hitched in silent, soft little sobs and I just let her go.

I understood a few things about growing pains. I'd watched Everleigh raise some butterflies in her little she-shed at one point, babying these fuckin' caterpillars that were supposed to be super rare or some shit, feeding them all the things they liked best, patiently watching and waiting for them to spin themselves into their little cocoons.

There was a butterfly house at the conservatory she was beekeeping at, and she'd taken on the butterfly watching duty as a favor to one of the entomologists that worked and researched there.

I guess the public going in among the butterflies for a fee was some sort of educational fundraising schtick or whatever. One of those academic ecosystems of researching, education, and the funding to do it all – but I digress…

The thing I learned with that little escapade of my best friend's girl that may be applied here to Teresia too, was the part where, these brand-fuckin'-new butterflies were emerging from those cocoons.

It looked messy, and painful, and Everleigh had been glued to watching them and taking notes and shit, filming them for this researcher on vacation or doing whatever the hell she was off doing. I had asked, *why don't you help pry them out if these things are so damn important?*

She'd told me that would cripple them – that's why, and I'd been right and properly fuckin' confused by that.

She'd patiently explained that the struggle to emerge was what forced something like their circulatory system to fuckin' cooperate and get moving, forcing fluid into the delicate veins of their wings or something, making the wings unfurl and flatten out eventually.

What I saw was these ugly ass bugs struggling like a motherfucker covered in goo and misshapen, dragging themselves out of the muck and bindings. The transformation wasn't pretty, but the end result? After the struggle was over, and they'd been given enough time to rest and reset into their new little bodies?

Nothing short of magical.

As to the woman in my arms? That's what this felt like. Like I was watching that same kind of visceral struggle. Only she was pulling herself out of her past and into the present, and as much as I wanted to help her, to pull her through and placate her or whatever – I wouldn't be doing anything exceptionally useful. I could, in fact, despite my best intentions, inhibit her growth and I didn't want to do that.

She was a beautiful creature to begin with and I had full confidence that when she found her grip and wrenched herself free of whatever invisible chains of expectations or whatever was holding her back, she would be the most stunning thing to ever walk this earth. She just had to be allowed to get there in her own time.

Not going to lie, the moment we were having was a little shattered by the soundtrack of Narcos railing Everleigh upstairs, her feral cries both sexy and sweet, floating out over our heads and down toward the babbling river.

Teresia sniffed and wiped at her eyes and laughed a little. I couldn't help but chuckle myself.

"At least somebody is having a good time," she said dryly, and I felt my grin grow just a little bit bigger.

"Get up here and kiss me and lets just see what happens from there, eh?" I kept my tone mockingly surly and it had the desired effect. She shivered beneath the thin blanket covering her, and I knew it didn't have anything to do with cold. It was a modesty thing. She was wearing one of my shirts and nothing else, and that was just the way I liked it.

When we'd returned from swimming, it'd been swelteringly hot in and around the cabin. It'd taken some convincing for her to just put the shirt on, and nothing else. She'd relented once Everleigh had pointed out we'd all just been skinny dipping and in a cuddle pile and that no one was just going to roll on up through here unannounced. We were in literal BFE which was the whole fucking point of this place. Cut off from everything and everyone – no phone service, no emails, or texts or social media.

All the noise of the city left in the city.

This was our place to take a respite from it all if and when we needed to.

I think Teresia had picked up on the vibe, because she shifted against me, putting her hands against my chest and swinging a leg over my hips to straddle me in the dark.

Backlit by the fire, her silhouette became a shadow. Her hair golden and bright became flame and as she drew my shirt up and off from over her head, it did something visceral to me. I felt my gut clench, my cock jump in my shorts, and even though the evening air was cool against my shirtless chest, I warmed all the way through.

"God, you're fucking beautiful," I murmured and I know my voice held awe, because I was in awe.

I smoothed my hands over her hips, up the hourglass curve of her body, and leaned up, pulling her down to me, tangling my hands in all that thick, luxurious hair of hers, to press her mouth to mine.

She hummed out in pleasure, her arms going around my shoulders as she kissed me back from her unusual height above me from this angle. I was used to being the taller one by now, even though we'd only been around each other such a short time.

"Oh, fuck, baby, *yes*," I moaned as she parted my fly and reached into my shorts to stroke up and down my shaft. She managed even though our mouths were locked together, and the angle was a little weird. I was so hard, so stiff, my hips rising and falling unbidden off the hard wood of the sturdy, wide, Adirondack chaise we were on.

"God," I grunted against her mouth. "I want to be inside of you."

She moaned into my mouth like that was the best thing she'd heard all damn day. With a little bit of awkward wiggling to get my shorts down, she put me at her entrance and slid down my length agonizingly slow, an exquisite torture.

She moved above me, graceful, and yet with purpose, and I bit my bottom lip and held on, desperate for her to finish before me. I felt like I literally had *everything* working against me in that moment to that end.

She was gorgeous. She was wild and so tangibly *real* and *raw* and *beautiful* in that moment that I went from zero to fuckin' sixty in the first or second grind of her luscious hips against me. Her pussy was so fucking hot and wet, wrapped around my cock, I almost forgot to fucking breathe for a moment.

She was elegant in every movement she made, a masterpiece of sinew and bone, wrapped in the most delectable and soft flesh. So ethereal, so magical, a fuckin' goddess-made flesh and I was just the poor fuckin' mortal sod lucky enough to receive her benevolent benediction.

She was pure poetry in motion, the way she made love to me and I loved *her* for it. The way she looked down at me, the way she moved so deliberately, that spark deep in her blue eyes as she let her carefully clutched inhibitions go for me. Shit, that was hot.

She rode me under the star-laden sky, by the light of the fire, under the eyes of God and any other nighttime creature taking in the show. Fuck if it didn't make me feel powerful, almighty in my own right, my hips rising to meet her downward momentum as she stroked my cock deep up inside of her.

I pressed my hand against her stomach, down low, pressing my thumb against her clit and slicking it through the wetness between us. She moaned, sighing out, clutching the back of the seat above my head. I hadn't even remembered slouching down, but I had, giving her free rein.

"Yes!" she moaned out, her movements becoming more frenetic as I teased her clit with the pad of my thumb.

I could feel her clench tight and tighter around me, and I grunted. My cock jumping, I spilled inside of her, but she was close, so close, and somewhere between the second and third jet of my hot cum inside of her, she spasmed around me. She took her own plunge over the shining fall of sensation into the deep pool of bliss I was already in – arms outstretched to catch her.

I JOLTED AWAKE AT NARCOS' touch to my shoulder and immediately looked down to check on Teresia, resting atop my chest. All I could see was some of her messy blonde hair from this angle, but the slight touch of a smile on my partner's lips told me all I needed to know. She was sleeping soundly and hadn't been disturbed by my jolting awake.

"What's up?" I asked quietly.

"Should head into town, check any messages, get a status report," he said, and I nodded.

"Take the girls for breakfast or bring the breakfast back to the girls?" he asked.

"Shit, I don't know," I answered truthfully.

"Bring breakfast back to the girls," Teresia moaned sleepily, and I chuckled.

Narcos echoed the sentiment and leaned down, pressing his lips to my girl's bare shoulder.

"Gonna have to get off 'im, baby," he told her and she moaned again, this time with a whining edge to it.

"I got this," Everleigh muttered, and she appeared from behind Narcos and went around to my side of the bed.

"Get your big ass up," she ordered grumpily but the sparkle in her eyes belied any real hard feelings.

"Alright, alright," I declared and slid out from a whining and vociferous Teresia. Everleigh, in one of Narcos' tees, slid into the nice warm bed in my place and wrapped Teresia in her arms, kissing the top of her hair and cuddling in.

I exchanged a look with Narcos who gave me a deep and meaningful look like, *bro...* and I was right there with him. I wanted nothing more than to pile back into that bed, get naked, and not give up until all four of us were panting, sweating, and sated.

"Be back in a flash," Narcos said and leaned down to kiss Ev. As soon as he got out of the way, I did the same to Teresia.

"Back soon, baby. I promise."

"Okay," she murmured sleepily.

Fuck it was hard to climb down out of the loft, leaving the two women and the two cats in a cuddle pile on that bed. I longed for one of the king-sized beds that would fit all four of us and the cats comfortably if just a little bit cramped.

No... not cramped. Cozy.

God, that sounded so cozy.

I got dressed to ride, Narcos moving around and doing the same and we headed out. We didn't need to watch for the cats, those two boys wouldn't leave their mama for nothing. They never tried to pull any sort of runner unless she was heading out the door.

I'd never been so fuckin' jealous of however many pounds of fur as I was right then – comfy and cozy with the two women in the bed that *I* was supposed to be in.

When we got out front and over to the bikes, I mockingly glared at my best friend and grumbled, "We are not friends for at least five minutes, motherfucker."

He laughed, and it was one of those I genuinely had caught him off guard and cracked his ass up sort of laughs and I had to grin.

"Let's hurry our asses up, hit the general store and get back home, then."

"Yeah," I agreed.

The ride was beautiful, the sun dappling through the trees nice. It was still cool enough out with as early as it was and I could appreciate Narcos getting my ass out of bed early for that fact alone.

We pulled up outside the old general store and Narcos gave me a wave and went inside as I sat astride my bike, engine ticking intermittently between the drone of the ringing of the phone in my ear.

"Yeah?" Skids growled into my ear.

"What do you mean, 'yeah?'" I demanded gruffly.

"Shit, what time is it?" he asked, and I could hear him wincing, the bed creaking as he turned on his side or something.

"Early," I told him. "Have to run all the way into town. We wanted to beat the heat," I told him.

"Oh."

"Nothing new I take it." I couldn't keep the discouraged tone out of my voice.

"No," he said. "Close according to Youngblood and Yale, but we ain't passing out cigars yet."

"Well, shit. Keep your eye on the prize, I guess."

"Look," he said. "Things change, I'll send a rider out there to meet y'all. You ain't gotta worry."

"You ain't have to do that, Skids. It's too fuckin' far. We'll check back in tomorrow, man."

"Sure," he said. "Anytime."

I knew he meant that. Never too early or too late.

I called in to my captain next and got much the same. Nothing yet, but there were some rumblings. His words, not mine.

"Rumblings?" I asked.

"Yeah, like how your stomach rumbles right before you gotta take a shit," he said in that Texas drawl of his. "Same fuckin' principle at this point, son."

I couldn't help but laugh and said, "I'll be in touch."

"You do that," he said. "Be safe."

"Oh, trust me. Ain't no place safer," I told him.

I ended the call. Sure, it could be triangulated or whatever but all that shit leaves a trail and the cabin was well out of town. Hard as fuck to find anything out in these hollers, which is why we were here and not home.

I followed Narcos into the general store to help get the shopping over with so we could get back to the girls.

23

*T*eresia...

I woke up cuddled up with Everleigh, and for half a second it felt strange to be so intimate with a woman. But I stopped myself and really sort of tore into that a little bit. I finally settled on it wasn't strange because *woman*, it was simply something I wasn't all that exposed to. It was just strange as in *new*, if that made any sense at all.

She traced some of my hair behind my ear and kissed my forehead. I giggled a little bit and opened my eyes.

"Morning," she said with a Cheshire cat's grin.

"Good morning," I murmured and sighed happily. It was so good to be cuddled and held and had been so nice to be accepted and held fast by all three of them in the pool the day before.

"Can I kiss you?" she asked gently, and I smiled.

"I'd like that," I murmured.

"Yeah?" She grinned, pleased, and then her lips were on mine – so gentle, so delicate and soft. I kissed her back and smiled at the slight taste of cotton candy lip balm. So out of place. I expected mint, honey, pomegranate, or any other number of natural flavors. Hell, cherry Chapstick! But no, she tasted like candy floss and sunshine and I found myself pressing my thighs together beneath the sheets.

A small sound escaped my throat, and she scooted closer, her hand finding my bare hip underneath the sheet and giving it a squeeze, her tongue flickering against mine so quick, it was like heat lightning through the clouds that invaded my brain, making all coherent thought leave me for the moment.

We made out for a little while and it was like sparklers or effervescent bubbles played along my scalp in a wash down my back, radiating from where her hands touched my skin. Before I even realized it, I was touching her, too, my hand on her thigh, sliding up under the tee that she wore.

Finally, she drew back and murmured, "Can I confess something?"

"Mm?" I acquiesced with the small sound, curious as to what she would say.

"It's dirty," she warned, and I snickered.

"Just tell me. It's alright," I said.

"I want to watch…" she said. "You and Driller, and Narcos. I want to watch them fuck you so bad."

"Really?" I asked quietly, my brow furrowing.

She nodded enthusiastically. "I think you're beautiful," she said. "I know you excite Driller, and I know you excite Narcos. I want to watch their cocks disappear into your pretty little pussy and I want to touch myself while I watch and maybe even kiss you or lick your clit while they fuck you if you'll let me."

Holy shit.

"Yeah, that's dirty alright," I said breathy. "But it also sounds so hot and sexy. I just... I just don't know how to start," I confessed right back.

"Close your eyes," she said, and I did. Her lips found mine again in a light kiss. "Keep them closed," she whispered, and I heard and felt the rustle of cloth.

"Would you let me fuck you at some point?" she asked.

I swallowed hard. "Yes," I said. I jumped slightly when her fingertips grazed between my thighs and parted my legs slightly to give her questing fingers better access.

She kissed me again and touched my pussy. I gasped, my hands finding her waist which was barren of the tee she'd been wearing. I slid my hands over her skin and she teased me with her fingertips. I parted my legs a little more, and she slipped them between my pussy lips.

She moaned into my mouth when she found me wet and plunged a finger up inside me.

I gasped, and let my legs fall open completely as her kiss intensified and she fitted another finger inside me, her other hand massaging my breast. I gripped her hip with my one hand and mirrored her, palming her breast with my other and her skin was so soft, so smooth. She wriggled her fingers in me and I jerked my head back, crying out.

She was a woman, so of course she knew just where to grope, just where to flick her fingers against inside of me.

"Mm, yeah," she praised, and I bucked my hips against her hand.

She teased my clit with her thumb and pinched my nipple almost savagely, but fuck, it felt so good.

"I want you to come on my hand, baby," she said, and I bit my bottom lip. "That's it, that's it, oh, good girl!" she cried, and I clapped my thighs together as my hips bucked, whimpering and moaning as my body jolted in a powerful orgasm while Everleigh laughed, delighted, and with almost... I don't know... pride?

I opened my eyes, and hers shone, her smile almost too big. She pecked a kiss to the tip of my nose and said, "You did terrific," as she pulled her hand away from my pussy.

"I-I've never tried to go down on a woman," I said and she bit her bottom lip through her grin.

"You want to experiment on me?" she asked.

I nodded.

She lazily rolled onto her back and parted her legs. After a moment, I pushed myself up into a sitting position and kneeled between her knees.

"It's okay if it's not for you," she said, but the heat in her gaze told me just how much she wanted me to touch her.

I nodded and traced my fingertips up her inner thighs. She shuddered and let her head fall back, closing her eyes. I was encouraged by the sight of her back arching, her tits thrust high toward the low ceiling.

I leaned over her and worked my nerve up by kissing down her body, her pussy a pale pink and her lips wet and glistening. I touched her, petting her, teasing her carefully, and she moaned. I worked my middle and longest finger inside of her and swished it back and forth inside her, pressing up against the roof of her channel and finding it enticingly slick and rough at the same time.

I mean, I had touched myself plenty of times, but you could never really get your fingers into yourself this deep without a bit of a contortionist's pose to do it.

She gasped, and I went over that spot again. She writhed a bit and gripped the sheets at her hips. I lowered my face slowly, flicking my tongue against the little kernel of pleasure in the slight nest of hair at the top of her sex. She preferred the little trimmed landing strip, where I was au natural and simply just trimmed.

I put my other hand at the top of her sex and pressed down slightly while dragging up just enough to reveal her clit more fully, flicking my tongue against it, not really tasting so much as pleasuring her with it, manipulating that bud of flesh with it to work at bringing her to orgasm as she'd brought me just moments before.

"Oh, bullshit! You're a liar. You've totally done this before!" she gasped and writhed a little and I could tell she was struggling to hold still.

A fission of joy went through me at her words and pleased I was doing a good job. Her panting becoming more frantic and her body movements tighter and more controlled, I thrust my fingers up tighter and higher inside her and changed tactic with my tongue, sucking her clit into my mouth.

Bingo!

She cried out and shivered beneath me the way I had beneath her just moments before. I sat up as her legs damn near closed on my head and kept working her from the inside with my fingers, smearing my other fingertips in my saliva on her clit until her voice echoed down from the rafters in a cry that verged on panic from my having overwhelmed her.

I leaned up over her, bringing my mouth back to hers for more impassioned kissing and jumped when I heard Narcos' voice say, "Please, stay just like that and say I can stick my dick inside you."

Uh-oh, was my first thought. *The jig is up.*

"Babe, whatever you say goes, but I would fucking love to watch that," I heard from downstairs.

I turned my head to look in Narcos' direction and nodded, but that was all I could do, because Everleigh's hands were to either side of my face, turning it back to her so that we could kiss passionately once more.

I heard a thump as Narcos cleared the ladder, or so I thought, but then there was a second thump and I realized with the sound of his zipper right after that it was his other boot being kicked off. Another rustle of fabric and I felt his tee slip along the outside of my thigh as he tossed it down. With a grunt, he was kneeling behind me, his hands on my hips, drawing me up and back just enough to get me where he needed me.

Everleigh never stopped kissing me, her tongue twining with mine, and then he was slicking the head of his cock, hot and thick against my wetness. With a moan into Everleigh's mouth, he was pushing his way inside of me, sucking in a breath between his teeth.

I heard clothing being dropped and tore my mouth from Ev's to cry out as Narcos thrust in all the way deep, and *fuck yes,* it felt good.

"Oh, shit, that's good," he declared. "That's a good girl. Fuck yeah."

"Mm, pull me down," Everleigh ordered and then with a gleeful little yip, she disappeared some and her tongue was on my clit as her man thrust inside me.

"Gonna fuck you while you and your man fuck *her,*" I heard, and then Everleigh moaned against my body. I jumped slightly as she started moving back and forth, her mouth sucking at me, her man's cock filling me as I clutched the sheets in front of me. I arched down low to the bed and just gave myself over to the sensations of it all.

Oh my God. This was a pleasure and a freedom I'd never known, and if it was somehow wrong, I didn't want to be right.

I closed my eyes, squeezing them tightly shut as Narcos thrust powerfully inside me, the softness of Everleigh's mouth in counterpoint, driving me wild until I clutched the sheets and howled my pleasure. I lost myself completely to the racking waves of orgasm sweeping through me.

By the time I came back to myself, Everleigh was gone, Narcos was moving slower, smoother, hands sweeping over my skin in firm but gentle strokes as he intensely, voice low and purring with appreciation, praised me.

Praised me?

I-I hadn't done anything that I was aware of. Yet all the same, he murmured his praise to the stuffy cabin air, telling me how good I felt, how wet, how wonderfully my pussy squeezed his cock with my orgasm, and I reveled in it, carried along the warm effervescent river of afterglow. My senses dulled with deep pleasure as I heard in the background a grunt and Everleigh's singsong moan of her own pleasure which made me... happy.

So very happy that everyone had gotten what they needed, and I felt like I had most of all.

24

*D*riller...

It was hot and sticky up here, but that was okay. I didn't want to move Teresia off of me. If ever there was a sort of factory reset performed through sex, I think the four of us had accomplished it for her. She was dozing against me, and after how mind-blowing shit had been, I couldn't blame her.

She stirred after a bit and I smiled.

"Hey," I murmured and kissed her forehead.

"Hi," she rasped slightly.

"You doing okay?" I asked.

"Hmm, better than okay," she said with a smile that was like the cat that'd eaten the canary.

I laughed a little, and she pushed herself up and looked around. "Where are Narcos and Everleigh?"

"They weren't as wore out as you. They headed for the swimmin' hole to cool off."

"Oh, God, that sounds delightful," she said.

"Cool, we got some shit in town. Want to make up some sandwiches and take some beers with us?"

"Let's," she agreed eagerly.

"Okay."

She loved on one of her cats that was on the bed with us as she rose and I loved how languid and satisfied she looked.

"God, you're fuckin' stunning," I said, and she looked over at me from where she rooted through a backpack of her clothing for something suitable to make the short hike in.

"Really?" she asked skeptically.

"Really," I affirmed. "Probably one of, if not the most, beautiful woman I've ever had the pleasure to be with."

She colored a deep red and turned away and I pushed myself up into a sitting position.

"It really doesn't bother you that—"

"No. I loved watching you get railed. Made me hard as fuck," I said. "I fucking loved that we could all engage in some adult fun together and blow off steam. I don't get jealous when it comes to Narcos and Ev. We're a fucked-up sort of family according to the norm, but we like it that way. I'm glad you felt comfortable enough to share that with me," I told her.

"I don't really know what came over me," she stammered.

I lifted a shoulder in a shrug and said, "And that's okay. Did you have a good time?"

"Yes," she said.

"Would you do it again?" I asked.

"Ten out of ten would recommend," she said with a slow smile, and I grinned at her.

"That's my girl."

She laughed a little and said, "About that... you're sure you're not going to get bored or whatever once everything gets resolved?"

I chuckled and shook my head back and forth. "Fuck no. That's just when shit starts fixin' to get really started," I answered.

"How so?" she asked, sinking to sit on the area rug in front of our bags.

"Well, for starters, I'd like to spend more time together. Just you and me. Take you on a real and proper date. Maybe dancing again. I liked that," I said.

She smiled softly and nodded slowly. "I'd like that."

"Good." I said. "We'll figure everything out as we go along."

She nodded. "I'd like that. I mean, this is all so new, but really... I do like it. I just don't know how it all works."

"Our business is our business and fuck anybody else," I said with a blasé little one-shouldered shrug. I mean, for me, it really was that simple, but for a citizen, I could see how that could get complicated.

"I've never really done anything like this in my entire life," she said and I smiled.

"Just do what feels good, baby. And if something doesn't, don't hesitate to speak up about it."

She nodded, and that was that for the time being.

We went down out of the loft and she gave her other cat some lovin' while I went into the kitchen to throw together some sandwiches.

She took their litter box outside and scooped it for them while I finished up the lunches. I packed them up and put them away while she washed her hands thoroughly.

We chatted quietly, the silence between us a comfortable one, and I plied her with as many affectionate touches as I could get away with.

I liked touching her. She was so beautiful, and nothing at all like I thought she would be just from the few furtive glances I took during the trial. Certainly, she wasn't at all what I thought she would be after that first day of interacting with her when I picked her up from the hospital.

She was this alluring amalgamation of strong and independent, while simultaneously being so adorably sheltered and insecure. Yet, through it all, she didn't hesitate to *try*.

I liked that about her. No, I loved that about her and I couldn't wait to see what would come next with truly getting to know her and all the pressure of the situation coming off her slight shoulders. Pressure and a burden she wore like a fuckin' supermodel, strutting down the runway like it weren't no thang.

It was impressive. *She* was impressive, and I couldn't wait to find out more.

I was past the point where I wanted to fuck around. I guessed, I really just wanted to find out this time. For once. There was just something about her that made me want those things more than I'd ever wanted anything before. Like this was a great renaissance of my life, and everything was about to be made new. I didn't want to reject any of it. I wanted to *embrace it*.

"So, I was talking to Narcos about it the other day and I sort of wanted to run something by you," I said and she looked up from where she was packing things away in the picnic basket at the table for me.

"Oh?" she inquired.

"I've been thinking a lot about it and… and I just don't think I'm comfortable being a cop anymore."

She lowered the sandwich she had in her hand back to the table and put both of those delicate looking hands of hers that gripped and stroked me so well onto the back of the chair in front of her.

"That's… a lot," she said a little awkwardly. "I mean, I know we haven't known each other very long, but… but wow. That's *a big thing*," she said, and she looked like she was trying to take it all in.

"It is." I nodded slowly, and she took in a slow deep breath and let it out even a little slower than that.

"Can I ask you what made you arrive at such a monumental decision?" she asked.

I told her. I told her how even if the brass hadn't thrown me under the bus, how fuckin' guilty I felt about everything. About how if a situation like it ever came up again, how I knew I would hesitate and how hesitation could get someone killed; be it me or one of the other guys.

She listened, her deep blue eyes empathetic, her silence resounding as she listened. And I do mean she *listened*. Really listened, and that did my heart some good.

"I mean, yeah," she said finally. "Those are all really valid points," she declared. "But have you thought about what you're going to do, you know, *after*? Like, what's next?"

I nodded.

"I have. I was thinking about taking up the training and making a lateral transfer so to speak to the ICFD."

"The fire department?" she asked and sounded surprised.

I nodded again.

"I'd still be in civil service," I said. "Which is important to me. I just... I feel like I need to run it by you, you know, because you're important to me and even though this is really new, I value your input. I want this to be something that lasts, you know?"

"You care what I think?" she asked, and she sounded so surprised.

"Well, yeah, babe."

She was silent, her gaze averted, and I blinked stupidly when her eyes glassed over with tears.

"Whoa, hey, what's this?" I asked, and I went for her. She sniffed, and practically dove into the hug I was offering.

"I don't think anyone has ever really cared what I thought," she said, and I sighed out, taking some of the burden of her pain, my shoulders slumping.

"Oh, babe," I murmured.

"I'm sorry," she warbled. "I don't know where all this stupid is coming from."

"Hey, it's not stupid, okay?" I took a step back and smoothed a hand over her hair, cupping her face, slouching down enough to make direct eye contact with her.

"It's not stupid," I reinforced. "You're safe, and you're allowed to feel however you wanna feel about anything. Nothing about that makes it stupid. Goll-y, man." I pulled her in tight and hugged her, tucking her head under my chin and pressing a hand to the back of it.

She hugged me back and took several deep gulping breaths to get it back under control, and it frustrated me slightly. I mean, she didn't have to shut it down or be strong all the fucking time – I was here for that – but at the same time, I got it. It was just a part of who she was.

"So, what do you think?" I asked quietly after she'd calmed. "Think you could handle being a fireman's girlfriend?"

She nodded against me. "I mean, the stress of being a cop's girlfriend or a fireman's girlfriend is going to be the same no matter what, right?"

I chuckled and leaned back to look at her, a light of determination in her eyes, which to be fair, she was going to need it. That was part of being a first responder's partner. It wasn't easy for the wives or girlfriends of one of us, I knew that. Maybe that was why I was so attracted to Teresia – that inner core of strength of hers.

I knew she could handle it.

After watching this whole tableau, after listening to that 9-1-1 call, I was pretty sure this woman could handle anything.

"Right," I told her, and she braved a smile for me.

"Glad we had this talk," she said, a little stronger and with a stiff nod, and I laughed.

"That mean I need to get my ass in gear so we can get out of here?" I asked.

"Yes," she said with another curt nod.

I laughed again.

"Okay."

We finished packing up and headed for the swimming hole.

WE SPENT the whole day cooling off, talking, liberally applying each other with sunscreen and just generally having a good time at the swimming hole. Despite our best efforts, the girls both burned. We made our way back to the cabin and found Skids in the river, whipping a rod back and forth, the line spooling out and the fly dropping like a dream onto the water's surface.

"Well, will you look at this shit!" Narcos, who was up ahead of us, cried.

"Oh, snap – when'd you get here?" I asked.

"Few hours, ain't no never mind. I just helped myself to some of your fishing equipment. Figured you all would be back whenever you got back. No big deal.

"Shit, you got news?" I asked, kissing Teresia's temple and letting her go with Everleigh. "Go on, babe, get that burn looked after," I said.

"If it's alright with you, if there is news, I'd like to hear it," she said pointedly and I quirked a smile.

"No, you're right," I said.

"Ev, c'mon, let's get the hammock out for Skids and get some dinner going." Narcos put a hand to Everleigh's back, and she nodded, looking to Teresia to make sure she was cool. Teresia nodded and smiled and Skids reeled in his line.

"Get a fire goin' while you're out here, yeah?" Narcos asked me and I gave a nod.

"You bet," I told him.

Teresia started gathering kindling without being asked, while Skids packed in his borrowed fishing equipment. When the three of us were gathered at the firepit and while I worked to get a fire going, Skids took a seat on one of the half log benches and sighed.

"So no sooner did I get off the fuckin' phone with you, I got a call from Youngblood," he said. "I figured I could wait until y'all called this morning, but then I thought – fuck it. I could use the ride and to relax for a bit."

"Good call," I said with a nod. "What's the word?"

"Whole thing unraveled thanks to your captain at your precinct," he said.

"Oh?" I asked.

Skids grunted an affirmative.

"He had a hunch about a few fellas, let slip where ya had Ms. Ehrling. They were smart, waited – but didn't wait long enough."

"They show up at the house?" I asked.

Skids nodded. "Just like we thought they would. Sometime last night. Youngblood was in questioning the shit out of 'em and didn't get out until after you woke my ass up."

"Ah." I nodded. Teresia listened quietly, rapt.

"Did they break anything? Burn anything down?" she asked quietly.

"Nah, they weren't given the chance," Skids said. "They were a tough nut to crack, but Youngblood's tougher."

"So, what's the deal?" I asked.

"Buncha white boys, like you figured, trying to pop shit off, make the anti-hate groups look like somethin' they weren't. Just like you suspected."

"Fuck, sometimes I hate being right," I said, sighing.

"Yeah, but we all knew shit was off."

"Way off," I agreed.

"So, what happens now?" Teresia asked softly.

It was a good question.

"Well, now you get to go home, in a few more days at least. There are still some arrests to be made but they'll be made swift."

She shuddered and looked off into the woods where the twilight was just starting to seep out from the cracks and crevices between the trees.

"None of this really seems real," she said unhappily.

"Oh, I get that," Skids said with a gusty sigh. "Believe you me."

"Why me?" she asked softly.

"You were just unlucky enough to pick the short straw and to get onto his jury," Skids said, and I winced and shot him a slightly dirty look. He shot me back an apologetic one, and said, "Just a few more days, though, and you'll be alright. Can start to build back better than you were before."

Teresia glanced at me, and that glanced lingered, growing warmer by the second as she searched my face. She gave a slight nod to indicate she was okay, and more importantly that *we* were okay, and said, "I think that makes both of us."

I knew she meant me, and when Skids looked up from his hands folded between his knees, his forearms braced atop his thighs, he caught her meaning sure enough and nodded.

"Sounds about right," he agreed, and then he looked to me. "What about you?" he asked. "How are you doing?"

I nodded. "Doing some soul searching," I told him. "All in all, I guess I'm doing as alright as can be expected."

He nodded slowly and said, "Not sure if that's good or bad. It was a hell of a thing you went through and I ain't really had the opportunity to touch base with you."

I chuckled. "I'm alright, Captain," and I shot Teresia a meaningful look without her knowing.

Skids raised his eyebrows and gave a nod and that was that for the time being.

Wasn't much longer before Everleigh showed up with a platter and some meat sitting on top of some butcher paper.

"What's this?" I asked.

"That would be me. Stopped in town on the way in at the butcher's shop there. Got us some steaks. Didn't want to show up empty-handed."

"Fuck yeah, rock on. Teresia, you wanna grab me the cowboy grill top just inside the garage?" I asked.

"What's that?" she asked, giving a funny face.

I laughed. "It's just the round grill top with the funny legs. Sits right over the top of the fire, here. Be careful and holler for help if you need it. It can be heavy."

She nodded, rolled her eyes at the last part and got up from her seat.

"Ev, why don't you go on up and get some aloe for my girl. She's got two colors, I swear to God."

"What might those be?" Skids asked.

"Glacier and Lobster," I answered, and he chuckled. Everleigh handed Skids the platter of steaks and rolling her eyes, wandered off back toward the cabin. She met Teresia halfway and took the other side of the big grill grate my girl was carrying just fine but was trying to avoid getting any of the black from previous grill sessions on her.

Ev took the other side, and they brought it the rest of the way, laughing a little and going back and forth. Their chatter was sweet to the ear like a babbling brook. I stood up from the fire I had starting and Skids took Teresia's side.

"Now go on and get that burn looked after," I ordered and she smiled at me and shook her head a little ruefully.

"Come on," Everleigh said with her usual sparkle. "He won't let it go until you do."

"Grabbing a shower," Teresia said, and I nodded.

"Take your time, baby," I said, poking at things under the grate, trying to get the fire to breathe a little.

I glanced up and saw Narcos through the porch screen, rigging up the hammock for our unexpected but welcome guest.

"So, you got something going with Ms. Thing, huh? Tearing a page out of your partner's playbook?"

I chuckled a little bit and nodded. "I guess so," I said. I mean, that's sort of how Narcos and Everleigh had gotten started. She'd been under his protection at first from a notorious biker gang that'd done her dirty. She'd been all but mute back then, but with time and a lot of intensive therapy, that problem had almost all but resolved.

The mind did funny things to people under certain circumstances. No two people were alike in their response to trauma.

"Yeah, and how's that going?" he asked carefully, eying me. I couldn't help my smile and he gave a nod, chuckling once more, and said, "Well, alright. Good to hear it."

He caught me up on some of the grittier, gorier details of the hate group's master plan and we shared in some mutual disgust over how far said hate group had pretty much infiltrated the force.

By the time we got done discussing that little tidbit and how the brass was absolutely struggling to keep a lid on it, I felt like I was unequivocally making the right decision, considering moving over to fire. Still…

"Hey, Cap," I said after a lull in our conversation.

"Yeah, bud?" he asked me, dragging his eyes off the fire and fixing them on me.

"I've been thinking—"

"Well shit, usually that ain't led to nothing good," he said with a sparkle in his blue eyes. When the look on my face didn't change, he slowly lost his easy smile.

"Well, shit indeed," he said after a protracted silence. "What's on your mind, bud?"

I sighed. There wasn't really any easy way of saying it.

25

*T*eresia...

"This is going to feel so good," I said, fanning myself as I went in the back door of the cabin. Everleigh followed right behind me and Narcos peeked around the kitchen wall.

"What is? Am I getting a free show?" he asked.

Everleigh and I laughed, and I shook my head.

"Just heading in for a cool shower so Ev can slather on some aloe and try and calm this burn down," I said.

"Damnit," he said and snapped his fingers. "Also, you should take a hot shower, like as hot as you can stand it."

"What?" I asked. "That sounds crazy. Why would I do that?" I demanded.

"I don't recommend it," Everleigh said dubiously. "But Narcos seems to think when you get out, it makes everything out here feel cooler."

"It does!" he said, and I thought about it.

"I mean, it makes a certain amount of sense," I said. "It's like cultures from hotter desert climates drink hot beverages to stay cool. Same principle."

"Exactly!" Narcos said, and he sounded triumphant that someone was finally siding with him in this particular argument, which, whoa – I did not sign on for that!

So I said, "I mean, the science is there, but that doesn't mean I'm going to do it."

Everleigh burst out laughing and stuck her tongue out at Narcos.

"Should find a girlfriend, I said. It would be fun for me and Ev too, I said," Narcos' tone was mocking, but he winked at me and finished with, "I now have regrets."

I laughed and playfully flipped him off. He shot back with, "Shit, we got time? I'd love to rail that ass again." He bit his bottom lip and the way he looked at me had my nipples tightening beneath my tee and left the apex of my thighs tingling with want.

"Maybe later," I declared, and he winked at me. Everleigh just looked plain excited.

"I like it," he said and Everleigh grinned and gave me a little shove on my butt toward the little bathroom.

"Go," she said.

"Gonna wash my back?" I asked mischievously as I went into the bathroom and something clacked as if being set down or dropped in the kitchen. Narcos appeared around the corner and shoved Ev in my direction, and into the bathroom with me, and then leaned on the doorframe and crossed his arms.

"Well go on," he ordered to peals of mine and Everleigh's laughter.

She and I did end up showering together, making out and running our hands over each other's skin lightly, as we kissed and the lukewarm water pelted down.

Narcos watched, hungrily, and our fun was dissipated by the sound of the screen door banging shut from the back. Sam appeared over Narcos' shoulder and he said, "Holy shit. Why didn't you call me?"

Narcos snorted. "You're about to be unemployed for a bit of a stretch, giving you an all-access pass," he said. "Let me have a moment."

"Wait, unemployed? Why?" Everleigh dropped her hands from my waist and I looked up at her.

She looked vaguely hurt. Had he not told her?

"I was trying to find the right time to tell you," Sam said. "I'm thinking about quitting the force and moving over to Fire."

Everleigh's brow wrinkled, and she thought about it.

"I don't know if I like it," she murmured. "I mean, fire is dangerous," she said.

"So is being a cop." Sam's tone held a bit of defensiveness to it and I touched Everleigh's waist.

She looked at me, and I said, "Look at the big picture."

She thought about it, her green eyes locked with mine, the gears and cogs turning behind them, and she admitted finally, "I maybe can't see the forest for the trees."

"And that's okay," I said. "It's a conversation for all of us but maybe later. We don't want to keep our guest waiting, do we?"

"Exactly why I'm up here. Was fixing to ask what we were planning to have with these steaks?"

"Sorry, brother, I got distracted by a pair of minxes," Narcos declared. With a wink at me and Everleigh, he backed out of the doorway and went back around to the kitchen, swearing softly under his breath and adjusting himself in his shorts.

"Nothing has to be decided now," Sam said gently and Everleigh frowned a little more.

She said, "Don't you patronize me or try to placate me, honey. You've already made up your mind. I'm just a little butt hurt that I'm last to know," she said, and he smiled.

"That's fair," he said. "And technically, you aren't the last. I mean, I did just get done talking it out with Skids and the rest of the boys won't know until he calls 'em."

Everleigh cocked her head, and I was suddenly stiff and swallowing hard.

"I meant the last one in our household. And knowing that Skids got to know before me isn't helping your cause," she said, wilting just a little bit.

Meanwhile, I stood as though invisible and I hated that feeling. But at the same time, I couldn't help but reel from what she'd just said. *Our household* had certainly felt like it had just included me. It was paradoxical enough to drive me more than just a little bit nuts!

I felt both included and excluded at the same time and yet, I wasn't and both was upsetting at the same time. Like, I wanted to be hurt, but my logic brain was asking me seriously, *what for?* Meanwhile, my emotional center was just about all over the map and I still didn't really have an answer to the question of *what fucking for?*

Everleigh looked down at me when I dropped my hands from her waist and she cocked her head, raising a hand to cup my cheek.

"What's up?" she asked.

I swallowed hard, and as hard as it might be, I told the truth. "It's like you're both talking about me as I am both here and not here at the same time. I don't mean to be selfish right now but I'm confused, and it's really bothering me. I feel like I should be apologizing to you or something because I feel like Sam telling me first is stepping on your toes and—" She put a finger to my lips and frowned while sort of smiling at the same time.

"First of all, you're definitely included at this point when I say 'our household' and second of all, I'm sorry if I've hurt your feelings," she said.

"But?" I asked, and she shook her head.

"But nothing," she answered. "I'm sorry if I hurt your feelings, that's all. I mean, not that's all, I just really am."

I smiled and said, "I'm sorry if I hurt your feelings."

She shook her head. "You didn't!"

"I did?" Sam asked a little quietly.

"No, I don't think you did either," she said and sounded a little uneasy. "I think maybe I did. Like, I think I hurt my own feelings reading into shit I shouldn't have."

Sam cocked his head and said, "Legit, these talks have all been a sort of opportunity thing. You know I care about your input and what you think."

She smiled pleased and the tension in the small bathroom eased off. She turned back to me and pecked me on the nose. It was sudden and caught me off guard.

"I'm sorry I made everything uncomfortable," she said. "Sometimes my feelings come out of nowhere and catch me off guard. I didn't mean to make you uncomfortable."

"No, I get it," I said softly. "I mean, I'm new—"

She nodded slightly and said, "Adapt and overcome is a motto in this house and I think I zigged when I should have zagged on the adaptation part."

"It's okay," I murmured, and it was true. I mean, acceptance usually didn't come complete or absolute.

It usually took time.

"We cool?" Sam asked and I could tell he was asking both of us. I nodded immediately and Everleigh matched rather enthusiastically.

"Still new," she said. "Can we consider this growing pains?" she asked, and a relief swept through me.

"Growing pains, I like that," I said, and she smiled and hugged my nude body close to hers and *good Lord,* that felt good.

"Fuck," Sam said, thrusting himself back in the doorway, hand on his crotch, likewise adjusting himself in his shorts. Everleigh and I laughed together in shrill delight.

"They gonna kill us, brother," I heard Narcos declare and Sam just grunted in agreement.

The evening was pleasant, the conversations around the fire that night a little heavy and concerning next moves more than anything. Skids was a pleasant man, and introductions, when they were finally made, were made with profuse apologies at not having done it sooner and with a bit of uncomfortable laughter.

It turned out that Skids was a retired cop but was the leader of the Indigo Knights motorcycle club, which is why he was here. Everyone else was sort of busy with the unrest back in the city which I was a little disappointed in myself when I realized I hadn't put much thought behind all that. That there was an entire subset of the population being lost in all of this... lost yet again, and that they continued dying in the streets around this country with nary a thought or a prayer and for what?

For what?

There wasn't any denying that there was a problem, and a big one, in epidemic proportion that was going on in every U.S. city and town with no real end in sight. I just didn't know why, or how, we as a people, just couldn't seem to grow beyond any of it.

We all bled red, dammit; and yes, I know it was trite to say, but the whole damn thing left me just so very bone weary and exhausted. And that was *with* the privilege of my blonde hair, my blue eyes, and my white skin. I couldn't even begin to fathom what it was like to be anything else. The closest I could come to it in terms of discrimination was simply being a woman and even then... to be a woman of color out there?

Mm... my heart squeezed tight at the thought. That night, I couldn't get the tear-stained and anguished face of Témaël Etienne's mother out of my mind.

As I lay in the circle of Sam's arms in the dark of the cabin's loft that night, I couldn't imagine how he felt either. I knew he felt pain and guilt, and a myriad of other emotions but he was good at hiding them. Still, the photo of Témaël Etienne on his desk? The image of that haunted me too.

So much pain, and so much death, and so much heartache – the consciousness of the nation still so much a raw and aching wound – and the only answer I could come up with was evil.

It was pure fucking evil at work. The more I thought about it, the more the old saying of evil only triumphs when good men do nothing haunted me in ways I couldn't explain. I still wanted to believe that people were inherently good but the fact that these things kept happening... well... the irrefutable proof was in the proverbial pudding.

How good was humanity? I mean, really? It made me incredibly sad to think that we were honestly only as good as the evil and divisive men and women we allowed to walk among us without so much as a call out on their shitty behavior.

Did I think I could affect any change on the world? No, not really. Did I think I could affect change on my own little world? Yes, absolutely I could. I mastered the helm of my own destiny… so I would do better in any way that I could… and maybe, just maybe, if individuals like me straightened up and vowed to do better, things would catch on to the point that things would eventually *be* better somehow, some way.

Idealistic?

Absolutely, but it was the only thought I had that would allow me to even try to sleep tonight, and so I did.

Useless thoughts. I learned a long time ago just not to pray. That there was honestly no one listening.

The gods were either sleeping or didn't exist. I mean, how else could things have gotten this way?

I cuddled tighter against Sam who held me just that little bit more tightly in his sleep and let my thoughts chase themselves until I slept.

I didn't know what else I could honestly do.

I DON'T THINK I had ever been so happy to stop and be done traveling in my life as I was to pull into the driveway at Sam, Narcos and Everleigh's in the wee hours of the morning. We had ridden at night to both avoid cooking in our leathers and to protect the kitties with a bonus of avoiding what everyone had called cages. It had taken me a minute to figure out they were referring to cars.

I hated asking and looking stupid. Generally, I would wait and figure it out on my own until I just couldn't stand it anymore and had to give in.

I think it was one of my toxic traits.

"You alright?" Narcos asked as I wavered on my feet. I waved him off and Everleigh gave me a sympathetic look.

"Yeah, your woman needs a bed. We'll see you guys in the morning," Narcos said to Sam as he stood up from the bike with a groan.

"Want me to take Muninn?" Ev asked, and I shrugged out of the straps of my cat carrier backpack and handed him over so she could take him inside.

"Go on," Sam declared. "The rest of this shit can wait. I'm not dealing with it tonight."

I nodded wearily and followed Everleigh and Narcos into the house.

"Go get undressed and lie down as soon as you let the boys out," Sam ordered gently, and I raised an eyebrow.

"Where are you going?" I asked softly.

"Get the aloe out of the fridge for that burn of yours. You gotta be miserable."

I moaned. "The gods bless you and keep you," I said and let his soft chuckle drift from the kitchen as I set Muninn on the couch and let him out of his carrier. My poor boy leaped at the chance to get out and went to check on the more stressed Huginn.

"They'll be alright," Narcos reassured me at the look on my face.

"I just hate stressing them out. This isn't normal for them at *all*. Cats are creatures of habit. They don't like change for the most part."

"Could have fooled me," Narcos said, reaching out and scratching Muninn at the base of his tail. "Little fuzzy badasses have been taking everything like champs."

I rolled my eyes. "Right up until they don't and the crash can be pretty spectacular when they do. All sorts of stress-related problems and issues."

"Nah." Narcos waved me off. "They're tough just like their mamma. They've got this."

I smiled and moved to go past him down the hall and he caught me at the waist, leaned down and kissed my forehead.

"G'night squirrel," he said, and I blushed – but you probably couldn't see it for my sunburn.

I was beginning to think I was going to be stuck with that nickname. All because I had popped up from under the water at the swimming hole and had cried "Squirrel!" at the squirrel that had been by the pool. I don't know why. It had just been so unexpected, but something about it had just hit Narcos' funny bone, and the laughter had been contagious. And, well, here we were…

It was an honest to God, you had to have been there moment, at least to me. But it was still loads better than how Sam had gotten the name Driller. I'd been regaled with that tale when I'd asked around the campfire the night Skids had joined us.

All I knew, was that no matter how many other people called him Driller – I never would. Especially after finding out how he'd gotten the nickname. I also was *very* unsure about *ever* engaging in any anal after the story, because oh, my God… yuck.

"Hey," he murmured, slipping into his room and shutting the door behind us. To be honest, I was grateful to shut everyone and everything out tonight. Don't get me wrong, I adored Narcos and Everleigh… I just… it was nice to be just me and Sam tonight after being in such close quarters with other people for the last several days.

"Hey," I murmured back, and winced a bit as I tried to shrug out of the jacket I'd borrowed from Everleigh.

"Here, let me help you," he murmured, and he came to me and lifted the heavy leather off my screaming shoulders.

I sighed, and very nearly cried with relief after he relived me of my shirt and bra. I was *red*, even despite my best efforts at keeping up with the sunscreen.

Damn.

"Oh, baby. no, here, let me." He stopped me from bending over and went to his knees, helping me out of my boots, my socks, my jeans... just undressing me with undue care and tenderness. He made sure to pull the material of my clothing well away from any red bits before lifting it off me completely.

"Go lie down on your stomach in the center of the bed," he ordered gently.

"I'm going to get goo all over your sheets," I complained when he relocated the aloe gel from the top of his dresser to the closer bedside table.

"Stop, I don't care about that," he said. "I care about you and making you as comfortable as possible. I hate seeing you like this."

I scoffed. "I did it to myself," I tried to argue, and he snorted.

"So? You didn't do it on purpose."

I blinked and processed what he was saying. My mother wasn't like that. She gave no real quarter on that kind of thing. Neither did my grandmother. The only time they were nice about it is when I was suffering from something that was absolutely no fault of my own and couldn't be made my fault even with some mental gymnastics.

"You're too good to me," I said, and he laughed a little, pulling his shirt off over his head.

"You sound like you're complaining," he said, amused.

"God, no!" I cried and complied with his demands, climbing up onto the bed to lay face down so that he could tend to my sunburn.

He climbed up after me and sat by my hips, warning me, "Cold," before he dropped icy aloe across my heated back and shoulders.

I jumped, how could I not?

"Oh! Ho, ho, ho! Even with a warning, holy yikes!" I said, and he chuckled.

"Now for the not so fun part," he murmured, and he gently plied his fingertips to the goop to move it around.

I had to disagree. While it stung and felt overwarm where his fingertips touched, the lotion or gel or whatever you called it felt so damn good.

"Oh, that's nice," I moaned softly, and he hummed.

Eventually, he sucked in a breath between his teeth and I realized something… he was struggling.

"What's wrong?" I asked softly, trying to twist enough to have a look at him.

"You're just so fuckin' beautiful and tempting," he said and his words sent a shiver down my spine.

"You know what the best way to get rid of temptation is, right?" I whispered past the lump in my throat.

"Let me guess," he said, leaning down to kiss the base of my neck where my hair had protected it from getting burned. "Give into it?" he asked softly.

"Mm-hm."

"You sure?" he asked and his voice was husky, careful, and I nodded. "Okay, let me have this, and this." He took a couple of pillows from the top of the bed. "Now lift your hips for me, baby," he ordered, and I did, sort of pushing my butt up into the air as he awkwardly but efficiently shoved the pillows under my hips.

It left me prone, on my stomach, and in a weird way deliciously vulnerable. He settled his weight across my legs and I gasped as he put his hands on the globes of my ass, pressing forward and prying them apart, before his tongue dipped into the opening of my pussy.

I fisted the covers to either side of my shoulders and stiffened as he lavished attention on my pussy with his mouth, sucking at my pussy lips and darting his tongue in and out of me in a delectable cadence.

"Oh, God," I moaned, and he chuckled at me. It held a rich tone and coated my senses as though my soul had just been robed in dark chocolate and I was absolutely here for it.

"Mm, *God*." He sucked a breath in between his teeth and sounded like he was looking upon the sexiest, most beautiful thing he had ever laid eyes on. It almost made me turn to look for Everleigh but that was stupid. She wasn't in here. He was talking about *me*.

Me. Boring, plain, just… *me*…

It was almost unfathomable, and I didn't know what to do with it except be grateful, because clearly, he really did see me that way and *oh… shit…*

He cleverly short-circuited my brain by introducing what felt like his long middle finger into my cunt, massaging that fucking spot that made *everything* tingle.

I felt my ass rise and my hips push back, welcoming that finger inside of me and wanting desperately for *more*.

"That's it, baby." He sounded so pleased, his tone seductive and velvet. "I'm going to try something new. You trust me?" he asked.

"Mm, yeah, as long as this doesn't stop here," I said, and he chuckled anew.

"Not an icicle's chance in Hell," he said and moved away to the bedside table and opened up a drawer. I turned my head to look, but he was too quick, and I didn't see what he retrieved. I just heard the crinkle of a wrapper for a split second.

"Now, where were we?" he asked, and I reminded him, "Something new?"

"Oh, right, we'll get to that later, right now..." he went back down on me and I cried out as much from surprise as pleasure. I liked this, being at his mercy, not entirely sure what was going to happen from my prone position – but all the same, not caring.

Why would I care when it felt so damn good?

By the time he pressed his cock at my opening, I was *begging* to have him inside of me, and he slid right in as though he were *meant* to be there; and I do mean *all the way in.*

I cried out and pushed up off the bed slightly, arching my back low, my hips up and back onto his invading cock, loving how deep he went from this angle, how he bottomed out against my cervix in that sweet, spicy pain that was more pleasurable than anything. Like the spice of cinnamon, sweetly alluring, as opposed to the spicy burn of a hot pepper.

"Ooo, yeah," I moaned and I couldn't even be surprised at how this man made me sound and feel like a porn star.

I mean, I *liked* that he did. It made me feel uplifted, powerful, like I had some sort of secret identity that was sexy and cool. I loved the things he brought out in me, that no one ever could before. I loved how safe he made me feel, how I felt as though I were truly an equal with how we traded some of our deepest darkest hurts quietly in the deepest darkest parts of the night.

Confessing our sins, airing our hopes, revealing our fears, and how we both managed; despite our mutual dark sides, to *accept* each other.

It was something that still felt tenuous in its newness, but also, at the same time, so very *real.*

I could *trust* Samuel Stahl like I could trust no other, and I knew that – but I still flinched at the cracking noise of him opening a cap, the sharp sound sudden and loud over my soft panting and his quiet grunts of his appreciation.

"Trust me," he said, and it sounded like the plea came directly from his soul, so I relaxed.

The pad of one of his fingers, slick with something, touched my asshole and I bit down on my cry of surprise then surprisingly still, *melted* under that touch.

What the hell...

"Touch your clit for me baby," he ordered softly, and I buried my shoulder against the mattress and delved a hand deep between my body and the bed to comply.

I found my pussy soaking wet, and I gathered some of that wetness on my fingertips and gasped as I pressed them into my clit to rub firm but gentle circles.

"Oh, that's it," he praised as I felt my pussy tighten up around his cock, drawing him in, keeping him where I wanted him.

He rubbed circles with that fingertip around my asshole and I bit my bottom lip, trying to hold on and not come, not yet. I wanted to hold out a little longer. Everything felt so fucking *good*. If I came, I was half afraid the ride would be over and I didn't want it to end, not yet.

"That's it," he praised, and *fuck, shit, oh God,* I loved it when he did that. When he spoke to me so sweetly and *oh! Oh, oh, oh!*

His fingertip slid into my butt and he worked it back and forth, timing it with his thrusts. He pulled his finger out, his cock plunged in, and he started to withdraw from my cunt. He plunged his finger in that much further until I hissed from the sting.

"You okay?" he asked.

"Yeah," I breathed out. "Cinnamon, not pepper."

"What?" he asked.

I arched to take more of him and cried, "Cinnamon good, pepper bad!"

"Got it," he declared, and he gave me all of him – both his cock and whatever he was doing with my back door. I had to stop the motion of my fingers or I was going to come and I was going to come hard.

"No, don't stop that hand, baby. I want you to come. I want you to come for me and come hard."

I gasped and cried out and told him, "I don't want this to end."

He chuckled that decadent dark sound and I swear if that sound were manifest physical, it would feel like sable soft fur rubbing down my back.

"Ride's over when I *say* it's over," and *oh, God, oh fuck,* that was *so hot,* I couldn't help myself. The cracks in my veneer split. I stood on that razor's edge, on the precipice, staring down into that yawning maw of pleasure and when he added a second finger to my ass, stretching me just a little more, I fell.

Rushing silence enveloped me as I plunged into that warm bathwater abyss of pleasure, vaguely aware that my body left behind was twitching and convulsing of its own mind as mine seemed to get farther and farther away.

That sweet, fiery cinnamon burn in my ass disappeared momentarily, and I was vaguely aware of the sound of a wrapper again. I realized my pussy was vacant, and he was rolling a condom down his length before rocking on his knees and getting resituated.

"Breathe for me, baby," he murmured, and I sucked in a breath. "Hold it," he ordered, and he pressed the head of his cock where only his fingers had been before. "Let it out slow and push out," he said between gritted teeth and I did as he said automatically. He pushed against my asshole with the head of his cock, and I gasped as that cinnamon burn flared into ragged jalapeno heat for a mere moment and he stopped.

"Easy," he assured me. "Just take it easy. Rest here a while." He rubbed his hands over my hips and massaged my ass cheeks, my asshole pulsing around the strange sensation of his invading cock for a while. Unhappy at its presence before finally settling down into a mild grumble of disapproval.

Again that cracking noise of a flip top cap opening, cold, slimy and slick, he spread the lubricant around his cock and the rim of my asshole.

"Good girl, just relax. Yeah that's it," he murmured, and he slid in easily, just a little bit further and I went limp beneath him.

"Feel good?" he asked and I let out a breathy, "Yeah!" because it did. Oh, my God, did it. So new, so foreign, but so, so, good at the same time.

He worked himself in slowly, agonizingly slowly at first and once he was all the way in, he groaned in appreciation.

"Fuck yeah," he practically cried and then he was moving again, in a more natural rhythm. I could do nothing but let him take me for a fucking ride. My pussy was throbbing and pulsing, as though the orgasm of before had never fully quit, but had somehow become slower, gentler, the muscle spasms becoming more steady and almost timed with my heartbeat as he picked up his pace in fucking my ass.

I vaguely had the thought, as my eyes rolled back in my head, and I went limp beneath him, *and you thought you'd never...*

Bless this man for breaking down my walls and for gaining my trust enough to let him in, because this was fucking *wonderful*.

26

*D*riller...

Fuck, there was absolutely nothing hotter than tapping that ass. She bowed low to the bed, sticking it up in the air, pushing back to meet my thrusts and I was vaguely aware of the fluttering of her pussy against the bottom and base of my cock.

Yeah, that was good.

"Keep coming for me, baby. Just like that. Oh yeah, you're such a good girl for me," I whispered, and she just *ate up* the praise, sinking lower into the mattress, turning into a puddle under my touch and I loved that.

That she could be so vulnerable with me. That she trusted me to protect her. Fuck, that was so hot, so good, and the way her body gripped me tight at the base of my cock, the way her body massaged me, I was going to lose it if I wasn't careful, but I wasn't ready. Like her, I wanted this to go on forever. I wanted to come so hard I lost all vision but the vision of her, basking in the muted golden light of the bedside lamp, her beautiful body prone beneath my own, so accepting, bowed in almost worship of the pleasure I gave her.

Fuck me, Teresia made me feel like a god. Like no woman ever had before, and I wanted desperately to be the king to her queen.

I wanted her to grace my arm and the court of our very own kingdom, here by the sea, and I wanted the rest of the fucking peasants around us to be completely oblivious to the royalty that walked among them.

I felt a surge of powerfulness that felt like nothing I had ever felt before, my back tingling, my balls tightening, and before I could help myself, I was exploding inside her, exploding with the force of a thousand suns. Crying out with the force of it, how every nerve of my body racked up, stood at attention, and lit up like a fuckin' Christmas tree. I blazed for her. I burned for her, and I thought I would spontaneously combust at one point… but then, after the intense initial surge, everything faded into a comfortable warmth.

I came back to myself, lying over the top of her, pressing her into the bed, my taller frame cuddling her protectively into my chest as she moaned in soft appreciative pleasure beneath me, the sound almost a whimper.

"Oh, shit, your sunburn!" I sucked in a breath and made to push off of her but her fingers that had somehow found the spaces between mine locked, gripping my fingers between them, curling them over the back of her hand and toward her palm as her voice, clear and bright said, "No, stay! I don't care. Stay with me."

There was no denying my queen and her royal decree. I settled down, but I did pull myself out of her body, crying out as the sensation sent my cock twitching all over again but with nothing to shoot. I was fucking spent.

"Mmm…" she moaned and kissed my wrist which was the only thing close enough to her lips without her having to move more than a few scant millimeters.

"Fuck, that was good," I groaned and my voice was like gravel in my throat. She shuddered at the sound and I smiled to myself, feeling the appreciation radiate from her.

"The best," she murmured.

"Oh no," I corrected her. "The best is yet to come."

"Better than that?" She scoffed. "Impossible."

"Oh yeah, absolutely better than that. Imagine Narcos in that sweet pussy, me in that tight little asshole of yours, and Everleigh paying attention to whatever you've got left."

She froze beneath me and said, "Holy shit. For real?"

"Abso-fucking-lutely for real," I said, completely deadpan.

She wriggled beneath me, cuddled in close and said, "Sign me the fuck up."

I chuckled and said the only thing that was right in this particular scenario, "That's my girl."

She giggled fiercely and said something that was music to my ears. "Hopefully, for a very long time."

I kissed her neck behind her ear and whispered in her ear, "How does forever sound?"

She opened wide her one blue eye facing me and blinked. "Was-was that a proposal?" she asked.

"No," I told her. "If that ever comes, there will be a ring and I'll be down on one knee, but I don't much believe in the institution of marriage. I'm not much for religion and it seems to me it's just some kind of a tax grab or whatever."

She giggled, the sudden tension leaving her body, and she said, "I don't know that I'm even close to ready to be that serious."

I smiled and kissed her neck behind her ear once more and breathed her in deep. God, her scent was intoxicating.

"I'm in no rush, baby," I told her. "We got all the time in the world."

"You're sure?" she asked, and her voice held a timid hesitancy.

"Yeah, why?" I asked.

"I don't want to hurt your feelings..." she said and trailed off. I chuckled again.

"No hard feelings here. Believe me, I get it. We're both in a hard period of flux when it comes to our lives right now. I want to be here for you to make things *easier,* not harder for you."

She rocked back and forth beneath me, like a snuggly kitten getting comfortable and said, "Same. I don't want to make your life harder, either."

I smiled.

"Glad we're on the same page," I told her and kissed where I could reach that wasn't as red as a lobster.

"Me too," she said.

Eventually, I got up and retrieved the condom I'd pulled off and dropped aside when I'd gone soft and threw it away. I put the lube back where it belonged and helped her up. We were both so sticky with each other's fluids there wasn't anything for it. We both needed a quick rinse in the shower before bed. I lovingly washed her incredible body, and she did the same for me. The adoration clearly mutual, the respect as hard as granite.

I reapplied the aloe to her skin and turned out the light, both of us cuddling in together beneath a light blanket in the air-conditioned hush of the house.

"So, what happens now?" she asked after a protracted silence.

"Now, we take it one day at a time. We'll get the full meal deal on what arrests have been made. I'll make whatever threat assessments need to be made, and we'll get you home and go from there."

"I think I'm going to have a fight on my hands with the building owner and insurance and all of that," she said unhappily.

"Maybe, but maybe it won't be as bad as you think. One day at a time," I murmured and kissed her temple. "No need to borrow trouble that isn't even there yet. What may come, we've got this," I promised her. She held to me a little tighter in the dark and I had to smile.

She believed in me. I definitely believed in her. That was all that honestly really mattered.

27

Sometime Later...

*T*eresia...

"So, what happens now?" my mother asked, her eyes wide and a little bit frightened. My grandmother, who sat next to her and both across from me in a booth at the 10-13, echoed the sentiment on my mother's face... except my grandmother had an all-too familiar glint in her eye. One that read of equal parts anger and determination.

"Well, the owner doesn't *have* to lease the space back to me," I said. "Honestly, with things the way they are, I think they're looking to sell the building. Investors are willing to pay a lot of money these days."

"But the bakery, all your hard work!" My grandmother was growing upset. Everleigh gripped my hand under the table and looked over at me with pride.

"The insurance payout for the business was more than enough to put my plan in action," I said with a sniff. "I can still pay you the same rate with the new venture, but you'd have to work fewer hours."

"What?" my mother asked.

"What new venture?" my grandmother demanded.

"I bought a food truck," I said and let out a gusty breath.

"You did *what?*" my mother demanded.

"You heard me. We'll be operating out of a ghost kitchen in the morning, getting everything baked up and ready to go, so that's where I'll need your help. But as for the truck itself? I really need to be the only one manning the counter. I don't have a big space to maintain, so aside from a little kitchen cleanup, you'll both have the afternoons off—"

"Isn't this risky?" my mother demanded. "What if you can't make enough out of just a truck?"

"I'll cross that bridge when I come to it," I said and started getting defensive.

"What would *you* do?" Everleigh asked pointedly of my mother.

"With real estate like it is, and spaces in the city at a premium, this is far more low risk than starting all over in a brick-and-mortar establishment, Mom."

My grandmother reached across the table and put her hand over mine.

"I won't pretend to know how this will work, but if it's one thing I know about my granddaughter – she isn't one to take risks where her family is involved."

I smiled and shook my head. "Absolutely not. I've thought about it, and I plan to retool the bakery website so that people can preorder their breads and rolls so we only need to make just a little bit more above and beyond what we need. They can either pick them up from the truck or I can have them delivered through a third-party app. I'm still working out the details on that."

"I don't know," my mother – ever the drama queen – hedged.

"Hey." We all turned our heads, and I was suffused with a warm glow as Sam approached our table. Everleigh slid over so that I could slide too and make room for him at my side.

He sat down with us and my mother smiled wanly. "Hello, Detective," she said and her voice was a bit brittle.

"Sam," he said. "And 'detective' no longer. My last day on the force was last week."

"Oh, really?" my grandmother asked, intrigued. "What will you do?"

"Gram!" I complained, and she looked at me all wide eyed and false innocence.

"What?"

I gave her a look like *you know what*, and she pursed her lips, unhappy with me.

Sam laughed a little uneasily and said, "I'm not going to be an unemployed bum, if that's what you're asking. I just got done with the physical tests to become a firefighter."

"Oh, really?" my grandmother asked, perking up a bit.

"Isn't that dangerous?" my mother asked, glancing at me.

"Yes," I answered. "But probably no more dangerous than being a cop."

I sighed inwardly. I hadn't known why I'd expected any of this to go well. Heaven forbid, I do anything with my adult life that wouldn't send my mother and grandmother into a major round of second-guessing literally *every single decision* I made.

Fuck.

The rest of our late lunch was arduous at best and as much as I loved the two older women across from me that were pretty much the last of my living relatives, the more they picked at everything I was trying to accomplish and eroded my faith that I could actually do it, the more I just wanted to tell them that if they didn't want to help, they could get bent and I would do it myself.

The thing was, I was tired of doing it all by myself.

It was exhausting.

But then Everleigh gave my hand another squeeze at the same time Sam gave the top of my thigh a squeeze, and I realized that the old saying was true – *The blood of the covenant is thicker than the water of the womb* – meaning the chosen family I was building with Sam, Narcos, and Everleigh? Well, I would never be alone again. Nothing would have to be done all by myself, and that bolstered my spirits like nothing else.

"God, I thought they'd never leave," Everleigh said under her breath as my grandmother put her hand to my mother's back as they left out the front door.

I smiled and waved. Once they were out of sight down the street, I said, "Now do you see why just about every interaction with them can be exhausting?"

"It's like your mom is tried and determined to shit on your parade every which fuckin' way but sideways," a voice from behind us said. I blinked and Narcos got up and came around to sit down across from us where my mother and grandmother had been. He picked up a fry off my grandmother's plate and ate it.

"Where the fuck did you come from?" I demanded, and Everleigh stifled her giggle with a laugh.

"I saw him come in," she said dryly.

"What's with the super spy shit?" I demanded, but I was laughing. I couldn't help it.

"Eh, I wanted to be around in case you needed backup, Squirrel." I rolled my eyes at the nickname that had indeed stuck and had spread like wildfire through the rest of the club.

"You guys okay?" Skids asked, wandering over, tossing a bar towel over his shoulder.

"Right as rain," I declared. "More determined than ever."

"You look like you could use a drink," he said.

"Better make it champagne," Backdraft said, sliding into the seat next to Narcos.

"Oh, why's that?" Skids demanded.

"Somebody passed his shit with flying colors and is going to get an acceptance call and letter *very* soon," he said with a wink at Sam.

"What?" I exclaimed as Sam very nearly sagged with relief next to me.

"That's great! Way to go, man." Narcos' eyes shone with pride that pass or fail, I knew from experience, would be there anyway when it came to Sam.

I turned my face up to kiss him as Everleigh reached across my lap to grip his hand where it rested on top of my thigh. Her eyes were aglow with pride too, but somehow their expressive green depths managed to convey it was for the *both* of us.

A golden glow of pride burst forth under my breastbone and colored my cheeks a bright pink.

Sam groaned after glimpsing the look in my eyes and devoured my mouth with his. A little inappropriate at the table in a restaurant full of people, but I didn't care. I was just too happy for him. We turned back to Backdraft, who I remembered from the day of the fire at my bakery, who was grinning like a fool.

"Well alright, champagne it is!" Skids crowed. "Why don't y'all move on up to the fishbowl and I'll get the rest of the boys and their ol' ladies in here to have a proper celebration?"

"Sounds damn good, Cap," I declared.

And so, it went. We moved up to the fishbowl, which was a little weird as the women usually hung out outside of it and the space definitely had a "boys-only" vibe to it, but for tonight, it was as though Sam was king and he would accept nothing short of having me by his side as his queen.

I couldn't tell you how much I loved that.

Yale slid into a seat beside us sometime during the course of the evening and said, "Got an update for you if you'd like, or it can wait. Up to you," he said.

I glanced sideways at Sam who brought himself around out of the joking and ribbing conversation he was having with Golden and Oz. I smiled fondly at the memory of the first time he had brought me in here to meet the entire club and how everyone had quickly adapted and ushered me in to their inner circle. I felt like I had gone from very, very, few friends to more than I knew what to do with in the blink of an eye.

It was Yale's girl, Aly, who had put the idea of a food truck into my mind in the first place. And if all of this crazy shit worked out in my favor? I would be forever grateful.

"Shoot," Sam said without any prompting. He knew I wanted to know anything and everything about the people who had been behind the utter devastation to my business and the major upheaval of my life in general.

"Plea deals were struck with some of the lower players," he said. "None of them will be avoiding jail time, don't you worry, but it's a lot less than I would like." He sighed.

"How much less?" I asked.

"Two to five years minimum on each count. Some have multiple counts but they all turned and *boy* did they turn."

"Yeah?" Sam asked, eying Yale up and down.

"What?" I asked, not missing the look but definitely clueless on the significance.

"I can't say more," he said. "Domestic terrorism task force has the football. Just believe me when I say they're running down the field full tilt and it may take a while, but justice is definitely going to be served." He looked smug. I leaned back in my seat against Sam's arm.

"Holy shit. Nice," he declared after a low whistle.

"Yeah. As for the actual perp that smashed the windows and set your bakery on fire?" he said, leaving off the "with you in it" which really I didn't mind that part going unspoken. I had lived it, after all.

"Yeah?" I asked.

"We got him, too. No deal. I'm taking that one to trial. We've got that bastard dead to rights with his co-conspirator's testimony. I don't want that motherfucker on my streets." He leaned back.

"Who is he?" I asked, and he sighed.

"No one you know," he said. "Dylan Moore, real neo-nazi, KKK dick-sucking piece of work. Comes from a long and storied background of white supremacy and was born and bred into that lifestyle of hate. Should hear him. Proud as fuck his great-granddaddy was some high muckity muck in the Klan. It's unreal what's been crawling out from under the rocks this whole thing has lifted. But we're taking them down, domino effect."

Sam looked a bit withdrawn, lost in his own thoughts.

I had some of my own, but nothing I wanted to speak out loud for respect for the Etienne family... but I could see it etched into every line of Sam's face, the tightness around his eyes, the pain hidden in their dark depths.

I hoped that somehow, someway, the media would decide to actually do what it was intended to do and would report the actual news of these arrests as more than just a footnote on the evening news.

I didn't know about anyone else, but I, for one, was hoping that the legacy left behind from all of it – the shooting, the trial, just *all of it* – would be the destruction of hate and that somehow, someway, equality would win the day.

I knew it was wishful or hopeful thinking. Rarely, if ever did real change come out of an incident like this – an incident that was becoming all too common, played out in every major city all across America... but *fuck*. Maybe this time could and would be different. Maybe this time some form of justice would be served. I knew a lot of people wouldn't think that way, because Sam was out here, with me and not behind bars, but as I laced my fingers through his beneath the table and watched the pain recede, disappearing back behind the mask he so expertly put on for everyone else... this time, this one singular time, I knew *it had been an accident.*

Sam had genuinely thought he was returning fire on the man who had shot *him*, and he would carry that burden with him for the rest of his days.

There was no punishment greater than that, that could be visited on him.

Not a one.

"Thank you for telling me," I murmured. "And thank you for all your time and effort when it comes to my situation."

Yale smiled and gave a sharp nod.

"Just doing my job, Squirrel."

I made a face at the nickname and glared daggers through the glass at Narcos who was playing darts with Poe and Blaze to the track of Yale's laughter.

Men are so dumb sometimes, I thought to myself, but as Narcos winked back at me after catching my eye, I couldn't help but smile. I waved back to Everleigh whose eyes sparkled and tuned in to the fact that Sam was staring at me.

I looked up at him.

"What?" I asked.

"Confession time?" he asked, and it had sort of become our thing. A covert way of letting the other mentally and emotionally prepare for whatever was said next, that it had the potential to be a pretty big or triggering bombshell.

I nodded once, resolutely, and steeled myself for what it could be.

"I love you," he said, and that hadn't been what I'd been expecting.

"I love you, too," I blurted before I could think and it just sort of hung in the air between us.

"Fuck," he said, and he hooked a hand around the back of my head, his fingers tangling in my hair as his eyes glassed over with hearty emotion. He pressed a kiss to my forehead in an attempt to hide it. I smiled to myself.

Too late. I'd already seen it.

We hugged for a good long while, while everyone sipped champagne and talked boisterously around us. He whispered in my ear, "Ride back to my place with me?"

"Can we go now?" I asked.

"Fuck yes," he said.

A thrill of anticipation went through me at the low, sexy, gravel tone.

"What about my cage?" I asked, and he smirked at me.

"Ev can drive it home. Let's give her the keys."

"Alright," I agreed readily.

We made our way out. Everleigh was happy to take my keys, Narcos waving off my apologies and saying he'd see us later at home.

Yes, yes, he would.

28

*D*riller...

The ride home was a sweet one. The air still warm, summer only just starting to die out into fall. It was even better with Teresia's arms clamped around me, her body snug up against my back.

It'd been hard as hell taking her home when we'd been given the all-clear. Narcos and I had come and fixed her window with Backdraft's guidance. Saved her a gang of money on install doing it for her.

Everleigh had absolutely squealed over her yards, both front and back, and in the intervening weeks, I'd found Narcos' girl at my girl's place in the yard, since she'd pretty much run out of things to do in our own.

I liked that they bonded. That there was also an attraction there. That the times she came to our place, she was less and less afraid of joining in the fun and all four of us having a rockin' good time.

I don't think she realized how much she completed me, let alone *us*.

I was beginning to think she was getting a clearer and clearer picture day by day, though.

I loved that she practically attacked me the second I closed the front door behind us, her hands going for my tee beneath my jacket and cut.

It'd been a joy taking Everleigh shopping – she knew Teresia's sizes better than I could do – and had a better eye toward the feminine than I did for sure. We'd kitted her out pretty damn good with riding gear and had enjoyed the big Fourth of July run with the rest of the squad.

She fit into my life so seamlessly, and I worried sometimes if she felt like I fit hers, but all of that worry was dispelled when her mouth crashed against mine and her hands found my skin. Every. Time.

"Fuck, babe," I groaned against her mouth as she practically dragged me toward the bedroom.

"I need you to make love to me," she practically begged and I think it hit me, in a moment of clarity, she'd heard the words from me tonight and now she needed to feel it in my touch.

"God, I love you," I said, and I crushed my mouth over hers and poured every fucking ounce of how I felt for her into it, into my touch as I eradicated her clothing, piece by fucking piece, letting it fall where it may.

I think this silly squirrel of mine had it in her head that we'd done nothing but fuck this whole time and that couldn't be further from the truth. But now that I'd said the words, I think her mind was ready to accept it all the way, and I needed to show her just how really loved she was.

"Mm, Sam," she moaned as I tore my mouth from hers, gathered her in my arms, and pressed my mouth to that sweet spot on the side of her neck.

I walked her back to my bedroom and dropped clothing like bread-crumbs for Narcos and Everleigh to follow if they wanted to when they got home – but I would have my way with her first.

She leaped and wrapped her legs around me and I hitched her up, my boner pressing through my jeans, her pussy hot through hers.

We made out like wild things until I could throw her, giggling, down onto the bed. I immediately attacked her belt, pulling it free and practically ripping her jeans down her legs, spurred by my passion for her.

She gasped, and I shucked out of my own boots and jeans double time, climbing up onto the bed between those fucking thighs of her. We kissed, and she wriggled down into place for me, gripping me and stroking me with her hand, giving a delicate twist of her wrist as she did it, which had me faltering.

"Oh, fuck, *baby*," I groaned, and she gave me this wicked and delighted smile that made my insides turn liquid with fucking desire.

Fuck she was hot; so fucking hot, and she had *no idea.*

"Ah!" she cried out and her back arched as I pushed my way inside her hot, slick, waiting pussy.

I groaned at how she pulled me in, her hot little cunt gripping me tight, and fighting my withdraw.

I kissed her stupid, bent her to the point I bottomed out inside her and drew those feral little cries from her throat that set me on that fucking sweet-ass ledge. When I was sure she'd gotten hers, I plummeted over the side right along with her on her third, or was it fourth, round of coming around my cock and I tell you, I could *barely* hold back.

"Mmm," she hummed in something that was between satisfaction and relief.

"Mm-hm," was all I could muster, collapsing off to one side, drawing her snug against my side.

"That was hot," she murmured and somewhere out in the house I heard Narcos call, "It's about to get hotter. Make some fuckin' room."

She giggled, and we moved aside, Narcos and Everleigh slipping into my room both butt-ass naked and ready to play. Everleigh went for me, kissing me, her hand finding my dick and working me back to life. Narcos kissed my girl and got up to lie down on his back. He urged her to straddle him and slipped inside her easily.

I smiled and broke the kiss with Ev, who didn't hesitate, and went down on me, as I angled myself over to steal a kiss from my woman.

God, I wanted in her ass while Narcos fucked her. We hadn't gone there yet, just some anal play, plugs and the like, a little rimming while he fucked her like this. But tonight was definitely the night and with one traded look, Narcos raised an eyebrow. He was on board.

"Everleigh, come bring me that sweet-ass pussy," he growled, and Ev sat up from my now raging boner.

She smiled at me lasciviously and went to straddle Narcos' face and made out with my Teresia.

I went for the lube and a condom out of the bedside table.

"You better make her come a time or two more," I said and Narcos grunted, giving me a thumbs-up.

I got the condom on and got behind my girl, gripping her shoulders and shoving her forward, lowering my mouth to tease her into more readiness.

I don't know how to describe the feeling of fucking her with my best friend. The feel of his cock right up against mine through the thin veil of Teresia's body was so fucking hot. Like I seriously didn't even know what to say. He and I had fucked Ev like this countless times before but *shit...* this right here? With Teresia? This was something next level.

She moaned, in time with our see-sawing thrusting, and so enraptured was she, she couldn't even hold herself up. She lay over Narcos, and Everleigh's mouth found mine even as Narcos kissed my woman.

Pretty soon, Everleigh had positioned her pussy over his face to get in on some action, rather than just staying a spectator. He must have done something with his tongue that Ev found spectacular, because she cried out into my mouth which made me moan back into hers.

Fuck, I was glad I'd gotten off before they'd joined the party.

I felt like I could go like this for a *while*, which I knew was just prolonging the pleasure for my girl.

Narcos grunted in that familiar way that said he was about to fuckin' lose his shit and with a final grunt, he lost his rhythm and his hips jerked wildly. Teresia cried out somewhere between pleasure and pain and I rode things out, going easy on her, making love to her ass slow and even, keeping things steady as Narcos slowly started to go down inside her.

That was a sensation in and of itself, holy Christ.

He got Ev off with his mouth and when I thought she'd had enough, I slipped from Teresia, ditched the condom, and with a pleading look from Everleigh, got up inside her so she could finish with a cock inside her. I knew that's what she loved best – the full feeling of a rough fuck as she played with her pussy until she finished.

I managed to get off a second time, too – but damn, it wasn't the same. Not the same at all. Teresia's pussy was just magic – or I was just a fool in fucking love.

Narcos and I settled next to each other, our respective women draped over us as we relaxed in the dark, the lot of us sated and sticky. The best sex was always messy sex, and I was here for it every fuckin' time.

Narcos was the one to clear his throat and speak first.

"Ev and I were talking about your whole food truck thing, and I think I have an idea to, I don't know, buy you some more security or whatever until you find your rhythm."

"Oh, what's that?" Teresia asked dreamily, her voice faraway sounding.

"Move in with us," he said. "Rent your place out."

She went very still against me and I held my breath. I looked over to my best friend who was looking at me like *I dare you to argue with me, motherfucker.*

"Everleigh?" Teresia asked, uncertainly.

"Please?" Ev said. "Like, pretty please, with sugar on top."

Her silken hair stuck to my chest as she looked up at me. I looked down at her and said, "I didn't know nothing about this, but *fuck* do I want it."

"You *and* the damn cats," Narcos said. Everleigh smacked him in the chest.

"The truth!" Ev cried comically. "You just want the cats."

He snorted. "Yeah, that's it," he said. "The human with the bomb-ass pussy and mad-baking skills is just a bonus."

I groaned. "Yeah but the carbs…"

It was Teresia's turn to lightly slap *me.*

"You want me to move in or not?" she demanded, her smile belying her outraged tone.

"More than fucking anything," I told her and she snuggled into my side happily.

"With everything else going on, when do we start?" she asked, and Narcos laughed. I did too, and pulled her in tight, kissing the top of her hair.

"As soon as fucking possible, I say. I don't want another night without you right here where I can keep an eye on you."

She gripped me tight around my ribs, giving me a squeeze.

"Good, me either," she declared. "Just what to do with all my fucking furniture?" She groaned.

Everleigh laughed and so did I. Narcos said, "Sell some, store some, maybe take some down to the cabin?"

"That's going to be tough making up my mind on all of that," she said.

"We have time," Everleigh murmured around a yawn.

"That we do," Narcos agreed.

"Plenty of help, too. The boys and their ol' ladies will pitch in," I added.

Silence ensued for a little while.

"You're sure?" she asked us.

"Fuck yeah. I wouldn't suggest it otherwise," Narcos said.

I felt Everleigh's hand reach across him and take my girl's.

"We're sure," she said.

"Okay," she murmured, and I felt her lips curl into a smile against my chest.

"Okay?" I asked, wanting to make sure.

She laughed.

"Okay," she said.

"Fuck yeah," Narcos muttered and he and Everleigh traded a high-five.

Teresia laughed, and I chuckled. "Fucking dorks," I muttered.

"Yeah, but you love us," Narcos declared.

"Fuckin' right I do," I said, and I gave Teresia an extra squeeze.

She cuddled up closer and sighed in contentment.

"Me too," she said.

"Me three," Everleigh declared.

"Me fuckin' four," Narcos said, and I smiled.

Yeah, it felt really good to be dorks all together. Really damn good.

ALSO BY A.J. DOWNEY

Christmas with the Brotherhood

ABOUT A.J. DOWNEY

A.J. Downey is a Pacific Northwest girl living in an East Tennessee world who finds inspiration from her surroundings, through the people she meets, and likely as a byproduct of way too much caffeine. She specializes in real and relatable romance stories featuring that real-life kind of love that everyone craves.

Stalker Information:

Website
www.ajdowney.com

Sign up for her newsletter at
http://eepurl.com/dkQiIH

Facebook Group - AJ's Sacred Circle
https://www.facebook.com/groups/authorajdowney/

f facebook.com/authorajdowney
🐦 twitter.com/authorajdowney
📷 instagram.com/ajdowney
BB bookbub.com/authors/a-j-downey